D0369007

THE
Reserve

Also by Russell Banks

The Darling

The Angel on the Roof

Cloudsplitter

Rule of the Bone

The Sweet Hereafter

Affliction

Success Stories

Continental Drift

The Relation of My Imprisonment

Trailerpark

The Book of Jamaica

The New World

Hamilton Stark

Family Life

Searching for Survivors

THE
Reserve

A NOVEL

Russell Banks

HARPER

An Imprint of HarperCollins*Publishers*
www.harpercollins.com

THE RESERVE. Copyright © 2008 by Russell Banks. All rights reserved. Printed in the United States of America. No part of this book may be used or reproduced in any manner whatsoever without written permission except in the case of brief quotations embodied in critical articles and reviews. For information, address HarperCollins Publishers, 10 East 53rd Street, New York, NY 10022.

HarperCollins books may be purchased for educational, business, or sales promotional use. For information, please write: Special Markets Department, HarperCollins Publishers, 10 East 53rd Street, New York, NY 10022.

Designed by Jessica Shatan Heslin/Studio Shatan, Inc.

Library of Congress Cataloging-in-Publication Data

Banks, Russell
  The Reserve: a novel / Russell Banks.—1st ed.
    p. cm.

ISBN: 978-0-06-143025-1
ISBN-10: 0-06-143025-0
1. Rich people—Fiction. 2. Adirondack Mountains (N.Y.)—Fiction. 3. New York (State)—Fiction. 4. United States—History—1933–1945—Fiction. I. Title.

PS3552.A49R47 2008

813'.54—dc22

08 09 10 11 12 ID/RRD 10 9 8 7 6 5 4

For Chase, the Beloved

I am beautiful as a dream of stone.

— BAUDELAIRE

THE
Reserve

WHEN FINALLY NO ONE WAS WATCHING HER ANYMORE, THE beautiful young woman extracted herself from her parents and their friends and left the living room. She passed through the screened porch and crossed the deck and barefoot walked softly over the pine needles in front of the sprawling log building downhill toward the sheared ledges along the edge of the lake.

She knew that shortly the others would notice, not that Vanessa had left her father's party, but that the light in the room had suddenly faded, and though it was still late afternoon and not yet dusk, they would see that the sun, because of the looming proximity of the Great Range, was about to slip behind the mountains. The Second Tamarack Lake was deep and long and narrow, like a Norwegian fiord, scraped by glaciers out of the north- and south-running Great Range of steep, granitic mountains, and the view from the eastern shore of the Second Lake at this hour in high summer was famous. Most of the group would take their freshened drinks in hand and, following Vanessa, would stroll from the living room down to the shore to watch the brassy edges of the clouds turn to molten gold, and then, turning their backs to the sky and lake, to compliment the way the pine and spruce woods on the slopes behind the camp shifted in the dwindling alpenglow from blue-green to rose and from rose to lavender, as if merely observing the phenomenon helped cause it.

After a few moments, when the alpenglow had faded, they would turn again and gaze at the lake and admire in silence the smooth surface of the water shimmering in metallic light reflected off the burnished clouds. And then at last they would notice Vanessa Cole standing alone on one of the tipped ledges that slipped into the water just beyond the gravelly beach. With her long, narrow back to her parents and their friends, her fingertips raised and barely touching the sides of her slender, pale, uplifted throat, Vanessa, gazing in dark and lonely Nordic thoughtfulness into the whole vast enclosed space between lake and forest and mountain and sky, would seem to be situated at the exact center of the wilderness, its very locus, the only meaningful point of it. For her parents and their friends, for an interesting moment, the drama of the disappearing sun would be Vanessa Cole's.

There were nine people at the party, Dr. Cole's 1936 annual Fourth of July celebration at the Second Lake—Vanessa and her parents, Carter and Evelyn Cole; Red Ralston and his wife, Adele; Harry and Jennifer Armstrong; and Bunny and Celia Tinsdale. The men had been classmates at Yale, Skull and Bones, class of 1908. Their wives, respectively, had gone to Smith, Bryn Mawr, Vassar, and Mount Holyoke. All four couples had married young and had in their twenties borne their children, and their children, except for Vanessa, had in turn done the same. During the previous decades the men had made a great deal of money buying and selling stocks and bonds and real estate and from the practice of their professions—Dr. Cole was an internationally renowned, if somewhat controversial, brain surgeon; Red Ralston, Vanessa's godfather, was a corporate lawyer who specialized in bankruptcies; Harry Armstrong owned a company that manufactured automobile tires; Bunny Tinsdale ran his father's steel company—and husbands and wives both were old enough now to have found themselves in the process of inheriting homes and family fortunes from their dying parents. They and their parents and their children and grandchildren had not been much affected by the Great Depression.

Every year on the Fourth of July—other than during the war years, when Dr. Cole and Bunny Tinsdale were army officers stationed in France—the four families gathered together here at Rangeview, the Cole family's Adirondack camp, to drink and fish and hike in rustic splendor and to celebrate their loyalties to one another, to their families, and to their nation. This year, except for Vanessa, all the children and grandchildren were spending the holiday elsewhere—on islands, as someone in the group had noticed, Mount Desert Isle, Long Island's North Shore, Martha's Vineyard—which had somewhat diminished the occasion in importance and intensity, although no one said as much. They acted as if the absence of their offspring were both desired by them and planned and were not, as it appeared, a changing of the guard. The Coles so far had no grandchildren. Their only child, Vanessa, was adopted and at thirty had been married and divorced twice, but had remained childless—"barren," as she put it.

It was nearly silent there by the shore—low waves washing the rocks at Vanessa's feet, a soft wind sifting the tall pines behind her—and she could hear her thoughts clearly, for they were cold and came to her in words and sentences, rather than feelings, as if she were silently reciting a list or a recipe she'd memorized years ago. She was not happy, Vanessa told herself, not one bit, and she wished that she had stayed in Manhattan. It was always the same here, year after year, her mother and father's annual Fourth of July show, and though it was more her father's show than her mother's, that didn't make it any better. Not for her. Everyone had a show, she believed, and this was not hers, not anymore, if it ever had been, when she heard in the distance a low humming sound, a light, intermittent drone that rose and fell, surged and lapsed back almost into silence and then returned and grew louder.

She realized that it was an airplane. She had never before heard or seen an airplane at the Second Lake. Rangeview was the largest of only a half-dozen rough-hewn log camps, a few of which were elaborately luxurious, located in the forty-thousand-acre privately owned wilderness, the Tamarack Wilderness Reserve. Vanessa's grandfather Cole had been one of the original shareholders. When shareholders in the Reserve—*members,* they were called—or their invited guests flew up from Boston or New York City in a private airplane, which they sometimes did, as it was a long, arduous day trip on the Delaware & Hudson train to Westport and by automobile from there, they came up the Hudson Valley and flew in from Lake Champlain north of the mountain called Goliath. They landed their airplane in a broad, mowed pasture over in the village of Tunbridge, three miles west, where they were met by a car sent from the Reserve clubhouse, so that an internal-combustion engine was never heard nor an airplane seen inside or above the Reserve itself or even above the Tamarack clubhouse and golf course. The mountains and forests and the lakes and streams were held for the exclusive use and enjoyment of members and their guests, most of whom, at least those who did not have their own camp on the Second Lake, stayed at the grand, hotel-like clubhouse and the cottages that surrounded it. The mountains and forests and lakes and streams were off-limits to strangers, tourists, and the inhabitants of the several hamlets in the region—except of course for the local people lucky enough to be employed by the members at their camps or at the associated clubhouse, cottages, and golf course as servants, caretakers, cooks, caddies, and guides. They were allowed onto the Reserve and club grounds, but only to work, and not to fish or hunt or hike on their own.

Now Vanessa could hear the airplane clearly and steadily. Though she could not see it, she knew it was coming in from the north, flying low, tracing the Tamarack River to the First Lake and on to its headwaters here at the Second. Suddenly the airplane appeared in the northern sky just above a line of black silhouetted spruce trees. It was rising in the distance over the water quickly, its gleaming belly exposed to the waning sun, as if the pilot had decided to take in the view of the entire lake and surrounding mountains and the darkening sky, when she heard the engine cut back. The airplane—a pale gray biplane with scarlet trim and two open cockpits, a goggled, hatless pilot in the forward cockpit, the other empty—slowed there, seeming almost to pause in flight and hover, when it banked to the west, heading toward the mountain wall that plunged straight into the glittering water.

It was a seaplane with two large pontoons, and she thought she was watching a man about to crash his airplane deliberately against the thousand-foot vertical slab of gray granite, and she forgot her cold thoughts and grew almost excited, for she had never seen anyone kill himself and realized that in some small way she'd always wanted to and was surprised by it. The pilot seemed about to smash the airplane against the rock face of the mountain, when, less than a hundred yards from it, he banked hard to the left, dipped the wings back to horizontal, cut the engine speed nearly to stopping, and swiftly descended toward the water. The airplane touched down at the far side of the lake, broke the surface, and slid into the water, unfolding high fans of silver spray behind the pontoons. Vanessa was relieved, of course, but felt a flicker of disappointment, too.

Her parents and their friends stood smiling on the near shore in front of the camp. They clapped their hands appreciatively and gazed across in a welcoming way at the pilot of the airplane. Near them four Adirondack guide boats had been drawn up onto the bank and turned over to dry. Vanessa's mother sat gracefully on one hull, her barefoot legs crossed at the ankles, and sipped champagne from a crystal flute. From her distance, Vanessa admired her mother's gentle, slightly dreamy poise, and decided that it was the dress, a cream-colored, low-necked, beltless frock by Muriel King that hung straight from the shoulders. Her mother was in her early fifties, too old to look that good, Vanessa thought. It was the stylish designer dress and the simple gold bracelet, she decided. And the bare feet. The other women and the men, though they would no doubt dress more or less formally for dinner tonight, wore what they thought were north-woods hunting and fishing apparel—wool slacks, checked flannel shirts, rubber-soled boots: rugged Abercrombie & Fitch camp wear. Vanessa herself had on a pale blue sleeveless cotton blouse and a white pleated skirt that pointed nicely to her long, tanned legs and narrow feet. She wasn't so much competitive with her mother's appearance as wanting to distinguish it from hers, just as her mother, even if she had to wear dresses from Greta Garbo's personal designer here at camp and go barefoot, seemed to want to distinguish her appearance from that of the other women, who were her oldest, dearest friends. More than either of them thought, however, or wanted to think, Vanessa Cole and her mother were alike.

At the far side of the lake in the cool shadow of the overhanging rock wall, the pilot pushed his goggles to his forehead, squinted, and peered across at the cluster of people standing by the overturned guide boats and, half hidden in the ancient pines behind them, the wide deck and screened porch and outbuildings of the camp. The airplane rocked gently in the water. The camp was a low structure made of barked, hand-sawn logs, a nice-looking place, larger and more lavish than he'd expected, and a lot less rustic. But he should have known: Dr. Cole was old New York and Connecticut money, piles of it. The pilot counted eight people—then, when he noticed the tall, slender figure of a woman standing a couple of hundred yards from the others, nine—and was surprised and a little downcast. When he'd accepted Dr. Cole's invitation to come to the Second Lake and see his collection of Heldons, he had hoped for something a little more private. He hated having people watch him when he looked at pictures and wait expectantly for his remarks, which, despite his reluctance to say anything at all, he always felt compelled to make. Actually, what he hated was his inability to say nothing, simply to look at the pictures in thoughtful silence.

He saw Dr. Cole lift his cocktail glass in the air and extend it toward the airplane, and the pilot waved back. He inched the throttle forward, punched the pedal under his right foot and turned the pontoon rudders, bringing the airplane around to starboard. Gradually he increased engine speed and drove the aircraft out of the shade of the mountain into the twilight, thumping it through the low, dappled ripples and across the lake as if the aircraft were a motorboat. He knew it was forbidden to run a motorboat on the Tamarack Lakes—nothing allowed on the water but genuine, silent, handmade Adirondack guide boats—and wondered if there were rules against seaplanes. Not yet, but now that he'd flown his four-year-old Waco biplane in, give them a week and there would be.

The pilot scouted along the shore below the camp for a shallow beach and found it close by the young woman standing away from the others. She seemed lost in thought, in a blue mood, and did not look at him, but did not seem to be avoiding him, either. She was like an exhibit, a piece of sculpture set at the edge of the lake—part of the view. She was very pretty, he noticed when he drew near shore. Beautiful, even. She had high, almost Andean cheekbones and sharp, precise features, bright blue eyes, and full lips. She wore no makeup, or none that he could discern, and her long, gingery hair hung loosely over her shoulders. Broad shoulders for a slender woman, he noticed. She must be an athlete, a swimmer or a serious canoeist. Maybe she's an actress, he thought. She looks like an actress. Her face was vaguely familiar to him, and then he remembered who she was.

He pulled the throttle back, shoved the rudders full left, and brought the airplane around and into the wind to keep it from slithering while anchored and getting itself all weather cocked. It would be nice if the Coles had a dock to tie up to, but there were rules, of course, against lakeside structures, other than the camps themselves, which had to be built a certain distance from the water and be as invisible from the lake as possible, and strictly on the Second Lake. The illusion of wilderness was as important to maintain as the reality. The pilot's wife sometimes called the Reserve a zoo for trees, but that was extreme, he thought, a particularly European point of view.

Cutting the engine, the pilot stood in the cockpit, took off his goggles altogether, and scanned the slate blue lake from one end to the other in the near dark, quickly memorizing its dimensions and the ins and outs of its shoreline. He had meant to get over here earlier in the day but had made the mistake of ducking into his studio after breakfast and by the time he checked his watch it was nearly four thirty. Alicia had been right, it was a national holiday, and he should have allowed himself to forget his politics for once and enjoy the holiday like everyone else in America today, go down to the river with her and the boys for a Fourth of July picnic and then, while they were napping, fly over to the Reserve, see the doctor's collection of Heldons, and be home before nightfall, in time to drive Alicia and the boys to watch the fireworks with the rest of the locals. But instead he'd worked late.

He eased himself from the cockpit and stepped onto the left pontoon, tossed his mud-hook anchors into the water, tugged at the lines until he knew they were snagged in the lake bottom, and kneeled and tied the lines tightly to cleats. The woman had turned and was watching him, still with the same distant, broody expression on her exquisite face. She had very smooth, white skin that shone. He glanced up at her. A world-class beauty who knows it, he thought. Nothing but trouble. He had recognized her face from photographs he'd been shown by Alicia. He knew she was Dr. Cole's daughter, Vanessa, the one-time Countess de Moussegorsky or something like that. For years, ever since she'd been presented to society, both in New York and in Washington, she had been the subject of much gossip, local, national, and international, although the pilot was more familiar with the local than the rest, except for when Alicia from time to time called his attention to a piece in one of the glossy women's magazines or *Vanity Fair* or the *New Yorker* or the society pages of one of the New York papers. Her celebrity was of a type that mattered more to Alicia than it did to him. The woman was nothing more than a socialite, for God's sake. A parasite. Come the revolution, no more socialites.

He eased himself down from the pontoon into the shallow water and strode ashore, wetting his boots and his trousers to the knees and seeming not to care. Vanessa smiled and brought her hand to her mouth to cover it. The pilot's easy, unselfconscious directness was a sudden relief to her, and all her gloom lifted. He wore a collarless leather jacket with ribbed cuffs and waistband and under it a white dress shirt open at the throat. The pilot was a large man, in his early forties, tall and broad, with big, square hands, and moved with the grace of a man who liked the feel and appearance of his own body, although he did not seem to be vain. His black straight hair fell loosely forward over his brow and gave him a harried, slightly worried look. Because of the goggles he wore when flying and his permanently tousled hair, his fair skin was unevenly tanned. He had very dark, almost black, deep-set eyes, and a prominent, long arc of a nose, and his face was wide, with a jutting chin, slightly underslung. He was not a remarkably handsome man, but to Vanessa—because of his size, his physical grace, intense coloring, and prominent, symmetrical features— an extremely attractive one nonetheless.

He stamped his boots on the ground and said hello to the woman, turned to the others in the distance and waved in a loosely friendly way and started walking toward them.

"Who are you?" the woman asked. Her voice was low and husky, a smoker's voice.

He turned back to her and smiled. "Jordan Groves. From over in Petersburg. Who are you?"

"I'm not sure you're allowed to bring an airplane in here," she said.

"Me neither. Your father invited me over. He and I met on the train the other day coming up from the city."

"So you know who I am."

"Yeah, sorry." He hesitated. "You're Vanessa . . ."

"Von Heidenstamm."

"Von Heidenstamm. Née . . . Cole."

"Right. And you're . . ."

"Jordan Groves."

"The famous artist."

"So they tell me."

"Né . . . ?"

"Groves."

"Well, aren't we something, then?" she said and came forward and, smiling up at him, hooked his arm with hers and walked him toward the others, who had waited for him by the shore until Vanessa seemed to have taken possession of the visitor and then they had moved away from the nearly darkened lake and were now making their leisurely way back up the piney embankment, returning to the camp.

As they walked, Jordan Groves glanced at her bare arms and said, "Aren't you a little cold?"

"Yes," she said. "I am. Let me have your jacket until we get inside."

He shrugged out of his jacket and draped it over her shoulders. She smiled gratefully and walked ahead of him, while he lagged a few steps behind and admired her long, confident strides and straight back and head held high as if she'd just done something to be proud of. A damned beautiful animal, he said to himself. But a woman to watch is all. Not to touch. Maybe to paint is all. Definitely a woman to be careful of. The way she walked reminded him of a woman he had met in Budapest many years ago, and her figure was like that of another he'd met in Toronto just last year. He hadn't painted either woman and was glad of it, but he'd touched both, and both had left him feeling badly used—more by himself than by them.

When they reached the camp, Vanessa hooked the artist's arm firmly with hers, and once inside proceeded to introduce him to the people there one by one, even to her father, as if Jordan Groves were her guest and not her father's.

"Jordan Groves and I are practically old friends," Dr. Cole said. "Am I right, Jordan?"

"Yes. Practically."

There was a fire crackling in the huge stone fireplace. Mrs. Cole had lit the kerosene lamps and a few candles, and the room glowed in soft, rust-colored light. It was a large, handsome room, and the interior of the house smelled like the forest that surrounded it. Except for Dr. Cole and his wife, Evelyn, Jordan Groves forgot the names and faces of the houseguests as quickly as they were given to him. They each shook his hand and stepped away. Plutocrats, he decided at once. Leisure-class Republicans. People with inherited wealth and no real education and, except for the doctor, no useful skills. Not Groves's sort, he knew, and they knew it, too, and were no more curious about him than he about them.

A seaplane landing in the lake, however—that was fairly intriguing. Quite a sight, way out here. The fellow probably thinks the rules are made for other people, though, not him. Another of Carter's left-wing artist types. Among his friends and colleagues, Dr. Cole was himself a left-wing artist type—although he was certainly no supporter of Franklin Roosevelt and his so-called New Deal and was not an artist, merely a man who, since college, appreciated art and enjoyed a little amateur sketching and watercolor painting and photography. They thought of their old friend as harmlessly creative.

Mrs. Cole went to the bar to fix Jordan a whiskey. Dr. Cole said, "So glad you could make it, Jordan. Quite an entrance, I must say," he said and laughed appreciatively. The doctor was nearly a foot shorter than Jordan, with the beginnings of a humped back that made him seem even shorter than he was. His pale face and round body were soft, jellied, but he had beautiful white hands with long, slender fingers. Of course, a surgeon's hands, Jordan thought. The doctor's grip was quick and careful, in and out, with no friendly squeeze or masculine shake. In another man, Jordan would have thought the handshake effeminate. With this man, merely careful. Protecting his tools.

"Yes, well, sorry about that," Jordan said and looked around the large, high-ceilinged living room for the Heldons. After Jordan Groves himself, the most famous artist residing in the region was James Heldon. In fact, the two were among the best-known living artists in the country, at least among Americans. In those years the truly famous artists, the painters and sculptors prized by museums and serious collectors, were European. Though often linked by critics and reviewers, mainly because they both were figurative artists and American and resided at least part-time in the Adirondack mountains of northern New York, Groves and Heldon, as artists, were very different. Heldon's oils and pastels were mostly transcendental, expressionistic landscapes of the north country—the mountains, lakes, and skies that the artist had lived among part-time for decades—and blurred, etherealized nudes of his wife. He was very popular in New York City and Philadelphia art circles. His paintings, in spite of being rather small, for he painted in the forest and on the mountains *en plein air,* sold for many thousands of dollars. The tonier and more academic critics loved him. Jordan Groves, on the other hand, was valued and known mainly for his graphic work—woodcuts, etchings, prints—although he also, but only occasionally, painted in oils and pastels and had done a number of celebrated murals for the WPA. He had become known increasingly, both in the United States and the Soviet Union, notoriously here, lovingly there, for his politics. Thus he was often compared to the great Mexican muralists Orozco, Sequeiros, and Diego Rivera. In recent years, however, he had become famous for his commissioned illustrations of limited-edition books—classics like *The Scarlet Letter* and *Huckleberry Finn* and *Aesop's Fables*—for which he was paid large sums of money. While Jordan Groves admired James Heldon's work, he had a nagging suspicion that Heldon, who was nearly the same age as he and whom he had so far avoided meeting, did not consider him a serious artist and thought of him as merely an illustrator and left-wing propagandist. As Jordan saw it, the problem, the crucial difference between the two north country artists, was political, not aesthetic.

Even so, James Heldon was himself viewed as a man of the left—at least by the critics and general public. He had spoken out often in support of the workers and any number of Roosevelt's domestic programs, but he had always been careful to avoid being connected with causes and positions taken up by the Communist Party, the Comintern. Which was not Jordan's way. Though Jordan had refused to join the party—he was not a joiner, he often said, but as long as the battle was just, didn't care who fought alongside him—he had donated a group of his most valuable pictures to the Soviet people and had painted several murals in Moscow honoring the workers' heroic role in the revolution. He wondered where Heldon would come down on this Spanish thing. The Italians were in the war now, and in spite of getting thrashed in March by the Spanish Republicans at Guadalajara, they were spoiling for a second go-round. Bombing Ethiopia in May had bolstered their confidence and had probably improved their flying skills.

Dr. Cole led Jordan Groves from painting to painting. Hanging on the varnished plank walls of Rangeview were more than a dozen small Heldon landscapes that he had purchased over the years from the artist himself, with a dozen more hanging in his Park Avenue apartment and their home in Tuxedo Park. Vanessa followed the two men, but kept a few feet behind them, silent and watching and listening, like a reluctantly roused predator, operating more on instinct than need. She liked the artist's hard concentration, how he stood before each painting and literally stared at it for long minutes, as if it were alive and moving and changing shape and color before his eyes; and she liked that he offered no comment, no praise, compliment, or critique; just looked and looked and said nothing and moved on to the next, until he had seen them all, then returned to three or four of the landscapes for a second long look.

Her father, to his credit, did not ask Jordan's opinion or evaluation of the pictures, although he was justly proud of having purchased them and proud of his personal friendship with James Heldon— who was, after all, practically an Adirondack neighbor and a fellow second-generation member of the Reserve—and confident of the long-term value of the pictures in the art market. Dr. Cole collected paintings that he loved to look at, but he also made sure that they were sound investments. He owned three John Marin watercolors that had been painted when Marin visited the region in 1912 and '13, a large Jonas Lie, two very fine Winslow Homers, and a landscape by William Merritt Chase that he had inherited from his mother. They were the nucleus of a small, but tasteful and increasingly valuable collection. He insisted that his focus was solely on paintings of his beloved Adirondacks, but in Vanessa's view her father collected art in order to collect artists, because he himself was not one and wished he were. And now, apparently, he was collecting Jordan Groves.

She reached out and touched Jordan on the shoulder. "Do you want your jacket back?"

"Thanks, yes," he said and watched her slip it off her shoulders and allowed her to drape it over his. "Wouldn't mind another whiskey, either," he said and handed her his glass.

She went to the bar, and he drifted along behind, enjoying that particular perspective, and Dr. Cole followed him. Without looking at him, Jordan said to the doctor, "Those are fine pictures. Heldon is a lousy painter, you know, but a wonderful artist. It's probably lucky for him that he can't paint," he said, and instantly regretted it. He knew that he was showing off for the girl. He should have said nothing, but once begun, it was hard to stop. "If he could paint, he'd be a lousy artist and merely a wonderful painter. Lucky for him he can't. Lucky for you, too. Since you've bought so many of them,"

"What do you mean, 'If he could paint, he'd be a lousy artist'?" Dr. Cole asked.

"He's religious. Heldon is a forest Christian."

"I don't quite understand."

"If he could paint, he'd lose his religion, and he wouldn't have anything to replace it with, except technique. And technique alone won't hold value."

"Daddy," Vanessa said, "you shouldn't expect one artist to praise another. Especially when he's afraid the other artist is better than he is. You are, aren't you, Mr. Groves? A little?"

"What?"

"Afraid."

"Afraid of you, maybe. But not James Heldon."

"Come, come, Vanessa," Dr. Cole said. "Don't get started. Here, while you're doing that for Mr. Groves, refill my drink, too, will you?" He handed her his empty glass and stepped between his daughter and his guest.

Vanessa obeyed, but glanced back at Jordan like a cat who'd been interrupted at her meal and would soon return.

Timidly, a little reluctantly, the others in the group, once the artist had taken a seat by the fire and appeared to open himself to them, gathered near him and one by one made a polite effort to draw him into light conversation. Red Ralston's suggestion that he ought to paint the early sunset, catch the alpenglow here at the Second Lake, went nowhere, and Ralston slipped off to the porch to smoke a cigar in the gloaming. Jennifer Armstrong asked Jordan if he'd ever been to the Second Lake before, and he said no, and she offered him a canapé, which he accepted. "But isn't it lovely?" she asked him.

"What?"

"The Second Lake."

He agreed, the Second Lake was lovely.

"What about the Reserve?" she asked.

"What about it?"

"Isn't it lovely?"

He said yes, the Reserve was lovely.

"We're damned fortunate Carter's held on to the old family homestead," said Harry Armstrong.

Dr. Cole laughed at that. "Yes, the 'homestead'! Not quite, Harry. That's still the family farm in Greenwich, and as soon as my mother goes, it goes, too."

"Carter, really," Mrs. Cole exclaimed.

Harry Armstrong said to Jordan, "I mean, we're lucky because, even though we're members, we can't build our own camps out here on the lake. Not anymore. Got to preserve the Reserve, I guess. But at least we get to use Carter's Rangeview. The Reserve's put a freeze on any new construction up here, you know."

Jordan said that he didn't know.

Bunny Tinsdale was curious about Jordan's airplane, was it his own?

"It's a 1932 Waco," Jordan told him. He'd bought it new at the factory in Troy, Ohio, four years ago and had flown it to

Lake Placid, where he'd had it fitted out with pontoons. Then he had flown to his home on the Tamarack River, where he'd landed on water for the first time. "Nearly dumped the damned thing."

"Interesting," Tinsdale said. And how long had he been flying?

"Since I was a kid," Jordan said. He took a sip from his drink. He didn't want to talk about flying with this crowd.

"And where did you learn to fly?"

"Well, I took the army flying course at Ashburn Airport on Chicago's South Side."

"So you were in the war?"

"Yes. Late. In 1918. I was in the Ninety-fourth Aero Squadron."

"You flew under Eddie Rickenbacker?" Dr. Cole said.

"Briefly."

"Did you shoot down any Germans?" Vanessa asked and smiled.

"Yes. Two. Both on the same day."

"And what day was that?" she asked.

"April 4, 1918."

"Must have been quite a day," she said.

He didn't answer, and she smiled.

Bunny Tinsdale wanted to know about flying a plane with pontoons. "Is it harder than flying a regular plane? You know, with wheels?"

In the air the pontoons were deadweight and slowed the airplane down, Jordan explained, but in the water it wasn't much different from running a motorboat. Once you got the hang of it.

"Where the heck do you actually *fly*?" Jennifer Armstrong wondered. "I mean, with those things on it, pontoons. What do you actually *use* it for?"

"Transportation," Jordan said. He flew it mainly here and there in the north country.

"Interesting."

But he was thinking of taking a trip to Greenland soon, Jordan told them, and would fly it there. He wanted to make some pictures of the glaciers to illustrate a book. An account of his previous travels there.

"Your own book? One you wrote yourself?"

"Yes."

"Interesting," Jennifer Armstrong said and got up to make herself another drink.

"You'll stay for dinner, won't you, Mr. Groves?" Evelyn Cole said. "We have a dozen lake trout from this morning's expedition. Our boys are *very* good providers."

The pilot felt suddenly physically fatigued, as if he'd been running. He took a few seconds to answer, then said, "I don't think so. It's getting dark, and I'm expected at home. But thanks." He wondered if her "boys" were the doctor and his friends, or the local men working in the kitchen shack out back. His friend, Hubert St. Germain, was the regular guide and caretaker for the Coles. He wondered if Hubert was the good provider.

Maybe he ought to stay for dinner, Jordan thought. He was as aware as Vanessa that the good doctor collected artists, but the man also collected art, and Jordan had a few small, unsold Adirondack landscapes and a dozen woodcuts that he wouldn't mind placing in Dr. Cole's collection. They might make the doctor reconsider his passion for James Heldon. Jordan was conscious of Vanessa standing behind him, and he waited for her to say something that he would have to defend himself against without at the same time alienating her father. It was not easy for him to be polite to these people.

But Vanessa said nothing. It amused her to see the degree to which her parents and their friends bored and slightly irritated the artist and the ways he did the same back to them. She left the room for a moment and returned wearing a pale linen jacket over her blouse. She made herself a martini and again took up her position behind Jordan, who was slumped in a wide, cushioned chair made of wrist-thick branches of a birch tree with the bark left on for rustic effect. It was an uncomfortable chair, and she could tell from his glum expression that to Jordan it was also ugly and pretentious, and so it was to her now, too. Most of the furniture was of that type—it was the desired style, meant to look handmade, cumbersome, rough, as if built by a local woodsman with ax and adze, which was in fact the case—but up until this moment she had seen it only through her parents' and their friends' admiring eyes.

She leaned down and placed her face next to Jordan's and whispered, "I won't be happy until you take me for a ride in your airplane." Her cheek nearly brushed his, then pulled away. The others seemed not to notice. They were discussing the annual fireworks display at the Tamarack clubhouse tonight, which they could not see from the camp unless they rowed out to the far side of the lake in the guide boats around nine o'clock and faced the northeast sky above the distant clubhouse and golf course. They wondered whether it would be worth the effort.

"When?" Jordan asked her.

"Now," Vanessa said.

Jennifer Armstrong said, "I hate to complain, but every year I'm rather disappointed. The fireworks are really mostly for the locals, I think."

"Good public relations," Bunny Tinsdale said. "Bread and circuses for the hoi polloi."

Jordan stood and declared that he had to leave. He thanked the doctor for his hospitality and for showing him the Heldons, nodded to the group, and quickly departed from the room. The sun had disappeared entirely behind the Great Range, and the lake was black, and the temperature was dropping fast. Outside on the deck he stopped to roll and light a cigarette and checked the wind. In the west, above the sooty mountains, the sky had faded from lemon to silken gray. The air was still smooth, he noted. The blue-black eastern sky was clear, with swatches of stars already visible, and over the treetops behind the camp a half-moon was rising. The pilot smoked his cigarette and made his way in the gathering darkness down the path to the lake and walked along the shore to his anchored airplane.

She was waiting for him when he got there. She stood barefoot on the rocky beach in her white skirt and linen jacket, looking eager and elegant and brave. Jordan said nothing to the woman, and she said nothing to him. He stepped into the water and she followed. Grabbing a wing strut with one hand, he swung himself onto the nearer pontoon, turned, and extended his other hand to her. Refusing his help, she stepped gracefully onto the pontoon and made her way along the lower wing to the aft cockpit and situated herself there.

Jordan untied and retrieved first one anchor, then the other, and quickly seated himself in the forward cockpit. He switched on the ignition, double-checked fuel and oil-pressure gauges, and started the large radial engine. The propeller rotated feebly for a few seconds, then the engine coughed, grumbled, and came to life. Jordan cut the float rudders to starboard, bringing the airplane around, facing it into the light northeast wind. He nudged the throttle forward, and the aircraft began to accelerate, bumping across the low ripples of the lake on a bearing that took it gradually away from shore, toward the farther side of the narrow lake.

As the airplane passed the camp, Jordan glanced to his right and saw that Dr. Cole and his guests had come out onto the deck. They watched the airplane reach the far side of the lake where it had first touched down and thought they saw a passenger in the cockpit behind the pilot, but couldn't make out who it was.

Without breaking speed, the pilot brought the airplane around to starboard again, carving a tight turn into the northeast, heading it directly into the wind, then pushed the throttle ahead another notch, accelerating as it came out of the turn. At about forty knots, the airplane squarely hit the step, the gathering surge of water just ahead of the pontoons. As the nose of the airplane rose, the pilot pulled back on the control yoke and pushed the throttle all the way forward. For a few seconds the airplane fought the water, working its way up and over the step, until it leveled off, and then it was airborne and climbing.

From the deck of the camp, Dr. Cole and his wife and their friends watched the airplane rise off the surface of the lake and soar overhead and disappear into the night sky behind them, and when they turned to go back inside and get dressed for dinner, they realized almost as one that the artist's passenger was Dr. Cole's daughter, Vanessa. No one said it aloud until the couples were in their respective bedrooms—Dr. Cole and his wife in the master suite, a large, high-ceilinged bedroom just off the living room, with its own fireplace, and the others in the guest quarters, a low structure called the Lodge that was attached to the main building by a roofed-over walkway—when husband and wife said to each other, "Well, *that* was fast," and, "I don't know where she gets the nerve . . . ," and, "I didn't even see her leave the room."

Dr. Cole pulled on his dinner jacket, brushed his lapels, and shot his cuffs. Checking himself in the mirror, he straightened his bow tie and said to his wife, "What do you think? Is she all right?"

"No, of course not! When has Vanessa ever been 'all right,' Carter?"

The doctor sat down heavily on the bed and placed his right hand over the left side of his chest and winced. His face had gone pale, and he was sweating.

"What's wrong?" his wife said.

"Nothing."

"You don't look right."

"I'm fine, damn it! Leave me alone! It's just . . ." He grabbed his left arm, high up.

"No, you're not fine. Are you in pain?" She came over to him and put her hands on his shoulders and stared at him.

"It's . . . it's just indigestion. Heartburn is all. Leave me alone," he said and shook her off him. "Jesus Christ," he muttered through gritted teeth, "I'm a doctor, I know when something's wrong."

WITH THE ALTIMETER READING 2,250 FEET, JORDAN SLID THE wheel slowly, smoothly forward, pulled back the throttle, and stopped climbing. He put the airplane on a heading for the clubhouse grounds two miles away. Below them the black forest flashed past. Jordan turned in the cockpit and looked back at Vanessa. She was smiling broadly, her hair tossed wildly by the wind. She lifted her arms over her head and opened her hands wide.

"Can you fly an airplane?" he shouted above the roar of the engine and the wind.

"Of course not!"

"Put your hands on the wheel!"

"What?"

"You fly it! Hold on to the wheel!"

She grasped the control yoke with both hands, looked at him as if for approval, and he nodded. She's done this before, he thought.

"You're sure you've never flown an airplane?"

"Never!"

He said, "Okay. Five things to remember! Five precepts."

She laughed. "Only five?"

"*Observe! Think! Plan! Execute!* And *abandon!* You use *abandon* if *execute* doesn't work, and then you go back to *observe!*"

"Okay!" she shouted. "You're crazy, you know!"

He let go of the yoke, and suddenly Vanessa was flying the aircraft. She seemed too eager to take the controls, too fearless. He kept his hands loosely on the yoke, not giving the airplane over entirely to her. He was not convinced that she had never flown before. He turned back and asked her to repeat the five precepts.

"Observe!" she began. "Think! Plan . . . and what?"

"Execute!"

"Right, execute! And abandon!"

"Good! So what do you observe?"

"Oh, Christ! *Everything!*"

"Start with altitude, bearing, speed!"

"Okay, okay, okay!" she yelled and looked down at the gauges. "Altitude! I've got the altitude! And the compass, so that's bearing! And here's speed!"

"Good! What else can you observe?"

She peered around his broad shoulders and over the cowling and saw in the distance the moonlit roof of the clubhouse and some other smaller buildings nearby and the broad expanse of the golf course and then more dark forest and beyond the forest the mountains, Sentinel and the big one, Goliath. "Oh, my God! Mountains coming up!"

"Right! So *think*! Precept two!"

"We're not high enough."

"Right! So *plan*! Precept three!"

She nodded soberly and said nothing. Jordan smiled and waited for her to try gaining altitude on her own. They passed over the rambling rooftops of the Tamarack clubhouse and cottages and outbuildings, the automobiles and trucks and horse-drawn buggies parked along the roadway and in the oval drive, and the large crowd of people waiting on the side of the eighth fairway for the fireworks to begin, their faces all upturned, gazing at the biplane as it soared over them and on into the Adirondack night.

He felt the yoke under his hands move slowly, steadily back, felt the nose lift slightly as the airplane lost speed and gained altitude, and knew that she was executing. Not enough speed, though, and not enough lift. "Give it some more power!" he shouted. A few seconds later the engine noise grew louder, and they began climbing faster. The airplane rose up and over the treeless cliffs of the summit of Sentinel, topping it by less than five hundred feet. Now they were passing over Bream Pond, toward Goliath, but the airplane needed to gain another fifteen hundred feet quickly to avoid slamming into the broad, granite shoulder of the mountain, and there was not enough time to do it at this speed, unless she abandoned her plan and cut hard to starboard, bringing the airplane back toward Bream Pond, Sentinel, and the Tamarack clubhouse and grounds. He waited five seconds, ten, and figured he had five more before he'd take over the airplane, when he felt the yoke turn in his hands a few degrees to the right, from twelve o'clock to two. The airplane dipped to the right, but was losing altitude. Then gaining speed, fighting torque, and pulling out of the turn. But it was too low now and headed for a stand of tall pines on a bluff east of the mountain, unless she saw the notch ahead and slightly to the right and aimed for it.

"Observe!" he yelled and pointed at the notch, a cleft between the pine-topped bluff and the cliffs on the south side of Bream Pond.

She righted the airplane and brought it slowly around, flashing through the notch and missing the trees below by barely a hundred feet. Suddenly they were flying over the still, moon-silvered waters of Bream Pond. Jordan tightened his grip on the controls and took over the aircraft.

"Hey!" she shouted. She tried to turn the wheel left and right, pushed it forward and back. Nothing happened. The airplane was his again. "I'm not *through* yet!" she yelled.

"Yes, you are," he said, and he slowed the plane to ninety knots, then seventy, and looped around at the far end of the pond, and came back up its length, where he dropped it into the water a few hundred yards from shore. He taxied back to a short, sandy beach and let the airplane drift to a halt in shallow water, and shut down the engine. The world was suddenly silent, except for the dying waves from the airplane's wake lightly slapping the pontoons.

"This is a good place to watch the fireworks," he said to her and pointed back the way they had come. "You can sit here and see them through the notch."

"Brilliant!" she exclaimed. "But better from the shore," she said, and hitching her skirt to her long white thighs, she climbed out of the cockpit and splashed to the beach. "Come on! Follow me!" She made her way quickly up the slope, to where an overgrown lumber road passed the pond, and waved to him from there. "C'mon! There's a grassy clearing I know just down the road where the view is truly splendid. I walk up here lots to swim in the pond and picnic and get away from the family. We can lie on our backs and see the whole valley and sky from there!"

Jordan watched her as she disappeared behind a stand of white birches gleaming in the moonlight. She reappeared seconds later on the far side of the trees, striding down the narrow dirt road toward the opening to the valley and the clear view of the Tamarack clubhouse and golf course below. He watched her walk out of moonlight into darkness, and he knew what would happen if he followed. He started the engine, and the airplane drifted down shore a ways, where he brought it around to face the wind and open water.

"Hey! Where the hell are you going?" she hollered.

"Home! It's late!"

"What? You're leaving me here?"

"You left me, remember? Once you abandon ship, there's no getting back aboard!"

"You *bastard!*"

He didn't answer. He shoved the stick forward and quickly moved across the smooth water, hit the step, and accelerated across the skin of the pond as if on skids on ice. Then the airplane lifted free of the water and rose with a roar into the darkness. He was flying through the notch at about twenty-five hundred feet, still climbing, and prepared to make the long, rising turn to the northeast, to pass over Goliath and on to Petersburg and the Tamarack River and his home, where he was late and his wife and sons awaited him, when he looked off to his left and saw the sky light up. A battery of hissing rockets sent long, fiery arcs of red, yellow, green, and blue into the blackness, like thunderbolts cast against the gods. High in the sky above the Reserve, the rockets finished their ascent, lost their force and floated for a second, and one after the other exploded with a luminous flash—gigantic flowers of light that instantly faded, crumpled, and dissolved in the night. Trails of sparks floated back to earth like brightly colored petals. A thunderous boom echoed across the valley, and the sky filled with darkness again.

Shortly after midnight on Monday, May 3, 1937, the night train from Zurich left Switzerland, passed through Liechtenstein, stopped at Bregenz in Austria, and traveled on to the eastern shore of Lake Constance, where Switzerland, Austria, and Germany converge. At 3:30 A.M. eastern European time, as the train rounded the lake, the sky brightened, and the passengers, those who were awake, turned in their seats and admired the glistening white peaks and the blue water. The train was not crowded. Most of the passengers were Swiss businessmen traveling to initiate or complete transactions with German manufacturers and government procurement agencies. Among the passengers were a Swiss doctor in his midthirties wearing a gray wool suit and white shirt and knotted silk necktie, indistinguishable from the businessmen, and a young American woman who slumped sleeping in her seat beside him. They were alone in their first-class compartment. The man had been reading a book and now gazed intently out the window. The woman wore a tailored, brown tweed jacket and skirt and a black, wide-brimmed, Lilly Daché hat with a veil that covered her forehead and half covered her pale face. She wore no jewelry or makeup, and her long auburn hair was disheveled and needed brushing. The man nudged the young woman and pointed out the window at the lake and the mountains. Very beautiful, he said in English. The woman opened her eyes and sat up straight in the seat. She squinted and peered out the window as instructed. Where are we? she asked. We are in Germany, he answered. The town of Friedrichshafen. He indicated the three most prominent mountains south of the lake and said, Hoher, Churfirsten, and Santis. After a few seconds she said, Oh, and slumped back in her seat again and closed her eyes under the veil. In seconds the woman appeared to be sleeping. The train followed the glittering waters of the Rhine north and west into the German heartland. At exactly 7:14 A.M. central European time, as scheduled, the night train from Zurich arrived at the Hauptbahnhof in Frankfurt.

AT SIX, WELL BEFORE THE REST OF THE FAMILY WOKE, JORDAN Groves left his bed. He shaved and dressed for work in loose, paint-spattered dungarees and sweatshirt and came down the wide front stairs to the living room and went into the kitchen and let the dogs out and the cats in. Most days he carried a chunk of cheese and some bread directly to his studio and made a pot of coffee there and sat contemplatively for an hour in front of yesterday's picture before setting to work on it. It was the best time of the day for him, best for thinking, best for work. Today, however, he lingered at the house. He built a fire in the kitchen stove, let the two dogs back inside and fed them and the four cats, and reloaded the wood box—normally Alicia and the boys' morning chores—and waited for the others to come down.

Around seven thirty Wolf, still in pajamas, padded down the back stairs from the children's wing and headed straight to the icebox for milk, when he realized that his father sat in the rocker by the bay window, looking out. Characteristically somber, the boy said good morning, and Jordan Groves smiled, said, "Hello, son," and, continuing to look out the window, resumed his thoughts. He was replaying the events of the previous evening, trying to recall exactly what was said and done and by whom and why. He was pretty sure he understood Dr. Cole and knew what his intentions and needs were. And the others he didn't linger over:

they were all who and what they seemed to be. The girl, though, Vanessa Von Heidenstamm, was pretty much a mystery to him. She was not who and what she seemed. But the one who was most mysterious to him, the one whose intentions and needs and behavior he understood not at all, was the man himself, Jordan Groves. Why had he taken her up in his airplane and let her fly it so dangerously close to the mountains at night? And why had he left her there at the pond, left her to walk alone back to her family's camp at the Second Lake?

The view from the window gave on to the Tamarack River where it swerved away from the house and grounds into a broad oxbow and widened and ran north for three hundred yards of smooth, slow-running, deep water—more a pond here than a river. Directly in the artist's line of sight was the wooden riverside hangar he had built the summer he bought his airplane. Four years later, he still liked the sturdy, wide, four-square look of the structure. He had come in last night by moonlight reflected off the river. He had winched the airplane out of the water and onto the ramp and into the boathouse, and by the time he got up to the house, Alicia and the boys were already in bed asleep. Jordan stayed downstairs in his study for a while and read the new Steinbeck, *In Dubious Battle,* and, as was his habit, didn't go up to bed himself until midnight, and when he slid in next to her, Alicia did not appear to waken, which relieved him.

Wolf was the younger of the boys, just turned six. His brother, whose name was Bear, was eight. When his sons were born, Jordan had insisted on naming them for animals he admired— despite considerable resistance from their mother and her Austrian family, who said it might be all right for red Indians to name their children after animals, but not for white people. If Bear had been a girl, Jordan would have named her Puma. Wolf he would have named Peregrine. He said he wanted his children to be inspired all their lives to live up to what they were called, and since he was a devout atheist he wasn't going to name them after saints. "No Christian names," he declared, and no family names. Aside from Jordan himself and Alicia, there was no one in either family worth emulating. If when they became adults his sons wished to go by their middle names, which as a compromise had been drawn from Alicia's and his genealogies, that would be all right with him. But he was sure it wouldn't happen. By then they will have *become* their names, he said. Just as, for better or worse, he had become Jordan, and their mother had become Alicia.

Wolf drank from the chilled jug of milk, put it back in the icebox, and crossed the large, open kitchen and climbed onto his father's lap. He nuzzled against Jordan's chest and inhaled deeply the familiar smell of turpentine and paint and chemicals from the studio, his father's own smell, as comforting to the boy as his father's face and voice. Jordan wrapped his arms around his son and held him there.

"Did you see the fireworks, Papa?" Wolf asked in a faraway voice.

"I saw them from the air. On my way home."

"That must have been great, to see them from the airplane."

"Yes. It was. I'm sorry I couldn't get back in time for you to see the fireworks," Jordan said. "I got talked into giving someone a flying lesson."

"Oh. That's okay. We had fun anyhow."

Jordan eased the boy off his lap and set about making breakfast for him. A few minutes later Bear made his way down the steep, narrow back stairway to the kitchen. He gave his father a friendly wave and made for the icebox and like his brother slurped milk straight from the jug. Kittens, Jordan thought. Cubs. They know exactly what they want, and it's the same as what they need.

"Hey, how come you're making breakfast, Papa?" Bear asked.

"How come you're not?" Jordan answered and smiled.

"I don't know."

"Go get washed up and dressed, boys. Then come back and eat. We'll do something special together today," he said, and the boys quickly disappeared up the stairs.

The boys' wing of the house—a shared bedroom, bathroom, and playroom—was separated from their parents' private quarters by a long, railed walkway that looked over the vast two-story living room below, where an entire wall was taken up by a stone fireplace and hearth and an oversize cast-iron woodstove. Between the two second-floor wings were a pair of guest rooms and a guest bath. Below, adjacent to the kitchen, was the dining room, where floor-to-ceiling windows and French doors gave onto a large brook-stone terrace that Jordan had constructed around a hundred-year-old oak tree and a head-high, three-ton, gray chunk of glacial rock with a deep split in it. Off the dining room was Jordan's study, which resembled the library of a gentlemen's private club that he had once visited in London—a male sanctuary reserved for reading, drinking fifty-year-old cognac, and smoking Cuban cigars. At least that was its intended use. The center of the house, the room most used by the family together, was the kitchen, designed after the large, open country kitchens Jordan had admired long ago in Brittany. From the kitchen a narrow, roofed-over breezeway led to Jordan's studio. The breezeway was open to the elements, and in winter, to get from the house to the studio, he had to wear a coat and boots and kept them on until the fire in the studio stove got the building warm. It was a minor discomfort, but an inconvenience that Jordan liked, as if it were a daily test and proof of his willingness to work.

The house was an attractive, sprawling, physically comfortable, but essentially masculine structure. Jordan had designed it, in consultation with Alicia, naturally, and had done most of the construction himself, in the process teaching himself basic plumbing, wiring, and masonry. Carpentry had been his father's trade, and Jordan, an only child, had learned it working alongside him as an adolescent and, briefly, after he came home from the war. The unconventional layout of the house and the strict use of local materials and even the fine details of the interior—banister rails made from interwoven deer antlers, yellow birch cabinets with birch bark glued to the facing, hidden dressers built into the walls, and elaborately contrived storage units, with no clutter anywhere and minimal furniture—reflected almost entirely Jordan's taste and requirements, not Alicia's. None of the windows had curtains or drapes or even shades to block the light, and during the daytime the house seemed almost to be a part of the forest that surrounded it. And at night the darkness outside rushed in. On every wall of the house, framed prints and paintings and drawings by Jordan Groves mingled indiscriminately with pictures and small sculptures and carvings that had been given to him over the years by fellow artists—John Curry, Tom Benton, and Ed Hopper, and a Lake George landscape by Georgia O'Keeffe—usually in exchange for a work of his. Jordan believed that an artist should not have to purchase art. Exchanging artworks with your fellow artists was a way of honoring and being honored by your peers.

Jordan had purchased the land—three hundred forested acres with a small mountain of its own and a half mile of frontage on the Tamarack—the year they were married, when his pictures and illustrations had begun to sell for large sums of money. He built the studio first, and they had lived in it for two years, until Bear was born and the house was ready to receive them. Then he put up a shed large enough to store his Studebaker truck and the Ford sedan and his tools and building supplies, and a few years later built the boathouse for his floatplane. Alicia had wanted to give their home a name and tried Asgaard on him and Valhalla, but Jordan said no, too pretentious. She tried north country names like Rivermede, Shadowbrook, and Splitrock. He shook his head no and grew impatient with her. The only people who gave names to their homes and put up fancy signs at the gate, he explained, were rich people with aristocratic pretensions. Summer people. People who wanted to distance themselves from the peasants. No one local gave a name to his house. "And all indications to the contrary," he said, "we're locals."

When the boys returned to the kitchen washed and dressed for the day, Alicia came down with them. At the sight of Jordan standing at the stove cooking bacon and eggs, she raised her eyebrows in mild surprise, filled a mug with coffee, and sat at the long table and watched him. Bear and Wolf slid onto the bench at their usual places and waited.

"You want some bacon and eggs, too?" Jordan asked his wife without turning from the stove. "There's plenty."

"Coffee's enough. I'll eat later."

They were silent for a moment. The boys looked from one parent to the other and remained silent also.

Her voice rising slightly, Alicia said, "When did you come home, Jordan?"

"Around ten. You were asleep already, so I didn't wake you."

"We waited for you, and then it was too late."

"You should've gone without me. I got talked into giving someone a flying lesson. Over at the Reserve. Cole's daughter," he said

and served the boys their food. "That famous socialite. Or debu-
tante. You know the one."

"Yes. I know the one."

Alicia had met Jordan in New York City when she was nineteen and had come to America to study art curatorship at the
Pratt Institute and he had been teaching a course in printmaking.
Ten years older than she, long divorced, and a onetime student
of the famous Charles Henri, he was broke and unknown. Alicia
was the only child of a wealthy Viennese manufacturer of glass-
ware and his doting wife. The girl was nearly six feet tall, with a
creamy complexion, blue eyes that were strikingly blue, the eyes
of an Alpine goddess, Jordan had thought, and white blond hair
cut fashionably short, like a flapper's. She was the most beautiful girl at the institute, perhaps the most beautiful girl Jordan
had ever met, and her accented English was like *lieder* to him.
Halfway into Alicia's second year at Pratt, Jordan held his first
one-man show at the Knoedler Gallery, and at the crowded opening, with nearly every picture in the show already sold, he asked
her to sleep with him. When she refused, he at once proposed
marriage to her. Certain he was joking, she accepted his proposal,
and later that same night, drunk on champagne and Jordan's new
celebrity, Alicia went with him to his Greenwich Village studio
and slept with him. The next day he quit his job at Pratt. To the
consternation of her parents, Alicia dropped out of school and
moved in with him, and three months later, to their dismay, she
and Jordan eloped to Edinburgh, where it was easy for a divorced
American man to marry again and where he had long wanted to
make pictures of the scoured landscapes and winter skies of the
ancient Gaelic north.

Jordan brought his own plate from the stove and sat opposite
the boys and, head down, began to eat. He hated these morn-

ing-after conversations, when he felt judged and convicted of a minor crime, but couldn't name exactly the thing that he had done wrong and therefore could not properly apologize and get it behind them. He was good at apologizing, as long as he knew what for, and thus he almost welcomed accusations. But he was rarely given the chance. Over the years there were times, indeed many times, when he had committed minor crimes against her, but he was almost never accused of these. He was not even sure they were crimes. Nearly everything he had done that ended up hurting or depriving her, he had done with her permission and full knowledge, and therefore he could not apologize for it. The months alone in Alaska, Canada, and Greenland; his solo excursions to Cuba and the Andes; his trip to Louisiana and Mississippi; his long stays in Manhattan, London, and Paris: for his work, he insisted. On these expeditions and trips he took care not to fall in love with other women. Therefore he did not believe that he should feel guilty—except for having drunk too much, for talking too loosely to people he regarded as fools and knaves, and for indulging himself in what he regarded as harmless flirtations and brief sexual liaisons that never went anywhere dangerous. These were minor crimes, yes, but only against himself, he felt, not her. They did not threaten the status quo. They did not oblige him to feel guilty. Ashamed, perhaps, but not guilty.

"You're not working today, I take it," she said. She rolled a cigarette, a practice she'd borrowed from him years ago, and lighted it.

"No, not this morning. I've got a package of materials from Sonnelier that's waiting at Shay's in town. Thought I'd drive in with the boys and pick it up and maybe go swimming with the dogs at Wappingers Falls. Make up for last night," he added weakly.

"Yes. Fine."

"Feel like joining us?"

"No," she said, a little too quickly. "So what did you think of the famous socialite?"

"A spoiled bitch."

"A beautiful spoiled bitch?"

"You could say that."

"And her father's paintings? The Heldons? Were they beautiful, too?"

"Not really. Little altars," he said. "Altars to nature. Not nature itself."

She nodded and looked away. "Nature itself" was what Jordan painted and drew. He rarely made pictures of scenery, however, and never without evidence of the dynamic presence of human beings. To Jordan, history and politics and economics were all parts of nature. Sex, work, play: it didn't matter. To him, human beings were no less a part of the natural world than the mountains and lakes and skies that enveloped them.

"What's on your program today?" he asked.

"I want to walk," she said. "And work in the garden. And I want to think, Jordan. I need some fresh thoughts. You know what I mean?"

He didn't answer. He did know what she meant. Her thoughts—and his, too—were growing old fast. Something big was coming their way. Something uninvited and unwanted was silently approaching them. Something unavoidable. And though they didn't know what it was, they both knew it was coming. The boys had finished their breakfast and stood at the soapstone sink rinsing their dishes under the pump. Jordan told them to meet him at the car as soon as they were done and got up from the table. He called the dogs and, without touching his wife or saying anything more to her, went outside.

IT WAS A COOL, CLOUDLESS MORNING, THE AIR SO DRY IT FELT like all the moisture had been wrung from it—what Jordan enjoyed calling a perfect Adirondack day, referring not to the season or the temperature, but to the brilliant light. Winter or summer, on days like this, under a cobalt blue sky, everything in his sight was sharply detailed, as if etched with acid, making him feel he could see and touch each and every leaf on each and every tree, every patch of lichen on every rock, every boulder glistening in the stream. He drove the Ford over Balsam Hill and down the long slope to the grassy pastures of Tunbridge below, and his vision felt microscopic. Who needs the forest, when you can see the individual leaves of the individual trees? he said to himself. Who needs the mountains, when you can see the very rocks that make them? In light this clear and bright, it was all there, the entire universe, no matter where in it he looked.

Now that he was out of the house and away from Alicia's hard gaze and driving to town in the rowdy company of his sons and the dogs, he felt exhilarated—he felt restored to himself. He told the boys to crank down the rear windows and let the dogs put their heads in the wind. They were Irish setters, littermates he'd bought as pups three years ago from a breeder of champion show dogs in Saratoga Springs. The boys had been begging for a dog for months, and one spring night when he came back from a week in the city, he showed up at the door with a pair of dark red male puppies in his arms, which, during the solitary three-hour train ride north from Saratoga Springs, he'd named himself. They were to be called Dayga and Gogan, named after two of his favorite artists, Degas and Gauguin, he explained to his sons.

He pulled in at Shay's, the combined general store and post

office at the center of the village, and went inside, followed by his sons, who ran to examine the jars of penny candy.

"Good morning, Darby," Jordan said. "You've got a package from France for me?"

The man behind the counter was both storekeeper and postmaster, a balding, middle-aged man with a face pointed like a fox's and a blotched, rust-colored complexion to match. He nodded and cast a cold glance at the boys, as if to urge the father to keep a suspicious eye on them while he was away from the candy counter, then ambled into the little room at the back of the cluttered store where the mail got sorted and distributed. He lugged the carton up to the counter and set it in front of Jordan and had him sign for it. "What've you got in there? French cheese?" Darby asked.

"Art supplies."

"Americans must make good art supplies, I'd think."

"They do. Just not as good as the French." Jordan slid a dime across the glass and said, "Give 'em each a nickel's worth of what they want."

"Gum balls! The red ones! Make mine all red ones!" Bear said.

"What about you?" Darby said to Wolf.

"Half licorice sticks and half gum balls. Any color."

"That's four for a penny, y' know," Darby said. "Ten cents worth of candy. That's quite a lot for just two kids."

"It'll last a while, I guess," Jordan said.

The storekeeper bagged the candy slowly, as if reluctant to sell it, and passed the sacks to the boys. Without looking at Jordan, he said, "Heard you flew that seaplane of yours into the Second Lake last night."

"You did?" Jordan said. "Well, news gets around fast, I guess."

"Small town."

"How'd you hear it?"

"Bunch of fellows from town had to go up there and bring out Dr. Cole from his camp."

"What? Why?"

"One of his friends that was staying with him, the man come all the way out in the dark by himself to get help. Lucky most of the volunteer boys was already up to the Tamarack clubhouse with the fire truck, on account of having to run the fireworks. So they got into the lake pretty quick. Not that it made much difference."

"What the hell happened?"

"Heart attack, I guess. He was a goner by the time they got out to the camp. The daughter, Countess whatzername, they come up on her walking in from the clubhouse just when they got the old man back down from their camp. She didn't know about her father yet, so they had to tell her. For a while there they thought they was going to have to haul her over to the hospital instead of the old man, the way she was carrying on. But like I said, he was a goner. She was the one told about you flying in," he added. "The daughter. Claimed you set her down and left her up at Bream Pond," he said and chuckled.

"That's only about half right," Jordan said.

"I expect so. Say, is she really a countess? I mean, do you get to keep the title and all after you divorce the count?"

"I don't know," Jordan answered. He asked Darby if Dr. Cole's daughter and wife were still at the clubhouse, but Darby wasn't sure. The doctor's body had been taken over to Clarkson's Funeral Home in Sam Dent, ten miles away, so he thought maybe they were still staying close by, either at the Moose Head Inn in Sam Dent or over here at the clubhouse. "You know, to make preparations and all, for getting the body back down to New York City. For the funeral and all. That's where they come from, isn't it?"

Jordan nodded without answering. He grabbed the carton and hustled the boys out of the store to the car. From town he drove south on the road to the Reserve and turned up the steep incline at the entrance to the clubhouse grounds and pulled in behind a tan Packard sedan parked in the oval driveway in front of the wide veranda. Several other cars were parked there also, all with their motors running, their cloth-capped drivers—men Jordan recognized as out-of-work local men hired for the occasion, his neighbors—loading suitcases and golf bags and specially encased, custom-made fly rods and tackle boxes or standing idly by, waiting to carry their passengers to the train at Westport. On the veranda Jordan saw Vanessa and her mother and some of the people he had met the night before. He recognized the Tinsdales and the Armstrongs, but couldn't remember their names.

Russell Kendall, the manager of the club, a small, almost delicate-looking man wearing a seersucker suit and bow tie and white shoes, was talking to the group, with large gestures and exaggerated facial expressions, as if in a stage play. Jordan knew Kendall only vaguely, having seen him a few times at the open-house cocktail parties that people tossed at their summer homes, parties attended by nearly everyone not considered strictly local. He'd also caught him having a recreational drink alone at the bar of the Moose Head Inn in Sam Dent. Slumming, as it seemed to Jordan. He had large red lips half covered by a drooping blond mustache, and Jordan believed that he was a homosexual. Each time they met, Jordan Groves had to be freshly introduced to Kendall, which irritated the artist.

Although the artist knew that he would enjoy the clubhouse facilities of the Reserve—the tennis courts, the dining fit for a luxury cruise ship, the comfortable bar with a bartender from Ireland who made a first-class martini, the golf course, and the hiking trails and trout-filled lakes and streams that ran through the vast holdings of the Reserve—Jordan was not a member, nor had he ever wanted to join. One night a few years ago he'd ended up drinking late at the Moose Head with a pair of members wearing dinner jackets, flush-faced fellows his age who'd undone their ties and gone into town after the club bar had closed, and they had naively offered to put him up for membership. He was a celebrity, after all. Known for being somewhat eccentric and temperamental and thought to be politically suspect, Jordan Groves was nonetheless a famous artist. He could obviously afford the fees, and he held his liquor like a gentleman. He had said, "No, thanks, fellows. I don't want to be the first Jewish member of the Tamarack club." His sponsors said they hadn't realized he was Jewish. "I'd also be the first Negro member," he added, and they saw that he was joking and knew not to press him any further on the subject. His visit to Dr. Cole's camp yesterday was the first time that he'd actually set foot on the Reserve, and today was the first time he'd parked his car in the clubhouse driveway.

He shut off the motor and sat there for a few seconds and watched Vanessa. She was in a group of perhaps ten people, but he saw no one else. She wore a calf-length black skirt and a dark gray silk blouse with billowing sleeves and over her broad shoulders a black crocheted shawl, and she looked even more beautiful to Jordan today than when he'd seen her yesterday in the fading, late-afternoon sunlight standing alone by the shore of the Second Lake. She had on bright red, almost scarlet lipstick, and mascara, and though she was pale and her face full of sorrow, she was luminous to him, enveloped by a light that seemed to emanate from inside her. He did not think that he had ever seen a woman with a visible field of light surrounding her like that, a gleaming halo wrapped around her entire body.

He told the boys to wait for him and got out of the car and walked toward the veranda. As he approached the group, the people ceased speaking and looked at him, and then, except for Vanessa, abruptly turned away. Russell Kendall took Evelyn Cole gently by the arm and led her along the veranda toward the steps at the far end of the long, open structure, past the Adirondack chairs and wicker settees and gliders, and the others followed, although Vanessa did not. She waited with a puzzled expression on her face, as if Jordan Groves were only a vaguely remembered acquaintance approaching.

He said to her, "I just now heard about your father. I want to say I'm sorry."

"Why don't you, then?"

"What?"

"Say that you're sorry."

"I'm sorry. I am."

He was filled with an unfamiliar longing. He wanted to reach up and touch her and realized that not once yesterday had he actually touched her skin. Though she had whispered in his ear, their cheeks had not brushed. He remembered extending his hand to help her when she stepped from the water to the airplane, and a few seconds later, when she got into the cockpit, reaching again to assist her, but she had ignored his offers and not even their fingertips had touched. He had only *seen* and *heard* her.

"Yes, well, you have much to be sorry for," she said, her voice almost a whisper. She knew without looking that at the far end of the veranda her mother and Mr. Kendall and the others had turned and were watching her. She could see over Jordan's shoulder that even the drivers were watching her. She decided not to slap him, although she wanted to, and he deserved it. But a slap would not create a scene so much as end one. No one could hear them, but everyone could see them, and she didn't want the scene to end just yet.

"Yes, you're right," he said. "I do. I do have much to be sorry for. I honestly don't know what I was thinking."

"I'm afraid that I do."

"Then tell me, please," he said, and meant it. He wanted to know what he had been thinking last night when he'd left her up there at Bream Pond, and he believed her, believed that she knew what he had been thinking.

"You wanted to make love to me. And couldn't."

He inhaled sharply. She stepped down from the veranda and walked toward him, and as she swept past he smelled her perfume, the faint odor of a rose. He had seen her and heard her, and now he had smelled her. But he still hadn't touched her. "Wait," he said and reached out and took her left hand into his.

"Excuse me," she said, "but I have to leave. I have to arrange for my father's funeral."

She tried to pull her hand free. He wouldn't release it. He held it tightly, but carefully, as if her hand were a small, captured bird, terrified and fragile, struggling to escape his powerful grip without injuring itself. He felt the delicate bones and tendons turning beneath the cool, smooth skin of her hand.

"You may be right," he said. "About what I was thinking."

She looked up at him. "Well, it doesn't matter now. Does it?"

"Yes, it matters. A lot. It matters to me."

He could not help himself, and meant no disrespect or mockery: he lifted her hand to his lips and kissed it lightly and released the bird into the air.

For a split second Vanessa glared at him, as if he had indeed mocked her. Then she turned and quickly strode toward the tan sedan parked in front of his Ford. She called her mother sharply to come along and got into the rear seat of the car. The driver—a man Jordan knew, Ben Kernhold, who had once owned a now defunct machine shop over in Tamarack Forks and had made polished aluminum picture frames for him—closed the car door, cast a quick glance at Jordan, and went around to the other side, where he waited for Vanessa's mother. One by one, Evelyn Cole and the others came down the far steps of the veranda and got into their vehicles.

Slowly, like a cortege, the vehicles pulled out of the clubhouse driveway in a line and departed. Jordan stood by his car and watched them go over the hill and down, until they had disappeared from sight. Finally, he turned and, startled, saw that the manager of the club, Russell Kendall, was standing next to him.

"Oh, hello, Kendall," he said.

"Mr. Groves, you should leave now."

"So you remember my name after all."

"Yes. And I know all about last night. You and your airplane at the Second Lake. You are not welcome here, sir. You should leave at once."

"I should leave at once, eh?" He could hear his blood roaring in his ears and knew that trouble was coming. "Well, you know, I'm not sure I'm quite ready to leave yet. I've got my two little boys here, and I was thinking of showing them this grand historic structure and taking a good look at it myself. I've never been up here before. I might want to become a member someday, you know." He swung open the rear door of his car and said to his sons, "C'mon out, boys. We're going to take the tour."

The boys, sensing something wrong in their father's voice, hesitated. The dogs, Dayga and Gogan, did not. They scrambled over the boys' laps, leaped from the car, and happily took off across the broad lawn. Like hounds in wild pursuit of a fox, they galloped in ever widening, intersecting loops through flower beds, across the manicured bowling green, and onto the adjacent eighth fairway of the golf course, where last night half the town had sat on the grass waiting to watch the fireworks when Vanessa flew Jordan's airplane across the night sky above and aimed it at Sentinel Mountain and Goliath.

Kendall shouted at Jordan, "Call those dogs! We can't have unleashed dogs!"

Jordan gazed at the sky, as if half expecting to see his airplane return. What a pretty sight it must have been from here, he thought. He wished he could keep thinking about that and could ignore what was happening here. He wished he could somehow avoid what he knew was about to happen.

"Mr. Groves, call those dogs!"

"Daddy, we'll get them," Bear said and got out of the car. He called, "C'mon, Wolf!" and his younger brother followed, and the two boys ran up the slope of the fairway after the dogs. A party of golfers waved angrily at the dogs and the boys and shouted at them and sent their caddies loping over the grassy bluffs after them, which only kept the dogs happily running in more elaborate and widening circles. On the veranda a half dozen of the clubhouse staff—waiters and the two desk clerks—had stepped outside to see what was happening, several with barely concealed smiles on their faces, cheered by the slightest sign of disorder. A groundsman came around from the rear of the building, stopped, folded his arms, and took in the scene.

Jordan recognized most of the crew—local folks. Friends of his, neighbors. And they recognized him. It was the artist, Jordan Groves, from over in Petersburg in a row with Mr. Kendall. They liked the sight of the artist towering over the manager, seeming cool and calm and apparently unfazed by the little man's rage.

They were used to Kendall's tirades. The artist they believed was a good man and meant well. But he was a troublemaker and didn't seem to be aware of it. They hoped he wasn't trying to organize some kind of workers' union again, not here at the Tamarack club, like he did a year ago at the paper mill in Tamarack Forks. It was Roosevelt's Wagner Act that had given him the idea that it was legal. Two months later the mill closed its doors and moved to one of those states down South. The Tamarack Club was practically the only private employer left in the region, and if you got hired here for the summer—despite the low wages, the long hours, and the rough treatment by the members and management—you counted yourself lucky. Except for the eight weeks of July and August when the Club was open, most people in town, unless they were able to hook on to one of the WPA projects or the Civilian Conservation Corps, stayed unemployed year-round and, as much as you could in this climate, lived off the land.

Kendall turned to his staff and ordered them to catch those damned dogs, and a pair of busboys and a waiter obeyed, jogging across the lawn and onto the golf course. Then, a moment later, Jordan's sons came over the rise, each boy leading a dog by its collar, with the three club employees and the golfers' caddies trooping along behind. The boys led the dogs to the car, opened the door on the far side and put them into it, and got in themselves.

Jordan, still standing a few feet from the manager, put a feeble smile on his face and tried to appear amused by the whole thing. But he was not amused. He was very angry. He could not quite say yet what had angered him, however. Not Vanessa, certainly. And not the dogs. And not even Kendall, who was only doing his job, enforcing the rules of the Reserve.

"If you don't leave the grounds at once," Kendall said to Jordan, "I'll have you physically restrained. I'll have you arrested."

"For what? I'm not doing anything illegal."

"For trespassing!"

Jordan leaned in on him. "I'm not sure you can have me physically restrained. Not you, certainly, and not these fellows here, whom I know. These men are friends of mine. But for the sake of argument, let's say you somehow manage to have me restrained. Then you'd be holding me against my will, and I'd hardly be guilty of trespassing. No, I'll leave in my own good time."

Kendall turned to the waiters and the groundsman, who stood a few feet behind him, listening. They were unsure about what was expected of them. They were only waiters and a groundsman, after all, not security officers or bouncers. "Put him in his car," Kendall ordered. "I'm going inside to call the sheriff." He turned and stalked up the wide veranda steps and disappeared into the clubhouse, leaving four men and a teenage boy to face Jordan Groves, who gave no sign of moving.

The groundsman, Murray Bigelow, said, "Prob'ly oughta do like he says, Groves. We got nothing against you, but . . ." He shrugged helplessly and shoved his hands into his pockets and looked away, as if embarrassed. Bigelow was a ruddy, ex-lumberjack in his fifties who had worked all his life for the Brown Paper Company. Three years ago the company had sold most of its eastern Adirondack holdings to the Reserve, and Bigelow had come in from the woods and gone to work for the Club.

"When Kendall goes off like that, he makes it hell for the rest of us, Jordan," a second man, Buddy Eastman, said. He was one of the waiters and had once been a plumber and five years ago had helped the artist put in his well. "Do us a favor and go home."

"Fellows, there's no way I'm going to let Kendall or anyone else talk to me that way."

"That's just how he is," Eastman said. "He talks to everyone that way."

"I doubt it," the artist said. "Look, if out of ignorance I broke one of his Club rules by landing my plane on his goddamn lake water, or my dogs got loose and ran across his goddamn golf course, then I'll say sorry and pay the fine or whatever. But that's it. It doesn't give him the right to talk to me like I'm a bum and put me off the place. You agree with that?"

"Yeah, I suppose I do. But, hell, Jordan, give us a break here," Eastman said.

The artist leaned back against the fender of his car and folded his arms across his chest. A number of members and guests had gathered on the veranda to watch, and more were coming from the dining room and from the tennis courts as word of the quarrel spread.

Inside the car, Bear moved close to the open window and said, "Papa, can we go now?"

"In a few minutes. I've got to settle something first."

"Please, Papa?"

"In a few minutes, I said."

Kendall came back out of the clubhouse and stood glowering at the top of the steps. "You men!" he called to them. "I told you men to put him in his car!"

Murray Bigelow stepped close to the artist and in a lowered voice said, "Look, Groves, this is getting complicated. Make it easier on all of us by just letting it go. It ain't worth it, fighting with Kendall. Let it go. Believe me, we know what he's like when he's crossed."

"I'm not afraid of crossing him," Jordan said.

"You don't work for him," the groundsman said.

"C'mon, Jordan," Eastman said, and he took the artist's arm.

The artist shoved the man's hand away and gave him a hard look. The others came forward then and surrounded Jordan Groves—Murray Bigelow and Rob Whitney, another of the waiters, a man Jordan's age who had lost his dairy farm to the bank, and Carl James, a onetime traveling salesman, soft and pink and in his early sixties, and the teenage boy, Kenny Shay, the skinny blond son of the storekeeper Darby Shay. By their squared, open stance and their hands held loosely at their sides they made it clear that they weren't physically threatening the artist so much as trying merely to herd him peacefully into his car.

Jordan Groves looked from one to the other and said, "Don't do this, fellows."

From the veranda Russell Kendall shouted, "I can't reach the sheriff, so you'll have to put him off the property!"

Carl James turned and said, "That's not really our job, Mr. Kendall."

"If you want a job, you'll do what I tell you!"

"Be reasonable, Jordan," Buddy Eastman said. "You ain't helping anybody this way. We got no choice but to do what he says."

The artist looked from one to the other—the three waiters, the groundsman, and the teenage boy—and slowly shook his head. "Then I'm afraid you're going to have to do what he says. If you're able."

Buddy Eastman grabbed Jordan by his left wrist and pulled him forward and threw an arm around his neck, and Murray Bigelow and the others jumped in. They wrestled Jordan around to the front of the car, cursing at him, while he cursed back and struggled to get free. He managed a sharp head butt across Bigelow's face, sending him staggering backward, blood spurting from his nostrils, and he disabled Rob Whitney by kneeing him hard in the groin. Whitney grabbed his crotch, let out a howl of pain, and sat on the ground like a sack of potatoes. The teenage boy, Kenny Shay, let go of Jordan and quickly danced away. Fighting with a very large, very angry grown man was not something the boy was ready for.

That left Buddy Eastman and the remaining waiter, Carl James, to handle Jordan Groves alone, and they were not up to it. The artist got one arm free of Carl James's grip and shoved the man off him. He threw two quick punches that landed on James's ear and throat, and the man, nearly falling, backed away, dropped his hands to his sides, and watched from a safe distance. Taller and heavier than his remaining opponent, the artist swung Buddy Eastman around and got his other arm free. He moved into a trained boxer's stance and said, "I'll take you apart, Buddy, if I have to!"

Eastman put up his fists for a second, glared at Jordan Groves, then lowered his hands and said, "Groves, for Christ's sake, get some sense! Go home!"

Both men were panting and red faced. Slowly the artist brought his fists down. He walked around the front of his car and opened the driver's door. For a few seconds he stood there and looked across the broad, mint green lawn to the clubhouse veranda, crowded now with gaping spectators, and he saw what a foolish, harmful thing he had done to these men, four men and a boy who were his neighbors and whom he regarded as friends. What kind of man was he? A common brawler? Fighting with men who were his friends and neighbors in front of his sons. It was a shameful thing to have done. He blamed the woman, Vanessa Von Heidenstamm, for it. It was her fault. He blamed what she had said to him and what she thought she knew about him. Most of all he blamed her because she had turned her back on him. That was what had made him act this way.

He got into the car and started the motor. Then he drove slowly away from the clubhouse. Halfway down the hill to the main road, he looked into the rearview mirror and saw the ashen faces of his sons in the backseat, both of them sucking furiously on candy. He said, "Let's go swimming at Wappingers Falls, boys."

"That's okay, Papa," Bear said. "We want to go home now."

"Home? Okay, we can go swimming at home instead."

"We don't need to go swimming or anything, Papa. We just want to go home."

"What about you, Wolf?"

"Yes. Let's go home," Wolf said.

Jordan sighed. "All right." Then, after a few seconds, he said to his sons, "What happened back there, it was bad, I know. Really bad. I'm sorry you had to see it. But when a person insults you, you can't put your tail between your legs and act like you deserve it."

"I know, Papa," Bear said.

"So I can't promise you that it won't happen again."

"I know, Papa," the boy repeated.

In the east, the Spanish border crossing was located a few miles northwest of the Catalan village of Portbou. On January 2, the daily train from Paris arrived at the crossing at 4:15 P.M., right on time. It was the winter of 1937, and the train from Paris was not much, a stubby six-wheel locomotive and tender and two rickety passenger cars. The sky above the leaden sea was mottled gray and the air was damp and cold, which was unusual here, even for January. There were only four passengers, four rumpled unshaven men. They stepped from the second car to the platform one after the other and stood there for a moment. One of the men was Spanish looking, in his early thirties, and wore a dark suit and necktie and snap-brim felt fedora. He carried a briefcase and a single suitcase, as if he were returning from a minor diplomatic mission. A second passenger had a shock of pale blond, nearly white hair across his forehead. He was in his midthirties and wore a brown corduroy sports jacket and dark blue shirt open at the throat. He carried a large, much-scuffed leather suitcase. The third man, also in his midthirties, was short and square shouldered and had a pie-shaped face. He wore a trench coat and beret. His baggage consisted of a small black foot-locker, which he handled with difficulty. The fourth passenger was noticeably taller than the others and a few years older. He lugged a large canvas duffel down the steps to the platform. He walked a few steps with it and stopped and swung the duffel onto his shoulder and carried it there. Compared to his three companions, he was a big man, big overall, and though he was as dark as the fellow in the suit and fedora, he did not look Spanish, and unlike the other two would not have passed for European. He wore a short, fleece-lined leather jacket, plaid flannel shirt, and tan slacks, and he was hatless. More so than the others, his relaxed, self-assured demeanor and his clothing marked him as an American or possibly Canadian or Australian. In recent months there had been many such men crossing from France into Spain at this place, and while they stood out they were no longer unexpected. The four walked to the end of the platform where the conductor from the train directed them into the railroad station. The waiting area was empty and there was no one behind the ticket seller's cage. There was only the conductor and the four passengers. In the near corner of the high-ceilinged room a coal fire in a round-bellied iron stove gave off a faintly sulphurous smell. The conductor led the men to a closed door next to a filigreed tin sign: ADMINISTRATION DES DOUANES. The conductor opened the door to a small, nearly dark room beyond and stepped aside and let them enter. There was a scarred desk at one end of the room. Behind the desk a bleary-eyed customs official with a long, narrow face smoked a cigarette and in the weak light from a single high window read a day-old copy of Le Temps. He slowly folded his newspaper and turned to the four travelers and held out his hand, palm up. One by one, they placed their passports into the customs officer's hand. All four passports had been issued by the government of the Republic of Spain—three of them by the ministry of foreign affairs in Madrid. These three the customs officer quickly stamped and returned to their owners. The fourth passport, the one belonging to the tall man in the leather jacket, had been issued at the Spanish embassy in Washington, D.C. It had been issued to Juan Fernandez Carreja. The customs officer studied the photograph for a moment and measured it against the face of the traveler. *C'est vous, monsieur?* The traveler said, *Oui. C'est moi.* The officer rubbed out his cigarette and lighted a fresh one and continued to examine the passport. Finally, he asked, *Quel est votre nom, monsieur?* The traveler said, *Je m'appelle . . . Juan . . . Juan Carreja.* The officer pursed his lips and shook his head no. That was not his name. Quickly, the Spaniard in the fedora stepped forward and whispered in the traveler's ear, and the traveler said, Juan Fernandez. *Je m'appelle Juan Fernandez.* The officer nodded. Yes, that was indeed the correct name correctly stated. He stamped the passport and gave it back to the man, who slipped it into the inside breast pocket of his jacket. The customs officer kept his hand out, palm up. The traveler looked at the man's hand for a few seconds, then reached down and shook it. *Merci beaucoup, monsieur,* he said. The customs officer said nothing, just swung his head from side to side, no again, and caught the eye of the Spaniard. *Avez-vous quelque chose pour moi, messieurs?* the officer asked him. The Spaniard nudged the traveler, who suddenly understood. He reached for his wallet and took out an American twenty-dollar bill. He folded it twice and shook the man's hand a second time, leaving the bill behind. Then the four carried their luggage outside to the platform. From there they crossed into Spain on foot. They walked along the railroad tracks a distance of one hundred yards to a second platform and train station and customs officer, Spanish this time instead of French. Here they were greeted with broad smiles and embraces by a small party of uniformed military officers and half a dozen civilians.

"Won't be no sign or mailbox there," the old fellow said, pumping gas into the tan Packard sedan. He was a scrawny man in his late sixties in coveralls, with a plum-size lump of tobacco in his cheek and stumped brown teeth. "Every time he puts one up, somebody comes along and knocks it down."

"Why is that?" Vanessa Cole asked him. A light rain had begun to fall. She stepped away from the car and stood under the gas station canopy and watched the old man pump gas.

The man shrugged and looked the Packard over bumper to bumper and pursed his lips as if about to whistle. Nice-looking vehicle. Nice-looking girl, too. "Can't say. 'Course, there's some folks that claims he's a Red. You know, a Commie."

"And is he?" She reached into her purse to pay for the gas.

"Could be. I keep out of it. Could be he's only what you call abnormal, if you know what I mean. Friend of yours?" he asked and winked at her.

"Aren't you the flirt," she said. Funny old man, she thought. She paid him and lay a gloved hand on his shoulder in a friendly way and gazed deeply into his wide-open eyes, startling and pleasing him. She thanked him for the directions and walked slowly around the front of the car and got in, letting him watch her.

By the time she'd driven the four and a half miles north on Route 19 as instructed by the funny man at the filling station, the rain was falling steadily in cold, wind-driven waves. Through flapping windshield wipers she caught sight of the red farmhouse and horse barn he'd said to look for and pulled off the road. She bumped onto the dirt lane that passed by the farm and drove through the adjacent field where a blue sprawl of chicory spread from the lane into the field. A few hundred yards beyond the farm, she crossed the river on a narrow wooden bridge and entered the woods. After a few seconds the rain briefly let up, and from the car she could see fresh chanterelles glowing like nuggets among the sodden leaves.

Then the rain resumed, and she had a hard time seeing where she was going. The lane wound uphill a ways, first through oak and maple trees, then through spruce and old red pines. After a while it dipped back toward the river again, ending at a large, two-story, cedar-shingled house situated on a rise in a hemlock grove. It overlooked an oxbow loop where the river slowed and widened into an eddy the size of a large mill pond. She parked as close to the front door as she could, removed her gloves, and dashed from the car up the wide stone steps and onto the front porch. She shook the raindrops from her hair and knocked on the door.

Carefully tended flowers decorated the yard—perennials and rose- and lilac bushes and pale-faced hydrangeas and thriving herb gardens. There was a two-bay garage at the side of the house and down by the eddy in the river a building that looked like a boathouse and must be where he keeps his airplane, she thought. On the flood plain beyond the boathouse she noticed a large vegetable garden protected by a head-high deer fence. The house and outbuildings and grounds impressed her. It was clearly the center of a serious, hardworking country life. She assumed the large structure with the skylights at the back of the house was his studio. Smoke curled from a stovepipe chimney and light glowed from inside. She knew he was there—the famous artist ensconced in his skylit studio, working alone through the cold, gray afternoon making pictures—and was eager to see the man in his natural element.

But first Vanessa Cole wanted to present herself to the woman of the house. She had learned the woman's name while in Manhattan these weeks since her father's funeral, but little else, for the artist's wife was rarely seen in New York. Vanessa was curious about her—she wondered what the woman looked like, her age, her personal style. She wondered what kind of woman held on to a man like Jordan Groves. Or if indeed it could be done at all.

The door came unlatched and opened in. A very tall woman, taller even than Vanessa and a few years older, stood behind the screened door. A country woman, she seemed, and strikingly attractive, with pale blue eyes and silken, straight blond hair cut shoulder length. Her plaid flannel shirt was open at the throat, with the sleeves rolled above her elbows, and her arms and face and neck had a gardener's tan, not a sunbather's. A pair of Irish setters paced restlessly in the shadows behind her.

Vanessa said, "I'm sorry to bother you. I'm Vanessa Von Heidenstamm."

"How do you do," Alicia said simply.

Vanessa hesitated, expecting the woman to invite her inside. Finally she asked, "Are you Mrs. Groves?"

"Yes."

"I was hoping to speak with your husband. We met . . . he came out to my parents' camp a few weeks ago. On the Fourth—"

"Yes. I know that. He told me," Alicia said. Then added, "I'm sorry about your father."

Vanessa thanked her. She had caught the slight accent and wondered if it was German or Russian. Probably Russian, she thought. And probably why the locals think the artist is a Red.

After a few seconds of silence, Alicia said, "Jordan's in his studio. He doesn't like to be interrupted when he's working."

"I understand. I'll come back another time, then. When would be a good time?" she asked.

Alicia looked at Vanessa Cole for a moment, as if taking her measure for the first time. Friend or foe? Neither, she decided. "The studio's out back," she said. "But it's raining, so come inside. There's a breezeway. You can get there from the kitchen without getting wet," she said and pushed the screened door back, letting the woman into her house.

Vanessa followed Alicia Groves into a warm, brightly lit kitchen that smelled of wood smoke and baking bread, and the dogs clattered along behind. Two blond boys, looking more like apprentice horticulturists than artists in training, sat at the long table with colored pencils and sketch pads, making careful botanical drawings of the thatch of wildflowers scattered before them. Theirs was a household guided by firm and fixed principles. Maybe the accent is German, Vanessa thought.

Alicia opened the back door for her and pointed in the direction of the studio. "If he doesn't wish to be disturbed, he will let you know," she said.

Vanessa walked along the breezeway to the windowless door of the studio and stopped there. The smell of wild thyme perfumed the air. Above the sound of the pounding rain she heard music inside—Ethel Waters, a sexy Negro singer whose plaintive voice she recognized, having heard her perform many times in uptown clubs back during Prohibition. Her ex-husband, the count, whom she liked to call Count No-Count, had been a fan of Negro music and bootleg gin, and back then so had she. Her divorce three years ago she associated with the end of Prohibition and Harlem nights and the beginning of her passion for swing and a taste for champagne. She waited for the song to end, then knocked.

"Yeah?" Jordan called.

"It's me. It's Vanessa . . . Vanessa Von Heidenstamm."

Silence. A few seconds passed, and the door swung open. A gust of dry heat from the big-bellied cast-iron stove in the corner hit her in the face. The artist wore an ink-smudged T-shirt and overalls and was smoking a cigar. He put the cigar between his lips and without a word turned away from her and went back to his bench, picked up his chisel and mallet, and continued working. He was carving into a large block of maple for a woodcut. Rain washed across the skylights overhead and drummed steadily against them. The large space of the studio was open to the roof and smelled of cigar smoke and burning wood and paint and turpentine. Vanessa inhaled deeply.

With his back to her, the artist said, "Well, Miss Von Heidenstamm, what brings you way out here on a day like this?"

Cabinets and counters and tool racks were neatly arranged up and down the length and width of the studio—everything orderly and squared and ready to hand. Drawings and sketches on paper were pinned to the four windowless walls and on easels and corkboards. Suspended above the workbench, paintings on canvas and board and boxes of prints had been carefully stored in a shallow loft. On a table next to the tin sink sat a hand-cranked wooden record player, one of the boxy new portable Victrolas, and racked stacks of glossy black records. An overstuffed red leather armchair and reading lamp and a tall shelf crowded with books and magazines took up a near corner of the studio. Vanessa walked to the armchair and sat down, crossed her long legs, and lighted a cigarette.

"My father's ashes," she said.

He turned and looked at her. "Say what?"

"In the backseat of my car there is a large ceramic jar. Chinese. Second-century BC. The Han era. The jar happens to have been one of my father's most treasured and valuable possessions, and inside it are his cremated remains."

"Very interesting," the artist said. "A little weird, though, if you want my opinion. Carting your father's ashes around like that."

"Daddy was a little weird. Anyhow, that's what brings me back up here. And brings me to you."

"What does?"

"My father's ashes," she said. "By the way, is the town called Petersburg because you live here and you're a Red, or do you live here because it's called Petersburg and you're a Red?"

"None of the above," he said and smiled. "It's only a happy coincidence. Once a year I urge the town fathers to change it to Leningrad. They always vote it down."

"I wondered. Anyhow, I have a favor to ask." She looked around the studio. "Do you have anything to drink? A little wine? I don't suppose you have any champagne. I'd love a glass of champagne."

"It gives me a headache. I've got rum. Want a taste of old Havana?"

She smiled brightly and like a child nodded yes, and he pulled a bottle and two shot glasses from a cabinet above the sink and poured.

"*Salud,*" he said and drank.

"*Salud.*" She drained her glass and set it on the floor, beside the chair. "I heard about your brawl at the Club. You must be a little crazy," she said.

"I don't take lightly to insults. Not from twits like Kendall. Not from beautiful women, either."

"Neither do I, Mr. Groves. I assume you're referring to me, but I don't recall insulting you. Quite the opposite. In any case, I'm quick to forgive and quick to forget. What about you?"

He didn't answer. He refilled their glasses, then walked to the Victrola, cranked the handle a half-dozen turns, and placed a record on the spindle. The music was fast and pleasant, a quartet of black men singing and a single guitar.

Vanessa listened for a moment, unsmiling. "That's real cute," she said sarcastically. "What is it?"

"The song? It's called 'My Old Man.' By some guys named the Spirits of Rhythm. It's a group I heard at a Harlem joint a couple of years ago. You don't remember cutting me cold at the Club that day?" The Spirits of Rhythm sang in the background, *"My old man, he's livin' in a garbage can. Put a bottle of gin there an' he'll get in there . . . My old man, he's only doin' the best he can. . . ."*

"So I gather you're not quick to forgive and forget. What if I said I'm sorry?"

"Quick to forgive. Apology accepted. Very slow to forget, however."

She said she was afraid of that, which was why she had been reluctant to come to him. But she felt she had no choice. He was the only person who could help her.

"You don't strike me as a girl who needs help from anybody. Least of all from me."

"My father wanted his ashes up here in the Adirondacks. In the Reserve. He wanted them scattered in the Second Lake. He was practically religious about it."

"Fine. Do it. What's the problem?"

"I can't," she said. "Not without help." Russell Kendall, the manager of the Reserve, had informed her that it was against the rules to inter a body on Reserve land. By the same token it was equally against the rules to scatter the ashes of a deceased member in any of the lakes or streams in the Reserve.

Jordan asked her why she didn't carry her old man's ashes up to the Second Lake in that Chinese jar and not tell anyone and just row out to the middle of the lake and empty the jar.

"Impossible," she said. Mr. Kendall had warned her against trying exactly that and had alerted the warden at the gate to check her belongings for Dr. Cole's ashes if she tried to hike up to the lake and take out one of the guide boats. "The manager dislikes me only a little less than he dislikes you. But my grandfather was one of the founders, so all he can do is harass me. He can't kick me off the place. We're shareholders, members. When Mother and I went into the Reserve to go up to Rangeview yesterday afternoon, he and the warden stopped us at the gate and went through our pack baskets and even our purses. Like we were suspected smugglers and they were customs officers. It was a total humiliation for Mother. Luckily, we were only on sort of a reconnaissance mission, and we'd left the ashes in the car, or Kendall probably would have locked Daddy in the clubhouse safe."

Jordan laughed. "So what do you want me to do?"

"I want you to fly me and Daddy to the Second Lake in your airplane. When you fly low over the water, I'll do what Daddy expected me to do. That's all."

"Nope," Jordan said. "Can't do it."

"Why not?" she asked. Then, pointing at the record player, "Look, I get the joke. Do we have to hear that song?"

"What do you want to hear?" He lifted the record off the spindle and slipped it into its paper jacket and reracked it.

"I want to hear you say you'll help me do right by my father. I'll pay you, if that's what you're worried about."

"I know, money's no object. Thanks, but no thanks."

"I'll give you one of those James Heldon paintings you seem to like so much."

"I don't like them, actually," he said. "No, that's not quite true. There were two or three there that I admired. And I can get a Heldon on my own, thanks. But it doesn't matter, I can't help you."

"You mean 'won't.' Why not?" She stood and laid a hand lightly on his shoulder. "I think you're more *afraid* of me than angry. Besides, that morning at the Club all I did was tell you the truth. That's not so bad, is it? You don't have to be afraid of me, Jordan Groves. I won't hurt you."

"Miss Von Heidenstamm . . . or is it Countess?"

"Miss."

"Miss Von Heidenstamm, for a man like me, you are nothing but trouble. As you have already noted. No, the best thing I can do for both of us is see you out and say thanks for the visit and good-bye."

Gently, the artist took her hand off his shoulder and led her to the door. He opened the door and let go of her hand, and she stepped outside. He closed the door and went back to his work-table. For a moment he stood there staring down at the block of maple he'd been carving for three full days. Then he reached for the bottle of rum and poured himself a drink. Glass in hand, he walked to the Victrola. He placed the record back onto the spindle, and the Spirits of Rhythm resumed singing, *"My old man, he's only doin' the best he can. . . ."*

AROUND MIDNIGHT WHEN JORDAN CAME IN TO BED, ALICIA was still awake, reading *Gone With the Wind*. It was the novel that everyone in America seemed to be reading that summer, sent to Jordan by the publisher in typescript six months earlier with a request that he illustrate an *hors commerce* limited edition for special friends of the publisher and author, numbered and signed. It was a lucrative offer, tempting. But after skimming the first few chapters, he'd pronounced it a ladies' antebellum fantasy novel and tossed the manuscript into the fireplace. Now the book had become a beloved best-seller and there was even talk of making a movie adaptation. He was a little sorry he'd turned the offer down—it would have been the first time he'd illustrated a popular book by a living author. It might have led to many rich commissions.

He went into the dressing room and pulled his clothes off, washed his face and brushed his teeth in the bathroom, and came quickly to bed. Alicia had already closed her book and snapped off the bedside lamp, and though she appeared to have gone straight to sleep, he knew that she was awake. Awake and waiting.

For a few moments he remained silent. Then he said, "That girl, Vanessa Von Heidenstamm, she came by the studio today."

"Yes, I know. I wondered if you were going to mention it."

"Why wouldn't I?"

"Why wouldn't you? Really, Jordan. She has her cap set for you. You know that."

"Well, that's nothing to me."

"Oh."

"She wanted me to do something weird for her."

"Oh."

"She wanted me to fly her and her father's ashes up to the Reserve, so she could scatter the ashes in the Second Lake. Pretty weird, eh?"

"No, I don't think so. Maybe the place was special to him," she said. "Will you do it?"

"Christ, no."

"Why not?"

"Because I don't particularly like the girl. Or her family, either." He rolled over and put his back to her. "People like that don't need help from me. They contaminate everything and everyone they touch. Besides, it's against Reserve rules."

"When did you start caring about rules?" she said and was silent for a moment. "'People like that.' They collect art, Jordan. They have nice big houses and apartments. They think artists are interesting, superior people. And you like all that, you know. And there's no reason you shouldn't like it, is there?"

"They don't collect art, except as an investment, as capital. They collect artists. So I deal with them only as much as I have to," he declared. "And there's no way she's going to collect me."

"Oh."

"What's the matter with you, anyway? Are you pissed off at me for something?"

"Have you done something lately that I should be angry about?"

"No. Not that I'm aware of, anyhow."

"Then I'm not angry at you, am I?"

"Jesus. Do we have to live like this? Aren't you able to forgive and forget, Alicia?"

"You have tested me on that. Many times. And I have passed the test of forgiving and forgetting. Many times."

"All right, then. So why are you still pissed off at me?"

"I'm not," she said. "Go to sleep, Jordan."

For a few moments they lay in silence, unmoving. Finally, he said, "Do you know how many nights we've let end like this?"

"Yes."

"Do you know how long it's been since we've made love, Alicia?"

"Do you want to make love to me?" she asked. "You can, if you want to."

"Jesus Christ, Alicia! I hate this. You act as if you've taken a lover. Have you? Do you have a lover?"

"That's a very strange question," she said. "Coming from you."

"Well, I mean it."

"No. Go to sleep, Jordan. Unless you want to make love to me."

He was silent again. Then after a few moments her breathing slowed, and he knew she was sleeping. He closed his eyes, and soon he was sleeping, too.

THE FOLLOWING DAY, WHEN HE'D PUT IN A FULL MORNING'S work in the studio, Jordan Groves decided around noon to drive into the village to pick up the mail and newspapers and maybe have lunch at the Moose Head over in Sam Dent. He wasn't feeling especially sociable, merely in the mood for a little public solitude and a meat-loaf sandwich and a cold bottle of beer. He wasn't free to linger: Alicia was working in the garden and had plans, if it cleared up later, to take the boys swimming at the falls and would need the car. He thought a moment about taking the truck instead, freeing him to set his own time for returning home, then decided against it. There was the unfinished woodblock, the set of lithographs he'd promised the publisher of his Greenland travel book, letters to write and accounts to update, a new studio assistant coming by later for instructions. He couldn't linger. There was always more work to do than time in which to do it. Jordan Groves believed that was a good thing.

It was a bright day, but still overcast. He strolled from the studio to the garage, drew the doors open, got the Ford started, and backed the sedan from the dark interior out to the driveway. In daylight he saw the jar. It sat on the passenger's seat—a tall, jade-green container about eighteen inches high with an overlapping cover. He stared at the jar, stunned and disbelieving, as if the object were a person, a stranger sitting beside him, unexpected and uninvited. The jar was very beautiful, softly rounded in the middle and narrow at the base and top, and elegantly proportioned, the force and gentleness of its ancient maker's hands and mind evident in the form of the jar and the cut surface and the brilliant green glaze.

Ten minutes later, he pushed his airplane from the hangar and slid it down the ramp and into the water. To keep the green jar from being jostled or tipped, he had strapped it with masking tape to the seat in the aft cockpit. He let the engine warm for half a minute, then taxied upstream fifty yards and brought the airplane around and into the fluttery wind. He headed on a diagonal across the rippled open water into the wide smooth belly of the river, picked up speed, hit the step, and, pulling back on the stick, lifted the airplane free of the water. It rose quickly over the trees that lined the farther bank. He fought the torque and dipped the left wing slightly, cutting the airplane back around to the south. As he flew over the garden, he looked down and saw his wife and sons peering up at him. The sun had come out, and they shaded their eyes against it with their hands, and the shadow of the airplane passed across them.

His heading was south-southwest, a route that followed the glittering ribbon of the Tamarack River upstream, then over Bream Pond and down into the village of Tunbridge, avoiding the Tamarack clubhouse grounds and golf course, where he banked to port. Holding steady at twenty-five hundred feet he followed the Tamarack River toward its headwaters, flying over rising unbroken forest into the Reserve.

He knew that she would be waiting for him at her father's camp—no more an actual camp than her father's Park Avenue apartment. But calling it a camp helped people like the Coles coddle their dream of living in a world in which they did no harm. It let them believe that for a few weeks or a month or two, even though their so-called camps were as elaborately luxurious as their homes elsewhere, they were roughing it, living like the locals, whom they hired as housekeepers, cooks, guides, and caretakers: the locals, who were thought by people like the Coles to be lucky—lucky to live year-round in such pristine isolation and beauty.

Crossing over the First Lake, Jordan spotted a pair of fishermen in a guide boat casting flies along the eastern shore. This isn't going to work, he thought and was relieved. And a moment later, at the headwaters, when he came over the rise and looked down the cowl and surveyed the length and breadth of the Second Lake and saw that there was no one out on the water or fishing from the banks, he was faintly disappointed. He put the airplane down in the middle of the lake and taxied toward the eastern shore, then brought it along the shore to the shallows just off the Coles' camp.

Vanessa, wearing a pale yellow head scarf and denim shirt and tan slacks, stood on the shore by an overturned guide boat. She was smoking a cigarette. Jordan shut the engine down and when the propeller had wheeled to a stop told her to come aboard and remove her precious cargo from his airplane.

"We need to scatter Daddy's ashes from the air," she said.

"From the air? No! Do it from the guide boat. I'm in a hurry."

"I can't hold the jar and row the boat at the same time. Those little wooden things are pretty to look at, maybe, but they're tippy."

"What about your mother? Let her row and you hug your father's jar. Or vice versa. I'm just making a delivery, Miss Von Heidenstamm."

Vanessa explained that, after the long walk from the clubhouse in to the First Lake and the trip across both lakes to camp, her mother wasn't feeling well enough to go out in the boat again. Besides, this was not something her mother wanted to participate in. It was just too sad for her even to contemplate. Vanessa didn't want to put her through it. She was doing this strictly for her father. His last wish.

"All right, then, let's get it done," he said and this time did not offer to help her step from the water to the pontoon and climb from there to the wing. She carefully advanced along the wing to the fuselage and saw the jar.

"Take off the tape and hold it in your lap," he said to her.

"Jordan, I can't tell you what this means to me," she said. "What it means to my mother. And to my father. Him, especially. I do hope you're not angry with me."

"For sticking me with a Chinese jug filled with your father's ashes? Trapping me into coming out here like this? Of *course* I'm angry with you."

"I don't think so. I think this is something you'll never forget, Jordan. Or regret." She slid into the cockpit, stripped the tape off the jar, and placed the jar on her lap.

"Miss Von Heidenstamm, I already regret it."

"You don't have to call me that."

"What?"

"It was my married name. And I'm no longer married to him. Call me Vanessa."

"I'm going to taxi out to the middle of the lake. When I get there, you dump the ashes over the side, and I'll bring you back. And then, Vanessa Von Heidenstamm, I'll be on my merry way."

"That's really very boring, you know."

"Yes, I guess it is."

"Much more interesting to scatter Daddy's ashes from the sky."

"True." Without turning, he instructed her to take off her head scarf and remove the top of the jar and cover the jar with the scarf.

"Why?"

"Because of the wind. I'll tell you when to empty it. Just be sure you hold the damn thing out to the side as far as you can, and don't remove the scarf until you upend the jar to dump it, or the wind and the prop wash will blow your daddy's ashes all over you and inside the plane. I damn sure don't want to have to clean Dr. Cole's remains out of my airplane."

She gave the back of his head a grim smile. He restarted the engine and took the airplane back out toward the middle of the lake, where he hit the throttle, gathered speed, and put it into the air. At about five hundred feet he leveled off and banked the airplane toward the headwaters of the lake. He cut the speed to seventy knots and dropped it down until it was barely a hundred feet above the water, following the axis of the long, narrow lake from south to north. When he spotted the Coles' camp coming up on his right, he slowed again and dropped another fifty feet, and hollered back, "Go ahead, do it now!"

Vanessa hefted the jar to her shoulder, steadied it there for a few seconds with both hands, and facing it away from the wash, quickly extended it out to the side as far as she could and removed the scarf and emptied it. A gray swash of ash and bits of bone exploded into the air behind the airplane and drifted slowly down to the water, when suddenly Vanessa cried, "Oh, no!"

Jordan jerked his head around and saw the jar drop from the airplane like a green stone. He watched it splash into the lake, where it sank almost at once. Vanessa's scarf fluttered slowly down to the lake behind it.

"I dropped the damn thing!" Vanessa cried. "I dropped it!"

Jordan brought the airplane around and flew across the spot where the jar had gone in, locating it on a bisected pair of lines running the width and length of the lake. He saw the yellow scarf floating southward on the dark water, like a pale hieroglyph. "Try to memorize the shore points on both sides of the lake and at the ends!" he shouted. "The scarf'll drift and sink anyhow, so don't look at it."

"It's gone, Jordan!"

"No, it's not! You can row out and dive for it!"

"You idiot, it's hundreds of feet deep there!"

He didn't respond. He brought the airplane in close to shore and splashed down a short ways below the camp, taxied back to where he'd picked her up, and cut the engine. For a moment they sat motionless in the silence, the airplane rocking gently on its pontoons. Finally Jordan said, "Hey, look, Vanessa, I'm sorry about the jar. Seriously. It was very beautiful."

"Thank you," she said.

"And I never said it to you right. I'm sorry about your father, too."

"No, it's probably the best thing. The jar, I mean. Daddy loved that old jar more than any other thing he owned. Except this camp."

"It's probably worth a fortune, though. The jar."

"Mother would never have sold it. No, it's only right that it's

still with him . . . and that they're both at the bottom of the lake."
Her eyes filled with tears.

"Yeah, well, I guess that's the best way to think about it," he
said gently.

"You're being so kind. That's nice."

"No, that's normal."

"Would you come up to the camp with me? I need to talk with
somebody."

"What about your mother?"

She shook her head. "No, no, I can't talk to her. Mother and I,
we're like . . . we're on different planets. Especially about Daddy."
She paused, and noted that he seemed to be waiting for her to
continue. "C'mon, I think I owe you a drink, anyhow," she said. "I
owe you a lot more than that, actually," she said and smiled sadly.

He nodded and got out of the cockpit and extended his hand
to her, and she took it and stepped onto the wing beside him.
He quickly anchored the airplane, and when it was secured, they
came ashore and, still holding hands, walked up the long slope,
through the grove of tall pines to the deck of the camp. She liked
the feel of his large callused hand around hers. It was a workman's
hand—which was natural, wasn't it, for he had spent years carving wood- and linoleum blocks and making copper etchings and
cutting lithographs. Even drawing and painting required the use
of his big hands; and he was probably a builder, too, judging from
his house and the outbuildings, which had seemed handmade to
her—skillfully done, but not by a firm of architects, engineers,
and contractors. And all that firewood stacked so neatly in the
open sheds alongside the garage and studio and in the breezeway—he cuts his own firewood to heat his house and studio. His
arduous travels to distant, difficult lands—Greenland, Alaska, the
Andes—were legendary. He was strong and lean and hardhanded.

Many of the men whom she had successfully seduced in the past were cut from the same social cloth as he—rich men; cosmopolitan men; even a few famous writers and artists; and sportsmen like her first husband, the Russian Boris Seversky, men who flew their own airplanes and traveled to exotic parts of the globe on three-month-long treks and safaris. She was rumored to have had affairs with Ernest Hemingway and Max Ernst and Baron von Blixen. But none of them had hands like his. Their bodies had been hardened by sport and exercise, not by physical work.

She knew she had managed to slip through his resistance to her, but wasn't sure what had done it or how long it would last. He was changeable and unpredictable, a man who could burst into flame one minute and just as quickly turn to ice. She asked him to make himself comfortable on the sofa by the fireplace, then knelt with her back to him and lit the fire she had laid earlier. When it began to crackle and burn, she stood and crossed the room to the bar, aware all the while that he was looking at her.

"What'll you have?" she asked. "I have rum, but it's not Cuban, I'm afraid. Jamaican. It's what I'm having."

He studied her carefully, more watchful than curious, as if she were more a danger to him than a puzzle. "I don't know, it's a little early. Yeah, rum's fine."

She poured them each three fingers and returned to the sofa by the fire and sat next to him.

"Where's your mother?" Jordan asked, looking around the large room. There seemed to be no one else at the camp, no guide or cook, no friends or family members. Which made sense, he decided, given the two women's private and slightly illicit reasons for being here. "I'm thinking I ought to make your mother some kind of apology, too," he said. "I should offer her my condolences."

Vanessa explained that her mother was still overcome by Dr. Cole's death. Her mother was somewhat frail anyhow, and the long drive up from Manhattan yesterday and then the hike and boat trip in to camp had left her weakened. But he needn't worry, she would convey his apology and condolences to her mother later.

Jordan pulled out his tobacco and papers and rolled a cigarette.

"I'm afraid I'm going to have to become Mother's caretaker, now that Daddy's gone. She depended on Daddy for everything," Vanessa said, watching his deft movements, fingertips, lips, tongue. "Can you show me how to do that?" she asked.

"She didn't seem particularly frail to me," he said.

"Mentally."

"Oh." He passed her a cigarette paper and sprinkled tobacco into it and, softly guiding her fingers with his, got it rolled into a lumpy tube. "Now wet the leading edge of the paper lightly," he said and sat back to watch. She ran the tip of her tongue across the paper, looked up at him and smiled, then skillfully—expertly, he noticed—finished making the cigarette.

"I feel you've done this before," he said.

"Not with tobacco."

She tucked her long legs under her and lighted the cigarette and smoked, and though Jordan knew she was showing off, he could not stop himself from admiring what appeared to be her nonchalant, natural grace. The room was flooded with tawny sunlight. Wood smoke from the fireplace, the brown sugar aroma of the rum in the glass, and the smell of burning tobacco—private, deeply familiar odors to Jordan—mingled and perfumed the room and somehow let him feel that he had known this woman for many years. She made him feel glad to be alive. It was a rare, simple-hearted pleasure just to sit back and look at her full, precisely formed mouth and listen to her low, husky voice.

She wanted to talk about her father, she told him, but not with anyone who knew her father well or was related to him or one of his friends, and definitely not with her mother. They wouldn't understand. When her father was alive Vanessa had spent a year talking about him to a world-famous Swiss psychiatrist, she said, and it hadn't helped in the slightest, because she had come away both adoring her father and despising him fully as much as she had at the start. And now that he was dead, she adored and despised him to an even greater degree than before. And she was troubled by this, she said, for it made it difficult for her to grieve over his death in a useful or even an honest way. She had hoped that bringing his ashes up here would help, but she could already tell that it hadn't made any difference at all. "It's painful, his death, naturally. But all the same, I feel false. I feel ungrateful."

"I can understand why you might adore your father. What the hell, he was your father. But why did you despise him? Why *do* you, I mean."

"You'd be better off asking why I adored him. Actually, either way, the answer would be the same. After a year on the good doctor's couch, I learned that much," she said. "One hates a person for the same reason one loves him. Especially if that person is one's parent." Her father and mother had adopted her when she was little more than an infant, she told him. An only child, she had been doted on, swaddled by their love and care—even spoiled, she admitted it. All her life she had been given everything she wanted. With one exception. Right up to the day her father died, he had refused to tell her who her real mother and father had been or how she had come to Dr. and Mrs. Cole for adoption. All he would say was that she had not been wanted by her real parents. "Our foundling," was how Dr. Cole had described her, even to strangers. "He so dominated Mother in this that, even now, with his ashes at the bottom of the lake, she still won't tell me where they 'found' me or who left me there. Daddy's wishes were and are and always will be her commands," she said. "For all I know, they could have kidnapped me."

"You didn't answer my question," Jordan said. "You can't despise your father just because he wouldn't tell you how you came to be adopted. There's got to be another reason. He may have had good motives for it. Rightly or wrongly, he may have felt he needed to protect you somehow. I mean, what if your real mother was a whore and your real father a drunken sailor on a weekend pass? He might reasonably want to keep that from you."

"You're right," she said. "The truth is, the great, beloved Dr. Carter Cole was not the man everyone thought he was," she said. "Not in private, not in secret. Not when he was alone with Mother and me. And alone with me . . ." She trailed off. "Well, let's just say he was *different*. A different man. He was not a nice man, Jordan."

"No one's the same when he's alone with his wife or his children. It's where you let your guard down, especially if, like your father, you're more or less a public figure."

She moved closer to him on the sofa. "You're a public figure, Jordan, and I know you're different when you're with your family alone. In private. I can tell from a single visit to your home that Jordan Groves in private is a nice man." She laughed lightly. "Actually, it's in *public,* with the whole world watching, that you're not a nice man. A brawler. You've punched critics in the jaw and given reviewers black eyes. You're an opinionated, drunken Red. And a famous womanizer. Oh, you have such a *dangerous* reputation, Jordan Groves! While you're up here in the mountains holed up in your studio and your sweet wife bakes bread and your sons study the local flora, people in New York City are talking. Or when you're off on one of your famous adventures in the Arctic or wherever it is you go alone for months at a time to paint and where it's clear from your pictures and writings that you sleep with the native women and probably participate in horrid native rituals, all the while, back here and in the cafés of Manhattan, tongues are wagging. No," she said, suddenly serious, "you're the opposite of my father." She reached out and brushed his cheek with her fingertips. "You didn't shave this morning, did you?"

He swiped at her hand and shoved it away and scowled. "Yes, I shaved."

"Why are you so violent with me?" she asked, her voice almost a whisper.

"What makes you think you know me?"

"You're answering a question with a question, Jordan," she said softly and touched his cheek a second time.

"Once I would have eaten you whole," he said and took her hand gently away from his face. "Right down to your beautiful white fingertips," he said, and he put her fingers into his mouth and held them there and touched them with his tongue.

She closed her eyes and inhaled deeply. After a moment, he withdrew her hand and placed it on her lap. "But not now," he said. "Not anymore." He put his glass on the table beside him and stood. "I know what people say about me. I know my reputation, and mostly I don't give a good goddamn. Listen, Vanessa, somebody once asked me in one of those dumb magazine interviews what I wanted out of life, and I told him the truth, I said, 'I want *all* of it.' And until recently that's pretty much how I've lived my life."

" 'Until recently.' "

"Yes. But now . . . now I'm starting to realize that I can't have all of it." He paused and looked above her and out the window at the lake and the mountains and the sky. "Some of the things we want cancel out other things we want. I'm not going into details," he said, "but I want my wife and my boys to be happy. I want them to be proud of me. And I want that more than I want certain other things," he said and turned back to her. "Even you."

"And you believe that? If you can have me, you *can't* have them? And vice versa, that if you *can't* have me, then you can have them? Are you sure?" she said. "Because I'm not."

"Look, you're not some pretty little Chilean dance hall girl showing me her tits, or a smiling round-faced Inuit girl lying naked under a bearskin blanket, or some doe-eyed model from the Art Students League dying to sleep with the famous artist. You're not one of those Fifth Avenue society hostesses looking for a discreet tumble in the maid's room after the party's over and the other guests have gone home. No, you're like me, Vanessa Von Heidenstamm. And people like you and me, we leave a lot of wreckage behind us. I don't want my family to be part of that wreckage. That's all I'm saying."

She stood next to him and put her hands on his shoulders and drew him to her. Leaning forward, she nestled her mouth next to his ear, and whispered something he barely heard, a slight hissing sound whose frequency rose and fell. Wordless, it sounded to him like a distress signal beamed through turbulence from a distant transmitter. He shoved her hands off his shoulders and pushed her away and raising his large right hand placed it hard against her chin and cheek, his fingers running all the way up her face to her brow, and he pressed it there for a moment, while she closed her eyes and pushed back and waited.

"I'm leaving now," he said and abruptly withdrew his hand. He backed several steps away, turned, and walked from the room.

She stood by the fire with her eyes closed. She did not open them until she heard the roar of his airplane engine. A few minutes later, when she could no longer hear the engine and knew that he was airborne and gone from the lake, she walked to the door of her parents' bedroom. Taking a key from her pocket, she unlocked the door, opened it, and peered in at her mother. The woman was sitting on the chaise, her hands and feet still tightly bound with rope, her mouth gagged with a white silk scarf, her blue eyes wild with fear.

Vanessa said, "If you promise to be quiet and not scream or shout at me anymore, I'll remove the scarf."

Her mother nodded her head rapidly up and down.

Vanessa reached around her and loosened the scarf. Pulling it free, she wound it carefully around her own throat, arranging the ends over the front of her shirt in a fetching way. She looked at herself in the dresser mirror and rearranged the scarf slightly. "And if you promise to stay here in the bedroom and not come out until I say it's time, I'll untie you." Again her mother nodded, and Vanessa released the woman's hands and feet and left the room, carrying the pieces of rope in her hands.

MILES AWAY, FLYING ON A NORTHEASTERLY HEADING, JORDAN Groves put the Reserve behind him and crossed above country villages and farms tucked into the valleys and clustered alongside the curling north-flowing streams. Shining in the distance, with the Green Mountains of Vermont humped up at the far horizon, was Lake Champlain, a glacial lake fourteen miles wide and one hundred twenty-five miles long—open water all the way to Quebec. Jordan was not ready to return home yet; to place himself in the bosom of his family again; to become the husband and father he had been this morning, before he backed his car from the garage and turned and discovered in the passenger's seat the green Chinese jar with the ashes of the late Dr. Cole inside. He was not ready to let go of Vanessa Von Heidenstamm. He wanted to get away from her and everything associated with her—the Reserve, the Tamarack Club, the Second Lake, her father's camp, the people she came from and the people she ran with. But he did not want to let her go.

Yesterday's Canadian front with its blowzy raw wind and rain had passed off to the southeast. The cloudless sky was deep blue, the temperature in the low sixties, even at altitude, and the forest a rich green blanket running all the way from the Reserve down to the pale, newly mown fields of the lakeside farms. A steady five-knot wind blew back from the direction the front had taken. No gusts. Perfect flying weather. He saw a hawk carving spirals in the air several hundred feet below him. A black Model T Ford like the one he owned the year he and Alicia first moved up from New York City crawled along the dirt road between the iron-mining village of Moriah and the lakeside shipping town of Port Henry.

At the southern end of the lake, he banked left, and cruised in a northerly direction over the bare bluffs of Crown Point and made his way along the scalloped western shoreline. Tiny white triangular sails dotted the dark blue waters and clustered in the coves and marinas of Port Henry and, a few miles farther north, the towns of Westport and Essex. Halfway across the lake a ferryboat the shape and, from this distance, the size of a shoe box made its slow way from New York state to Vermont. Off to his right a rocky islet no larger than a barn rose, as if from the deep, covered with hundreds, maybe thousands, of birds—swarms of gulls and petrels and loons. Jordan circled the rookery, wonder struck by its abundance, and when his gaze returned to the open water ahead, he looked up and was startled by what he saw. It was at least two miles away and a thousand feet above the surface of the lake—an enormous, round, silver object that appeared to be coming steadily toward him from the direction of Canada.

It was an aircraft—a dirigible, he quickly realized. One of those huge new zeppelins from Germany he'd been reading about. They fascinated him, and he'd been trying to figure a way to make a picture of one, a painting or even an etching that captured the enormity of the thing, without having to portray it tethered to the ground with tiny human beings standing nearby to show scale. He wanted to picture it in flight, nothing surrounding it but clouds and sky, the largest machine in the world. He swung off to the port side, out of the path of the oncoming monster, and cut his speed and dropped altitude for a better view as it approached. There were only two of these gargantuan aircraft in existence, the *Graf Zeppelin*, which kept to the European and South American routes, and the *Hindenburg*, which crossed the North Atlantic from Frankfurt to Lakehurst, New Jersey, by way of Montreal. For months, he had been hoping to catch sight of it, but, up to now, whenever the *Hindenburg* passed through the region, he had learned of it too late, days afterward, from the local newspapers or from a neighbor who was lucky enough to have been at Lake Champlain when the great shining airship plowed through the blue Adirondack sky. It was exciting to have caught sight of it, and what a break, he thought, to see the damned thing from the air!

It was enormous, over eight hundred feet long and shaped like a gigantic bomb. It was one hundred thirty-five feet in diameter, he remembered reading. Despite its incredible size and its speed, which Jordan estimated at eighty miles per hour, it seemed more animal than mechanical as it moved implacably through the air, more a living creature from another age than a twentieth-century man-made flying machine. He remembered a few more of its specifications—that it was powered by four huge 1,200 horsepower Mercedes-Benz engines, and that it was filled with seven million cubic feet of hydrogen. The airship was fitted out with formal dining rooms, lounges, luxurious staterooms, promenades, and even a smoking room, all located inside its shining hull instead of in an external gondola, as with conventional dirigibles. And he knew a little of its history—that the Zeppelin Company, threatened with bankruptcy, had accepted financial backing from the Nazi party. The United States was the only reliable source in the world for nonflammable helium, but Congress, mildly anxious over the rise of the Nazis, had forbade the sale of the gas to the Germans, forcing the Zeppelin Company to fill its airships instead with hydrogen. The *Hindenburg* had been fireproofed, he'd read, but even so, hydrogen was flammable, and this somehow made the dirigible all the more dangerously attractive to Jordan, all the more a living thing.

He drew close to the airship. Keeping several hundred yards off its starboard side, so as to avoid its powerful wash and wake, he flew his airplane along its length, a sixth of a mile. He was stunned by the sheer size of the machine. Stunned and moved. Its very scale was beautiful to Jordan, like a Greenland glacier seen for the first time—a thing too big for human beings to imagine, but, for all that, a natural and perfected part of the world that humans inhabit. Passengers peered from the windows and waved as he passed, and from the open cockpit of his tiny Waco biplane he waved back.

Toward the aft of the airship, where the hull narrowed slightly, four gigantic fins emerged, a dorsal fin and a fin on either side and a keel-like fin from the belly, and as Jordan flew past them he saw the enormous red-and-black swastikas emblazoned on the fins. He had not expected that. At once the zeppelin lost all its beauty. It became an ugly thing. He peeled sharply away from the airship, cut speed, and dropped down toward the surface of the lake, heading slowly, as if with shoulders hunched, for the shoreline, where he flew up and over the low wooded hills and put his airplane on a heading toward home.

The man ordered breakfast at the Hauptbahnhof restaurant for the young woman, and when she had been served, he left her alone at the railroad station and arranged to have her trunk and her two Mark Cross suitcases sent by taxi to the Frankfurter Hof hotel. She was to present her passport and her ticket at the hotel later in the afternoon and retrieve her luggage after it had been thoroughly inspected by the officials of the Zeppelin Company. They are very much afraid of sabotage, the man explained. For the remainder of the morning and into the afternoon, the two behaved as tourists, visiting the Museumsufer along the embankment of the river Main and the Palmengarten and St. Bartholomew's Gothic cathedral. The man seemed to enjoy explaining the history and importance of the sites to the woman, in spite of her apparent lack of interest or curiosity. At 4:00 P.M. they arrived by taxi at the Frankfurter Hof and were directed to the main dining room, which had been commandeered by the Zeppelin Company. The room was crowded with the thirty-eight other passengers and numerous family members and friends, all carefully watched by Waffen SS men. The SS men stood in pairs at parade rest along the four sides of the dining room, while Zeppelin security officers in dark blue uniforms weighed luggage and purses and briefcases, then opened and examined the contents of each piece. A line was forming before a long table at the farther end of the room, where an inspector collected the passengers' matches, cigarette lighters, batteries, flashlights, even photographic equipment and flashbulbs. A second inspector placed the items into small cloth bags tagged with the owner's name. The passengers were assured that when the trip was over their property would be returned. They could keep the bag as a souvenir. One of the passengers, a very short, compact American man with black dyed hair that came to a point at his forehead, was arguing with the inspector. He clutched a package the size of a shoe box and did not wish to submit it for examination. *I had it specially wrapped!* the man protested. Two of the SS officers came forward and stood behind the inspector, and the American gave in with no further argument. The inspector removed the bright wrapping paper, taking care not to rip it, and opened the box. Inside was a Dresden china doll. *It's for my daughter,* the American said. One of the SS officers stepped forward and removed the doll from the box and put it through the X-ray machine and returned with it. The inspector took the doll from the officer, lifted the dress, and smiled. *It's a girl, dummkopf,* the American said. *So I see,* the inspector said and handed the doll back. The young woman in the plain brown suit and black hat and veil had watched the argument and the examination of the doll, and the man accompanying the woman had watched her. He took her purse from her and placed it on the table. *We must hurry,* he said. *Soon the buses will come to take everyone to the hangar for the departure.* She asked him if he had seen the doll. He nodded yes. *She was pretty, wasn't she?* the woman said. *Yes, very pretty,* he said, and, taking her by the arm, he moved her down the table, away from the man with the doll.

VANESSA'S MOTHER, EVELYN COLE, HAD LONG FEARED THAT her daughter was insane, but Dr. Cole would not hear of it. For years they had fought over whether to have Vanessa committed: Mrs. Cole arguing that it would save not only their daughter's life but their marriage as well; Dr. Cole insisting that Vanessa's periodic threats and occasional attempts to kill herself and her wildly reckless behavior—the flagrant sexual involvements with married men, the arrests for public lewdness, the spending binges on clothes and jewelry and the shoplifting that often accompanied them, the drug and alcohol abuse, even the two sudden elopements and the divorces that quickly followed—were high drama designed mainly to gain attention.

"Attention from *whom*?" Evelyn would angrily demand.

"From us," he would say. And sigh, "Mainly from me, I suppose," confessing once again that he had failed Vanessa when she was a child, that he had been consumed in those years by his work and consequently had neglected his daughter. "Though she's brilliant and talented, a trained musician and actress, and a gifted writer, too, if she wanted to apply herself to it, mentally she's still a child," he explained to practically anyone who would listen, but especially, when they were alone, to his wife, who seemed determined to blame Vanessa's behavior on Vanessa herself.

As if invoking a higher authority, he would say to her, "People who are deprived of certain emotional necessities in childhood often remain stuck there." And then confessing yet again, as if it gave him hope, "When she was very young, I was mostly absent, physically and emotionally. Even you know that. Then, during the war, when she was only eleven and twelve, I was off in France and left her in your care. And you, my dear, were often ill yourself. You were drinking heavily then, as you'll recall. No, the servants raised our daughter. We were both off in our separate worlds. And you know it, and I know it. Nannies and housekeepers and babysitters raised Vanessa. First servants and then boarding school headmistresses and then college deans. And now there's no one left to raise her but us. And because she's an adult, it's too late. The difference between you and me is that you won't admit it. We reap what we sow, Evelyn."

But he insisted that he did not blame his wife; he blamed himself. Dr. Cole was not one to shrug off responsibility. Evelyn, as he liked to say, had her own problems, of which alcohol was only one. As a young woman in her twenties and thirties, Evelyn Cole had suffered from what was called nervous exhaustion and was subject to fainting spells and long periods of lassitude and depression, hypochondria and extreme mood swings, which her husband, the doctor, treated with small doses of paregoric and other drugs, and she treated with gin. It wasn't until four years ago when she was approaching fifty and on an extended European family vacation and could not stop weeping and could not leave her Zurich hotel room that she put herself in the care of Dr. Gunther Theobold, the famous Swiss psychoanalyst, who took her off all forms of medication, including alcohol. It was he who finally convinced Dr. Cole that Mrs. Cole was correct. For their sake and hers, he told them, their daughter should be institutionalized. "Not confined like a prisoner, but psychoanalyzed.

She will of course be required to reside at the institute for at least a year," he explained.

Dr. Cole warned Dr. Theobold that Vanessa's accounts of her childhood would doubtless sound bizarre and were likely to be wholly invented, but the psychoanalyst smiled and said that he had been told all kinds of fairy tales and listened not for the facts but for the truth. "When the patient learns the truth, the emotional truth, she will be freed of her delusions and will cease the behavior that has been based on those delusions." They followed his advice and committed her then and there to the Theobold Institute, where Vanessa was indeed confined, kept behind high brick walls until, after meeting with her daily for thirteen months, Dr. Theobold pronounced her cured, no longer a danger to herself or others, and sent her home to New York, bearing what she said were the manuscripts of a surrealist novel and a Shakespearean sonnet sequence that she had written at the institute.

But she was not cured. Dr. Theobold confided to his assistant, Dr. Reichold, that the girl was probably incurable, at least by conventional means. He would not be surprised if before long she was back. Within weeks of taking up residence in her parents' apartment, she was arrested at the Carlyle Hotel for refusing to leave the hallway outside the penthouse suite where her ex-husband, Count Von Heidenstamm, lived when in New York. The count, who had recently remarried, was in Monte Carlo on his honeymoon. Though there was no reason to think the newlyweds would return for months and the nickel-plated revolver found in her purse suggested otherwise, Vanessa insisted to the police that she only wanted to be there to congratulate the couple when they returned to New York.

Days later, she wrecked her father's Packard in Westport, Connecticut, driving home drunk at 3:00 A.M. from a party, given by the members of a secret society at Yale, where she had been the only female guest. She was arrested and spent the rest of the night in jail. The following morning Dr. Cole rushed by train to Westport. He posted bail for his daughter, purchased a replacement Packard, and drove her back to New York, relieved to learn that the party had been given by Wolf's Head, not Skull and Bones.

She told her friends and her parents and their friends and a reporter from the *New York Herald Tribune* that she had been asked by the American Olympic Committee to solo all forty-four national anthems in their native tongues at the upcoming winter Olympic Games in Garmisch-Partenkirchen, Germany, after which she would be doing a series of programs for the BBC on the "New American Opera." Later, she attributed her absence at the winter games to the Nazi party's insistence on having a German operatic soprano sing the national anthems. The BBC series, she claimed, was canceled when it was learned that Vanessa had once been a friend of Wallis Simpson, the American divorcée whose attachment to the new king Edward VIII was scandalizing all Britain. "Attractive American women need not apply," she explained.

At the Stork Club one night she told Walter Winchell that she was sleeping with Ernest Hemingway and had been invited to join him on safari in Kenya, and Winchell reported it in his column the following day, although he did not reveal her name or Hemingway's, merely referring to her as a "Gorgeous Gotham Gadabout" and the author as a "Titan of the Typewriter."

"Oh, for heaven's sake, there's nothing to it," Vanessa said when her parents challenged her on these and other outlandish stories. "It's only a goddamn joke. I'm tweaking their noses, that's all. Giving bored people something interesting to talk about."

But her dangerous, erratic behavior and wild exaggerations and outright lies kept Dr. and Mrs. Cole in a state of constant anxiety and dread—which did not altogether displease Vanessa. She enjoyed keeping them in that state. Consequently, when after a few months her parents began to ignore her reckless and threatening ways, as if they'd grown accustomed to them, she would suddenly turn into the good daughter again—a calm, lucid, sociable, and controlled young woman of the world. Soon the three Coles, father, mother, and daughter, were seen going out to dinner together again, spending weekends at the house in Tuxedo Park, entertaining friends and colleagues and distinguished New Yorkers from the worlds of art, medicine, and commerce at their apartment, and in early July heading north to the Adirondack wilderness for the annual Independence Day gathering of '08 Bonesmen and their families at Rangeview, the Cole camp on the Second Tamarack Lake.

But as soon as her parents appeared content, Vanessa found a new way to alarm or, better yet, embarrass them. Flying off in a seaplane that Fourth of July night with the artist Jordan Groves was hardly alarming to them and certainly was not embarrassing, but it may have raised Dr. Cole's blood pressure sufficiently to have contributed to his fatal heart attack. And when, five days later, at his funeral in Greenwich, Connecticut, Vanessa delivered an oration over his ashes that scandalized her mother and everyone else who had ever loved and admired Dr. Cole—a strange, tangled account of her relationship with her father, suggesting, but not stating explicitly, that when she was a little girl he had sexually abused her—her mother was both sufficiently alarmed and embarrassed that, after consulting Whitney Brodhead, the family attorney, and exchanging a series of cables with Dr. Theobold, she decided that she had no choice but to have Vanessa institutionalized a second time.

It took Evelyn Cole most of two weeks to make the arrangements. Finally, under the pretense of meeting at the Wall Street offices of Brodhead, Stevens, and Wyse to discuss Dr. Cole's will, and in the presence of Whitney Brodhead and Dr. Otto Reichold, Dr. Theobold's nice young assistant, Evelyn Cole informed her daughter, Vanessa, that she had become a danger to herself and others. The necessary papers had already been drawn up, she said. She hoped that Vanessa would see the wisdom and necessity of this decision and would cooperate.

Vanessa sat back in the leather chair and sighed heavily and closed her eyes. Her mother reached across from the chair beside her and patted her hand. No one said a word. The large, dim conference room was decorated with portraits of the firm's founders and furnished with oak tables, glass-fronted bookcases filled with law books, heavy leather-upholstered chairs, standing ashtrays, and a tufted leather sofa with gleaming brass trim. The only sound was the loud ticktock of the antique, burled-maple clock posted by the door.

Dr. Reichold, flaxen haired, handsome, sturdy, stood by the window on the other side of the room. He slowly filled his pipe with tobacco from a small round leather pouch and looked down from the tall window at the bowlers and umbrellas of the lunchtime throng of pedestrians ten floors below. He was eager to get home to Zurich, but if the girl did not go along willingly and sign the commitment papers, if she resisted, then the mother might want to take the case to court, which Dr. Theobold had instructed him to avoid at all costs. The institute was not recognized in the United States as a legally licensed mental institution; no American court would approve of sending Vanessa to Zurich against her will. And Dr. Theobold did not want the girl committed to one of those terrible American lunatic asylums where, he wrote to Mrs. Cole, she would be driven to suicide. If anyone was going to cure the daughter of Dr. Carter Cole, it would be he, Dr. Gunther Theobold.

"Don't you think it would be nice and okay for enjoying the autumn in Zurich, Vanessa?" Dr. Reichold said.

Seated at the end of the long conference table with a sheaf of papers in front of him, Mr. Brodhead, round as a medicine ball and hairless except for a curling shoal above his ears and a thick white mustache, scrutinized his navy blue pin-striped lapel and plucked a tiny white hair from it and set it carefully to the side, as if saving it for later. "It's really for the best, Vanessa," the attorney said without looking at her. An unpleasant piece of business, this. He hoped it would end quickly, without a scene. He hated scenes, especially when significant family estates were involved.

Vanessa opened her large blue eyes, and they were filled with tears. She said to her mother, "I suppose you have everything ready for me to sign. Like last time."

"Yes, dear. It's really only a formality."

" 'Only a formality.' "

"Essentially, all we're doing here is giving your mother power of attorney while you're in the care of Dr. Theobold," Mr. Brodhead said. "And naming your mother, myself, and U. S. Trust as executors of the several trust funds established for you by your grandparents and your late father. And, of course, a statement certifying that you're putting yourself in Dr. Theobold's care of your own free will, et cetera."

" 'Et cetera.' "

"Yes."

"Why do I have to give Mother power of attorney, and give her and you and the nice old men at U. S. Trust control of what's rightfully mine? I'm not a minor. I'm not certifiably crazy. Am I?"

"No, dear. It's only a temporary safeguard," her mother said and lightly nudged her on the arm, her writing arm, Vanessa noted.

"Against what?"

"It's merely a means of safeguarding and managing your holdings while you're incapacitated," the lawyer said.

" 'Incapacitated'? I'm not incapacitated."

"While you're abroad, I mean."

"I suppose, Mother, you've already booked passage for me."

"Yes."

"Of course. On the *Isle de France*, I hope?"

"Actually, I . . . ," her mother began. "No. I didn't."

"Oh, dear. Ernest has booked passage on the *Isle de France* for later this month, and it would be nice if we could travel together. At least until we must part in Paris."

"Ernest?"

"Hemingway, Mother. The writer. He's going to Spain, you know. To fight the Fascists and write about it for *Collier's*, I think he said. He invited me to join him in Madrid. But I guess now I can't do that, can I?" She sighed again. "He'll probably end up with that awful Gellhorn woman. He's left his wife, you know. Or is about to."

"Actually, I thought you'd like it better if I got you a stateroom on the wonderful new German dirigible, the *Hindenburg*! You seemed so excited talking about it the other day! It's quite luxurious. And expensive, I might add. Four hundred dollars, one way. But less than three days between New York and Frankfurt!" she said brightly. "Isn't that amazing? And Dr. Theobold has agreed to meet you in Frankfurt and personally accompany you by train to Zurich."

Dr. Reichold got his pipe ignited and sucked hard on it for a few seconds. "I will travel from America with you, Vanessa," he said between sucks. "For me it is the first time on the zeppelin, too. There is even a room for smoking. We can sit in it and talk together, and you can tell me all about this writer, Ernest, if you like."

"If I like."

"Yes, yes, if you like."

Her mother continued to pat Vanessa's hand. "It's for the best, dear. Don't you agree?"

Vanessa pulled her hand away, leaving her mother to pat the arm of the chair. She felt like an animal with its leg in a steel trap and no way to free itself without amputating the limb. The mother, the lawyer, and the doctor had feigned calm solicitude and reason, and now, with barely disguised vigilance, they watched Vanessa examine her trap and test its strength. She knew what they wanted and expected from her. They were waiting for Vanessa to erupt in furious opposition, to snap and howl at them and keep them at bay, while she yanked at the caught limb, tore at it, clawed and then chewed on it, so that finally, to save Vanessa from herself, they would be obliged to wrestle her to the floor and stick her with a needle and medicate her. It would make her pliant and predictable. And it would make their case. They could say they had no choice. She was clearly a danger to herself and others. "Yes, Mother, I agree," she said. "Whatever you want, whatever Daddy would have wanted, it's for the best. Whatever Dr. Theobold and Dr. Teutonic Pipe here and Whitney Mr. Brodbent Esquire, and all those trustworthy old men at U. S. Trust, whatever they want is for the best. Best for *whom*, though?"

"Why, for you, darling."

"All right, Mother." She stood up and walked to the conference table. "All right. As. You. Wish. Where do I sign?"

THE FOLLOWING MORNING, AT THEIR HOUSE IN TUXEDO PARK, Vanessa and her mother were packing Vanessa's trunk, when suddenly Vanessa left her mother alone in the bedroom. She went downstairs and into the basement laundry room, where she untied the laundress's clothesline and cut it into four pieces. When she returned to the bedroom, her mother was bent over the bed carefully folding sweaters. Her back was to Vanessa, and she was humming "A Fine Romance." Vanessa came up behind her and grabbed her by the wrists and wrenched her arms back and quickly tied them at the wrists and elbows. Too shocked and confused to cry out or even protest, her mother merely stared at her. She opened her mouth and inhaled deeply.

"Don't say a word. Just listen."

Her mother said, "Vanessa! What are you *doing?*"

Vanessa wrapped a nylon stocking around the older woman's mouth and knotted it. "I told you not to say a word," she said. Evelyn Cole shook her head from side to side, like a horse trying to spit the bit. "We're going for a drive together, Mother. The *Hindenburg* will have to leave without me. Instead, we're driving up to the Second Lake and scattering Daddy's ashes there. It's what he would have wanted," she said and slammed the half-filled trunk shut. "Not this."

Later in the week, when Vanessa did not show up in Parkhurst, New Jersey, for the departure of the *Hindenburg*, Dr. Reichold was not particularly disappointed. He was not fond of Vanessa personally and had not looked forward to spending thirty hours in close company with her, even on the *Hindenburg*. Nor, unlike most men, was he sexually attracted to her, as he preferred young blond male athletes and regretted having to miss the Berlin Olympic Games for this. But thanks to Mrs. Cole he had his return ticket to Frankfurt already paid for and in hand. He would simply report that Mrs. Cole had decided at the last minute not to commit her daughter, and Dr. Theobold would, as usual, stroke his beard and shrug and say, "In order to be helped, people must first come to me, Otto. I cannot go to them."

Vanessa was well aware that she had done a terrible, probably irreversible thing. But she had done terrible, irreversible things in the past, and the consequences had not been fatal or even life-threatening. In time they had merely become part of her biography, episodes in the ongoing story of Vanessa Cole, which she later embroidered and elaborated upon, making of it a shifting, regularly revised tale filled with surprises and contradictions that shocked, amused, and perplexed those who heard it. From Vanessa's perspective, this was the desired effect. Since hers was a story of ongoing beginnings, it was the best she could hope for. There were no necessary middles or inevitable endings to her life's story. She wasn't like other people, and she knew it. She hadn't chosen this plight, exactly; it seemed to have been thrust upon her. It was as if her personal and public past and future were not real, as if her past could be constantly altered and her future indefinitely postponed. She was free to start her life over, again and again—daily, if she wished—but by the same token she had no alternative.

To avoid keeping her mother bound and gagged during the long journey north to the Reserve, Vanessa convinced her—although it was untrue—that she had a gun in her purse, the same nickel-plated .38 she had been carrying at the Carlyle back when she wanted to shoot Count No-Count. She told her mother that if she tried to escape or called for help, Vanessa would shoot herself in the head immediately. "If you wish to be responsible for my death, Mother, if you wish to see me murdered before your very eyes and in effect by your hand, then all you have to do is give the guy at the toll booth a signal or whisper something to the man pumping gas or say a word to anyone at the Tamarack Club," she declared. "I won't hesitate for a second to blow my brains out in front of everybody, believe me," she said, and her mother did believe her.

Later, when she had her mother ensconced at the camp, she would not feel she had to bind and gag the woman—except when she left to chase down the artist Jordan Groves at his home in Petersburg and, of course, the following day, when he flew his seaplane to the Second Lake with Dr. Cole's ashes and briefly visited the camp afterward and Vanessa almost succeeded in seducing him. She bound and gagged her then. "You can have the run of the camp as long as we're here alone," she said. "But you can't go outside, Mother. And if someone comes up the lake in a boat or a hiker or someone from another camp stops by for a friendly chat, I'll do all the talking. Otherwise, I'll have to tie you up and lock you in the bedroom again and keep you there."

Vanessa's plan was not a plan; it was closer to a wild desire than a strategy. She wanted simply to avoid being institutionalized again, and she wanted somehow to regain control of the very large trust funds left to her by her grandparents and father that she had so placidly, so stupidly, placed in the hands of her mother, Mr. Brodhead, and U. S. Trust. She believed that the first of these desires would be satisfied if she did not willingly go to Zurich and her mother were kept from committing her elsewhere. The second would be satisfied only when her mother died of natural causes, highly unlikely at her age, or removed herself, Mr. Brodhead, and U. S. Trust as executors, also highly unlikely. Especially now. Vanessa's ultimate wish was that, until her mother died, no one except Vanessa herself would be allowed to see the woman or speak with her. For the time being, then, and for as long as possible, the two of them would stay here at the camp, not exactly unknown to the world, but in relative isolation and very difficult of access. After that . . . well, she'd figure out what to do when she actually had to do it.

Rangeview, at the Second Tamarack Lake, was located as far from other people as Vanessa could presently imagine, but to stay there for more than a few days she needed supplies—fresh and tinned food, kerosene for the lamps, cigarettes, and liquor—and someone to deliver it on a regular basis. She thought first of the artist and his seaplane, but realized at once that he would refuse to help her, at least for now. Then she remembered Hubert St. Germain, the local guide who for decades had been attached as caretaker to Dr. Cole's camp. Every July first, before the arrival of the Coles, Hubert opened the camp, stocked the larders, cut the firewood, and made the seasonal repairs to the roof and chimneys, tightened wind-loosened windowpanes and replaced torn screens, fixing whatever the hard Adirondack winter had broken. Vanessa liked and trusted Hubert St. Germain. He was very good looking, she thought, and shy and kept a discreet distance from his employers. You barely knew he'd been there, until you noticed a high stack of freshly cut firewood or saw that the broken steps to the deck had been replaced or opened the kitchen cupboard and realized that it had been restocked with oatmeal, soups, flour, sugar, and tinned beef, and in the icebox a large chunk of ice from the Tunbridge icehouse and a half-dozen freshly caught trout and a chilled bottle of Alsatian wine.

She would have to get to Hubert somehow; she would have to induce him to make weekly deliveries without having to come inside or hang around the camp, without having to see or speak with her mother.

"I'm sorry, Mother, but I'm going to lock you in the bedroom again." They were seated at the kitchen table eating a breakfast of canned pork and beans. After two nights and one full day, it was the last of their food. "It's going to be for four or five hours this time, so eat up. And you'd better use the bathroom before I leave."

"You won't tie my hands and feet and cover my mouth again, will you? Please don't. Please. It's an awful thing to do, Vanessa. Just awful," her mother said and began to cry quietly.

"I know. And I hate doing it. But, Mother . . . ," she said and paused. "I can't trust you, Mother. I just can't. If I don't keep you here, I know you'll get the men in white coats to carry me off to the loony bin. It's that simple. It really is. If Daddy were alive . . . well, if he were here, none of this would be necessary, that's all." She pushed her chair back and stood. "Ready?"

"I'm an old woman, Vanessa. Please don't do this. And I'm not well, you know that."

"You're fifty-three, and you're healthy as a horse. You'll probably live another twenty-five years. By then *I'll* be an old woman. Come on, I've got a lot to do today. We can't live on canned beans and spring water."

AN HOUR LATER, VANESSA HAD CROSSED THE SECOND LAKE and had made her way over the Carry, as the quarter-mile land bridge between the two lakes was called. She rowed the length of the First Lake, tied the guide boat at the dock, and quickly walked the gentle sloping trail back through the forest along the Tamarack River to the clubhouse, two miles away. There she went straight to the office of the manager, Russell Kendall, and entered without knocking.

He stood up abruptly, red faced, as if she had caught him doing something illicit. "I'd appreciate it if you knocked first, Vanessa. I could be having a confidential conversation with a member, you know."

"But you're not."

"No. Not at the moment." He wished he could make this girl just go away. The mother, too. These women, Evelyn and Vanessa Cole, or whatever she called herself now, were demanding and imperious. They were like a showgirl and her stage mother, he thought, and admired the thought. He was sorry the father had died. He had rather liked Dr. Cole, a gentle, gregarious man from an old Reserve family who liked to talk about Art and Nature. A man with a philosophical turn of mind. He tipped the staff well, and at Christmas, when the Tamarack Club was closed and Russell Kendall was in Augusta and the Reserve was the furthest thing from most members' minds, Dr. Cole always remembered to send Kendall a hundred-dollar holiday bonus, ten times a club cook's weekly pay.

"What can I do for you, Vanessa?" he asked.

"You can tell me how to get in touch with Hubert St. Germain. I need him to bring supplies up to Rangeview. Mother and I expect to be staying for longer than we had planned."

"Oh. How long? I thought you were here for only a few days," he said. "What happened with your father's . . . his ashes? I hope you didn't—"

"Don't worry," she interrupted. "I dumped them in the Tamarack River, but way over at Wappingers Falls. Not on Reserve property. By now Daddy's doing the backstroke in Lake Champlain, heading north to the St. Lawrence and on to the freezing waters of the North Atlantic."

"Vanessa, please," Kendall said. "He's your father."

"Was. But you're right," she said, suddenly shifting intent and tone. "I'm sorry. It's just . . . it's just that Mother and I are both terribly upset by his death. Especially Mother. We're mourning together. We're grieving over him at the camp. The Reserve was Daddy's most sacred place in the universe, you know. It was his true church. Somehow, even though we were forbidden by you to scatter his ashes at the Second Lake, we feel closer to him at the camp. So we've decided to stay for as long as his spirit lingers there. Possibly the rest of the summer. Possibly into the fall. It's why I need to speak with Hubert St. Germain. I hope he hasn't gone and arranged to take care of other camps and completely abandoned us. I know how popular he is, but he's always worked for us, and Daddy was very fond of him. I'd hate to lose him . . . now that my father's no longer here." She brushed away a tear.

Kendall sat down at his desk and drew a ledger from a drawer, opened it, and went down the list of guides and their assignments. "No, Hubert's free. He hasn't worked since you left for New York on July fifth. At least not here at the Club or for any of the other Second Lake camps. Of course, he may have found work elsewhere by now. I mean, among the locals. Unlikely, though, given the way things are. And given the way guides are," he added and smiled ruefully. "All the guides want is permission to hunt and fish in the Reserve, and they can't do it unless they're hunting or fishing for a member. Of course, they do it anyhow. In the off-season when we're not here. Honestly, I don't know how these people survive."

She asked him how she could contact Hubert, but it turned out he had no telephone. Very few local people had telephones, Kendall explained. She would have to drive into the village and go to his house, which was out beyond the old Clarkson farm, a log house he'd built himself and where he lived alone, with no one but his dog for company since his wife died—a nice enough young woman, very plain, but quite pleasant when she worked at the Club, killed a few winters ago in an automobile accident. "Most of us expected Hubert to remarry, as he hadn't been married long and had no children. But no. He is quite the ladies' man, if you know what I mean. At least the local ladies seem to think so, the housekeepers and kitchen help. They practically swoon when he comes around," Kendall nattered on. He was trying to sound like an intimate female friend, an equal, but it was hard for Kendall to be more than merely polite to Vanessa Cole. "Hubert is handsome, I suppose, in a rustic way. And very quiet. But you know what they say about the quiet ones," he said.

"No. What do they say?"

"Oh, still waters and all that." Kendall hoped he wouldn't have to see much of the Cole girl this summer, or her mother, either. But if the two women did end up staying at their camp till the end of August or even longer, Hubert St. Germain would help keep them out of the manager's hair. St. Germain was competent, independent, and discreet, a guide who kept things from getting complicated, and when he worked for one of the camps he made sure the owners didn't have reason to come to the clubhouse complaining to management. "I'll draw you a map to his house. It's a little hard to find. It's stuck over there beyond the village north of the Tamarack River, in the woods below Beede Mountain," he said and pulled out a sheet of club stationery and began to draw.

JORDAN GROVES'S NEW STUDIO ASSISTANT ARRIVED EARLY FOR her first day of work, surprising the artist and irritating him, for she had interrupted the start of a silly, sexually explicit fantasy, a detailed continuation of his most recent encounter with Vanessa Von Heidenstamm, revealing for his delectation what surely would have happened had he not turned away from the woman at the last possible second. Turning away was not unusual for Jordan Groves. He was good at it. Several times a year, sometimes more, he walked to the very edge of a precipice, looked over and down the cliff with a longing to step off it, then backed away, later to enjoy from a safe mental distance the terrible consequences of a near leap into domestic disaster. The fantasies gave him an ache that was oddly satisfying and provided a sexual charge that he believed enlivened him without endangering him or anyone else. The only women he actually made love to, other than his wife, of course, were women he was incapable of loving, and he never had sex with them more than once and almost never saw them again. The others he visited like this, in fantasy, telling himself little sex stories, over and over. In this way—perhaps it was the only way—he had managed all these years to avoid falling in love with anyone other than his wife, and, except for the fact that he knew it was an indulgence and would certainly not have wanted his wife to enjoy a similar indulgence, it left him guilt free.

This practice over the years had made the artist sexually incandescent to certain women. It made him behave in an invitational way, indicating that he was clearly available, even eager, to bed them, but would not do it. He was dangerous, and yet was unavailable, off-limits, safe. It did not hurt that he was a famous artist and handsome and healthy, a legendary adventurer and sportsman, a roistering world traveler with a loving family, leftist politics, and a lot of money. It did not hurt that he was the subject of much idle gossip. Certain women enjoyed having people think they were sleeping with Jordan Groves. The artist was aware of the source of his attractiveness to these women—he knew that his fantasies invoked theirs—and did nothing to discourage it.

Vanessa Von Heidenstamm had entered today's dreamy narrative so vividly that she had displaced everyone else. It was as if all those other women Jordan Groves could have fallen in love with, had he only let himself make love to them, in a flash had been completely forgotten, erased from memory. This was different. In the past, whenever mundane reality intruded—as in the early arrival of Frances Jacques, his newly hired studio assistant—he could simply put his little story down without feeling frustrated or deprived, the fictional dimension of his life blending easily with ordinary reality. But no longer. Closing the book on Vanessa Von Heidenstamm, even temporarily, made him cross.

"What the hell are you doing here now!" he barked at the girl. "I told you to come at noon. You're supposed to be here twelve to five, not eleven to four."

Frightened and embarrassed, the girl stood in the doorway and wrung her hands. "I thought, it being the first day and all, I thought I'd get here early, you know, to kind of get used to where things were and all. Gosh, I'm sorry, Mr. Groves," she said. "I'll go away and come back later." She was a local kid just out of high school, teachable, he had thought, though he'd been disappointed when she showed him the portfolio of awkward, amateurish drawings and paintings she'd made in art class. Not much talent there. But her teachers had spoken highly of her intelligence and character, and she seemed good natured and alert and physically strong, and besides, all she needed to do was keep the studio clean, take care of his tools and materials, stretch the occasional canvas, and when necessary pack and ship his work for him, most of which she could learn in a week. And she was from a poor family, the father jobless, the mother at home with four younger kids, and so on. That was in the girl's favor. Her job would at least put food on the family's table.

"No, forget it. Come in, I'll get you started," he said and waved her into the studio.

She was small but wiry, a farm kid used to physical labor. Her hair was a dark brown mass of thick curls, cut short more for ease of maintenance than appearance, and she wore no makeup or jewelry. She had dressed too carefully for the job, the artist noticed, like a secretary come to take dictation.

"Really, Mr. Groves, I'll go away and come back later," she practically pleaded.

He softened toward her then and smiled and apologized for being so grouchy. He liked her large dark eyes and rosy complexion and her sinewy forearms, unusual in a girl her age, and he wanted her to be happy and excited to be working for him. "Let's start over," he said. "Okay? You go back outside and knock on the door, and we'll take it from there."

Relieved, the girl smiled and did as she was told. She knocked, and the artist said, "Who's there?"

"It's me, Frances!"

"C'mon in, Frances!"

She opened the door and stepped inside, smiling broadly.

"Hey, Frances, good to see you. Came a little early, eh? To get the lay of the land before starting?"

"Y-yes. Is that all right? I can come back later if you like."

"No, no, that's fine. Usually I like to work alone till noon, but this morning I got in early myself. I was thinking of taking a break now anyhow."

"Oh, that's good!" she said, genuinely pleased and believing him.

"Before you do anything, though, you better get into some proper work clothes. I don't want you to ruin that pretty dress."

"Oh, dear. But . . . I didn't bring anything else."

"That's all right. Go to the house, and tell my wife that I need her to loan you some overalls and a sweatshirt. She's a bigger size than you, but it won't matter. You can roll up the sleeves and cuffs."

"She won't mind? You're sure?"

"Of course not, she'll be delighted. It's all boys around here, so she never gets to loan her stuff."

Frances said, "Thank you, Mr. Groves," and almost curtsied and quickly left the studio.

As soon as the door closed behind her, Jordan Groves returned to the story he had been telling himself when the girl had first knocked. He opened it at the page he'd marked. It was where he imagined Vanessa Von Heidenstamm sitting beside him on the sofa in the living room at Rangeview, the room lit by the golden light of the sun slipping behind the mountains across the lake. She places her glass down on the coffee table and looks up at him and says, "This must always be our secret, Jordan. We must never tell anyone that we have shown each other our scars. . . ." He is unsure of his answer. What would he say if she said that? What scars?

Following the club manager's map, Vanessa drove quickly through the village of Tunbridge to the Flats, turned onto the rutted dirt lane known locally as Clarkson Road, and wound uphill toward Beede Mountain. It was a bright sunshiny day with white towers of cumulus clouds stacked at the western horizon. Halfway up the mountain, a narrower, rougher lane split off to the left, ending five hundred yards farther at a single-story log structure, more a cabin than a house, with a wide stone chimney at one end and an open porch across the front. The yard was potted with tree stumps, and most of the forest downhill from the house had been clear-cut, leaving heaps of brush and tree scruff for burning. The place resembled the forest home of an early American pioneer.

She was greeted by a large dog, a butterscotch Labrador that careened off the porch and charged the driver's-side door of her car and stood there barking ferociously. Vanessa waved the dog off as if brushing away cobwebs and got out of the car. She ignored the dog, and it cringed and backed off and, with ears and tail lowered, went silent. Vanessa seemed not to notice its existence one way or the other. She walked past the animal and marched up the steps of the front porch, where she turned for a second and looked back at the entire Adirondack Great Range. It was a spectacular view of the mountains, running from Goliath and Sentinel all the way around to the south and then west to Mt. Marcy— 180 degrees of unbroken wilderness, millions of forested acres spreading south and east almost to the suburbs of Albany and Utica. As she raised her hand to knock on the rough-hewn door, she glanced at the battered Model A Ford coupe parked next to the cabin, a large wooden box in its trunk converting the vehicle from a car to a pickup, and then saw and recognized, half hidden in the pines just beyond, Jordan Groves's black Ford sedan.

Well, well, well, she thought.

She knocked on the door with freshened authority. The artist would be tempted to shove the guide aside and offer himself instead, she thought, once he saw her asking another man for help. Men were like that. She knocked a second time. Then called, "Hello! Hubert St. Germain! Are you there?"

The door opened a few inches and no farther. It was dark inside, but she could make out the guide's somber, craggy face. His shirt was unbuttoned and his suspenders dangled at his sides, and he was tousled and unshaven, as if just awakened. "Hello,

Miss Cole," he said. "Sorry . . . I was doing something in back and must not've heard you right off."

She said, "I'm sorry for coming unannounced. But I need to ask a very special favor of you, and it can't wait. May I come in?" Placing her hand flat against the door, she pushed lightly, intending to speak with Hubert St. Germain, but only in the immediate presence of Jordan Groves.

Hubert pushed back from the other side. "Is something wrong up at the lake, Miss Cole?" he asked, his face nearly expressionless—unreadable to Vanessa, but not mysterious. For her, there was no mystery to the man. He was compact and muscular, like most of the guides, and of average height, his hands and neck darkly tanned. Vanessa had never really thought of him as someone with a life of his own and therefore had never thought of him as someone who was unknowable. For years he had merely been the coolly detached, competent, always available guide, efficient and attractively designed, like one of those fine Adirondack guide boats he built and handled more expertly than any but the old legendary guides from her grandfather's day.

In the near darkness behind him she saw a silhouette of a person slip out of her line of sight into a bank of shadows deeper in the room. Hubert moved to come out onto the porch and close the door behind him.

"May I come inside?" Vanessa asked. The dog had followed her onto the porch and now stood beside her as if ready to escort her into the cabin. "I don't mean to interrupt, but I do need to speak personally with you." She wanted Jordan Groves to hear her plea and volunteer to help her in Hubert's place, and she resented to a small degree the artist's obvious avoidance of her. She intended to press herself on him, to make it impossible for him to ignore her specific need and rising desire. Confident since yesterday's encounter at the camp that his need and desire matched hers, she felt entitled, even invited, to risk being rejected by him. He was trying to run from that fact, and she had no intention of letting him.

Hubert said, "It's all a mess inside. We can talk out here on the porch. I . . . I've got a . . . ," he stammered uncomfortably.

Then a woman spoke from the darkness behind him. "I'm just leaving, if you want to have a private conversation," she said, and suddenly, standing in the doorway beside the guide, was Alicia Groves. "Hello, Miss Von Heidenstamm," the artist's wife said and pushed past them onto the porch. The dog backed out of her way, but otherwise made no fuss over her presence. Clearly, the animal was used to her.

Vanessa stepped out of her way, too, and watched in silence as Alicia Groves crossed the porch, hurried down the stairs, and walked from the yard to the pine grove where the Ford sedan was parked. Alicia's bright blond hair, Vanessa noticed, had been freshly brushed. Without looking back, Alicia got into the car and drove quickly down the hill and away.

Vanessa said to Hubert, "Well, I believe that now we can talk out here on the porch, if you like."

The guide gazed down the slope to the bend in the rough lane where the car had disappeared behind a stand of spruce trees, almost as if he expected Alicia Groves to return. "What is it you want me to do for you, Miss Cole?" he said without looking at her.

JORDAN BROUGHT HIS AIRPLANE INTO THE RESERVE FROM THE west this time, cutting a wide arc to avoid the clubhouse and the First Lake altogether, flying instead above the forested spine of the Great Range and coming in low over the swampy headwaters of the Tamarack River, where, except for a few solitary mountain climbers, he was least likely to be seen. A mile north of Dr. Cole's camp, he cut his speed as much as he dared and put the airplane into the water gently and taxied slowly along the shore. He anchored it in a shallow, protected inlet a mile or so above the beach where he had first seen Vanessa Von Heidenstamm. He came ashore there and went into the woods, making his way through low scrub alongside a small, rock-filled brook.

Soon the trees and brush thinned out, and he saw the roofs of the camp woodshed and the caretaker's shack. Avoiding the open ground in front of the camp, he walked through tall pines toward the guest quarters and approached the main building from the side. He passed the big stone fireplace chimney and was a few feet from the steps leading up to the deck when he stopped suddenly and stood stock-still, as if to hear the breeze stroking the high branches of the pine trees.

This is crazy, he thought. I'm a goddamn lunatic doing this, coming out here in the middle of the afternoon. I'm like a hound chasing a bitch in heat. It was his first conscious thought since he'd put Frances Jacques in charge of the boys. Alicia was in town, he knew, doing her thrice-weekly volunteer work at the little medical center there and picking up groceries afterward and would be home by three or so. He'd told Frances to inventory all his tools and brushes and to let the boys help her. That way she would learn where everything was located in the studio and what it was called. Just as his own father had done when he was a small boy, Jordan had taught his sons the names of the tools of his trade. It was the first step toward teaching them the trade itself. He gave the girl a pad and pencil and said that if she found a tool or a piece of equipment that neither she nor the boys could name, she was to make a drawing of it, and he would tell her later what it was called. He wanted her to memorize the location and name of every tool he owned, so that he could be like a surgeon and she his nurse, and all he'd have to do was ask for a particular brush or chisel, and she'd place it in his hand. He instructed her to go through all the drawers and look on every shelf and into the cabinets. He had nothing to hide. No secrets, he told her. He wanted her as familiar with every square inch of the studio as he was. Today was tool day, he said. Tomorrow they would inventory materials. Then he had left the studio for the hangar and his airplane, and until this moment, when he found himself in the Reserve at the Second Lake and about to step up onto the deck of the late Dr. Cole's camp, Rangeview, and quietly knock on the front door, he had no thoughts about what he was doing or why. He simply did it.

He realized that his silly sexual fantasy, not the woman herself, had gotten the best of him. Vanessa Von Heidenstamm was beautiful and provocative and intriguingly unpredictable, but she was flawed, terribly flawed, as if something inside her, a crucial, defining part of her mind, were permanently broken and made her dangerous to anyone foolish enough to get close to her. It wasn't a matter of liking or disliking Vanessa Von Heidenstamm. You were magnetically attracted to her or you were repelled, and in his case it was both. He glanced down the slope in front of the camp to the glittering water and noticed that the guide boat was not there. So she was gone, then.

He searched the lake for a moment and saw only a deer with her fawn stepping cautiously from the woods on the far side to drink. A pair of loons floated offshore a ways, bobbing in the low waves, disappearing abruptly underwater, reappearing a minute later fifty yards farther on, and Jordan wondered if, like swans, loons mated for life. Then suddenly the artist felt very foolish. He felt foolish and exposed, like a lovesick adolescent boy caught standing below the window of an inaccessible woman, a nobleman's young wife or daughter, and he merely the carpenter's son. Turning, he walked back along the side of the main building of the camp and into the woods and made his way downstream along the brook to the inlet where he had anchored his airplane.

The new American flyers flew formation drills at Los Alcázares twice a day for a week. The rest of the time they amused themselves pitching coins with their Spanish mechanics, tossing five peseta pieces the size of silver dollars. The tall American, the one they called Rembrandt, mostly kept himself apart from the others and made drawings of the blond hills. Finally one morning in early February, after they had been checked out and approved by their Spanish commander and a Russian colonel, they were sent to Valencia aboard an old Fokker trimotor transport. The Fokker landed at a half-constructed airfield in Manises, just outside the city, shortly after noon, and the Americans took a taxi to the Hotel Ingles, where they dropped their luggage and strolled to the nearby Vodka Café. They went there to meet the other foreign pilots based in Valencia, men who had been in Spain most of the fall of '36 and now the winter of '37. They were Allison and Koch and Brenner from the United States, and the Englishmen, Fairhead, Papps, and Loverseed. The three new arrivals were known to each other by their nicknames, taken earlier when they'd first arrived in Los Alcázares—Whitey, because of his pale hair, Chang, because of his round face and flat features, and Rembrandt, because back in the States he was a well-known artist—but they introduced themselves to the veteran pilots by their last names instead, Richardson, Collins, and Groves, as if somehow here in Valencia where there was a war on, nicknames seemed frivolous. Groves, the artist, asked, What've they got us flying out of here? All we had in Los Alcázares were a couple of old Polish Cojo-Jovens. Real clunkers, barely held together with tape and baling wire. Fairhead, who was the squadron commander, smiled and said they'd be flying even older 1925 Breguet 19s. Groves scowled. Christ, that crate was obsolete the day it came out of the factory, he said. The Englishman laughed. Oh, you'll get so you can squeeze enough out of it. It'll always get you home. Or nearly always. Every airplane has its virtues, Groves. Like women. You just have to learn how to locate them. Their virtues, I mean. And then how to get the bloody most out of them. Do you read me, Groves? he asked. Do you read me? The Englishman seemed drunk, and the American didn't answer. He moved away from the group and after a while left the café and went back to the hotel. The rest of the flyers kept drinking, and as the afternoon wore on they grew very loud and raucous, the veterans because they felt lucky to be still alive, the newcomers, Whitey and Chang, because they were afraid.

Trembling as if suddenly chilled, Alicia Groves drove rapidly downhill from Hubert St. Germain's cabin and said to herself that she hated this, lying like a child and hiding like a common criminal. And most of all, she hated having been exposed this way. Though it was probably a good thing, she thought. The exposure would allow her to end the deception. But not the guilt. No matter what Jordan did when he found out, the punishment would not be severe enough to end the guilt. And he *would* find out. And he would punish her. That girl will make sure he knows. She wants him for herself, Alicia thought, although she's probably already had him. Vanessa Von Heidenstamm was the kind of woman who takes a man away from his wife and children just because she can and then leaves him behind and moves on to steal another. Alicia hadn't known women like that, not personally, but she had read about them in novels and magazines.

It wasn't that way with Hubert. It was different with him, wasn't it? It had to be. That difference, however, was the source of her guilt. For she believed that she loved Hubert and he loved her, and she believed that Hubert had made her happier to be who she truly was than her husband ever had. In fact, it was Hubert who had shown her who she truly was. But there was a price to pay. A high, ongoing price. Regardless of what happened now, Alicia's happiness and freshened knowledge of who she truly was had corrupted her marriage, had tainted it forward and backward, from its beginning to the eventual end of it. It was as if she had been false to her husband all the years they were married and now was condemned to be false to him for the rest of her life. That's what Alicia believed.

Twice she felt the car begin to shudder and bump off the corrugated, switchbacking lane and had to yank the wheel and pull the vehicle away from the steep ditch at the side. And twice, lost in her thoughts, overwhelmed with guilt—and now dread, too, for she had seen herself through the calculating eyes of the other woman—she let the car coast almost to a stop before suddenly realizing it and accelerating back to a normal speed. Alicia had not intended to become involved with Hubert. Or with anyone else, for that matter. She told herself that she had not been looking for love outside the marriage, and she believed it. She and Jordan had often quarreled, of course, as all couples do, coming sometimes closer to violence, however, than most husbands and wives; and they had endured long periods of sullen detachment from each other, for Jordan was a difficult, demanding man with a roving eye and a permanent wanderlust and a need for constant forgiveness. But she had accommodated herself to his sharp, selfish ways, accepting them as an even trade for all the other ways in which he was large and exciting. Alicia believed that Jordan Groves had given her a bigger life than she ever could have acquired on her own or with a lesser man. Consequently, until she met and fell in love with Hubert St. Germain, Alicia had thought that, given her unique personality and desires, she was a happily married woman.

Over the years she had on several occasions been tempted to sleep with a man other than her husband—many men, usually friends or colleagues of Jordan's, had made themselves available,

especially when Jordan was off on one of his extended painting treks. But she had always turned them away with a gentle,
appreciative smile, glad for the attention, but unwilling to break
her marriage vows. Alicia had been raised a strict Catholic, and
though she had not been to confession or mass since arriving
in New York at the age of nineteen, and had said of herself in
the intervening years that she was, like her husband, an atheist,
and also like him was a Marxist, yes, but not a Communist, a
Trotskyite, maybe, but not a Leninist, she still took vows of any
kind seriously. It did not matter that she had made her marital
vows in a civil ceremony performed by a Scottish justice of the
peace with witnesses pulled in from the street. A sworn vow was
a promise that, regardless of changed circumstances, one kept.

Thus, even though throughout her marriage to Jordan Groves
there had been the usual crushes and flirtations, brief infatuations with men who resembled her husband not at all—short-
lived fantasies generated by mild sexual curiosity—they had never
come to anything. A few mixed signals and Alicia had quickly
backed off, relieved, her curiosity doused, her fantasies fading
fast and no longer able to excite her. In that way she had learned,
to her surprise, that she was attracted to quiet men, self-con-
tained, intelligent men who were modest about their accomplish-
ments, men whose small, compact bodies were not at all like her
husband's Viking body. She discovered that she was attracted to
men who knew things she didn't, who possessed skills she lacked,
and whose background and social status were radically different
from hers. Knowing this, she was able to stand slightly outside
her attractions and observe them dispassionately, even with mild
amusement, for she was married to and, as far as she knew then,
was still deeply in love with and made adequately happy by an
entirely different sort of man—a man physically large and ener-

getic and known to all the world for his turbulence and his frank outspokenness and egoism and his unquestioning belief in the importance of his life and work. A belief she had no difficulty in sharing with him.

In many ways they were, after all, a natural pair, Alicia and her husband, Jordan Groves. Jordan was educated in the arts, as she was, and like her was an only child raised by religious, politically conservative parents against whom he had rebelled early on—although his parents, of course, were American working class, Midwesterners, very blue collar, while hers were from the European *haute bourgeoisie*. And though they had made their home in a small farm village at the edge of the northern wilderness, Jordan and Alicia Groves were both cosmopolitan, worldly, sophisticated people. And they were rich. Together, but independently, and almost without trying—he by virtue of the immense early popularity of his work, she by virtue of being the daughter of well-to-do parents and the wife of Jordan Groves—the couple had become wealthy, renowned members of the *haute bourgeoisie* themselves. Thus she found it surprising and amusing and faintly ironic that, while she loved her husband for all the ways he and she were alike and in spite of the few ways they were different, she was periodically attracted to men like Hubert St. Germain for all the ways they were different and in spite of the few ways they were alike.

How they were different from each other was glaringly obvious to her. But until she had come to know the man intimately Alicia Groves could not have said how she and Hubert St. Germain were alike. There in his narrow bed in the furtive darkness of his small hand-built house, she learned that he was a man abandoned and lonely. She learned that he was a stoical man with low animal spirits, but one nonetheless eager to please in a sexual way and easy to please. And though essentially passive and trusting of all forms of authority, he was at bottom a man stubbornly independent of influence by others, especially in matters of right and wrong—ethical matters. And in that way she discovered that she, too, was all these things.

For she was abandoned and lonely. She had not been widowed like Hubert and was not childless and therefore was not, of course, abandoned and lonely in the same ways as he. But she was married to a man who was driven by powerful needs and desires, a man who for years had moved through her life like a hurricane, as if she were a single, small island in a vast archipelago, unable to alter his direction or diminish his force. After his storm had passed over and on, she always found herself alone, awaiting its return. Abandoned and lonely, then.

Also, her slow, gentle lovemaking with Hubert had taught her that she wanted to be held, not taken. She wanted to be touched with delicate precision by tongue and fingertip, not penetrated and lifted, awkward and off balance, unable to control her body herself, forced to give its leverage over to another. And she saw that, easy as she was to please, she was just as eager to give her lover pleasure back. She gave it, not as repayment, but as a gift outright, pure and simple, and the giving aroused and satisfied her.

They met in the fall and did not become lovers until the following spring. And all that spring, into the summer months, whenever she could steal away for a few hours, they made love and afterward walked in the woods and mountain meadows up behind his cabin, and there she discovered that she enjoyed deferring to Hubert's authority in matters where she was incompetent or ignorant, as in the names and natures of the trees of the forest that surrounded them and the Alpine flowers and the berries and bushes and the natural history of the land and the streams and the lakes. She admired his woodland skills, which to her were arcane, like hunting and fishing and building a house with little more than an ax, a splitting maul, and a buck saw. And she never lied to Hubert, never pretended to possess knowledge or experience that she lacked, the way she lied to her husband to keep him from instructing her. She did on occasion, however, give over to Hubert's authority in matters where she herself happened to be expert, such as gardening and cooking—skills she had learned from her Viennese mother and refined over the years of her marriage—but she did not believe that this was the same as lying to him. In these ways she learned that she was not vain or a liar by nature, as she had thought; she saw that she merely disliked conflict.

At the same time, when it came to matters of right and wrong, she believed that she was as stubbornly independent of Hubert's opinions as he was of hers. They did not, therefore, discuss politics or religion or money. Those subjects did not yet concern them and might never concern them, although she knew that he had voted for Herbert Hoover, that he was a practicing Methodist, and that he owned little more than his cabin and his old car and his rifles and dog and lived for the most part outside the cash economy. And Hubert believed what the other villagers believed—that Alicia and her husband were probably Communists, atheists, and rich, for they were "from away," as the locals said. Thus, when Alicia and Hubert spoke of right and wrong, ethical matters, they talked, not about their politics, religion, or money, but about the one thing more than any other that they shared—adultery.

In his bed, their faces pressed together, their hands laced and bare thighs touching, she said, "I don't believe in this, Hubert. Adultery. It's wrong. I don't mean the sex part, our secrets. I mean the lying. The deception. I'm scared of it."

"Why are you scared of it?"

"Because we'll pay dearly for this someday. Probably someday soon. It's not the same as having secrets. Everyone has secrets. It's like privacy. But whether Jordan finds out or not, lies and deception corrode your soul, Hubert. They turn you inside out and make you into a liar and deceiver. It's not just what you *do*, Hubert, it's who you *become*. Not to God, and not to other people, who don't know you're lying. To yourself. I don't want to become that person, Hubert."

He lifted his hand to her face and traced her lips with his fingertips and said, "You're wrong. It's not a terrible thing. Come on, now, it's a damned beautiful thing we're doing. A good thing, not a bad one. I loved only one other woman, Alicia, and she died. And now you. And to tell the truth, I didn't love her the same way as you. I loved her because I knew her so long and so well. It was love, yes, but it was different. It was *like* love. So nothing you say will make me think it's not a beautiful and good thing, Alicia. Nothing."

"Nothing, my darling? But it will come to nothing. It can't go on, and you know that as well as I."

"No," he said. "Don't think like that." And he kissed her again, and she closed her eyes and opened herself to him again.

AT THE BOTTOM OF BEEDE MOUNTAIN, ALICIA DROVE THE FORD past the Clarkson farm and made a wide, distracted turn onto the unpaved road and headed north toward the village of Tunbridge. The road wound through the valley of the Tamarack River, whose headwaters rose deep in the rugged mountains of the Reserve, among the brooks and muskegs that fed the Second Lake. Here below, surrounded by the peaks of the Great Range, the valley was broad and flat, with wide green meadows—a rich floodplain granted shortly after the Revolutionary War to New Hampshire and Vermont veterans of the war as payment for their services. For generations, in spite of the harsh climate, the inhabitants of the valley had managed until recent years to feed, clothe, and shelter themselves and their families through careful use and management of the region's few natural resources—soil good enough to support family farms and modest herds of livestock, a surplus of tall timber for export to Albany and Troy, and fast-running streams for powering small mills. For generations, the people of Tunbridge had been farmers, woodcutters, and mill workers.

Hubert St. Germain was one of the few local men who regarded themselves, not as simple working people, but as professionals. The guides were gruff, no-nonsense men whose skills and knowledge of the mountains, forests, lakes, and streams were essential to and much admired by people from the cities whose desire for a wilderness experience, starting in the mid-1800s, brought them north to the Adirondack region in increasing numbers. For many years, the visitors were paying guests at local farmhouses, eating homegrown produce and fresh game at the farmers' tables, playing cards and checkers in their parlors after supper, and swapping stories on their front porches. During the long summer days the people "from away" followed the hired guides into the forest and shot at deer and bear and other wild animals, killing them by the hundreds, and fished where they were told along the streams and on the lakes, where they caught trout by the thousands, and scrambled behind the guides up the steep, rocky, root-tangled trails to the bare mountaintops, there to quicken and refresh their sooty, urban souls with transcendental views of nature unadorned spreading out below to every horizon, as far as the human eye could see. The visitors were for the most part an educated, genteel lot, and many of them painted pictures of these scenes;

others wrote pastoral poetry; still others wrote long letters and kept copious journals in which they extolled the harsh beauty of this wild terrain and praised the warm generosity and independence of the people who lived in it year-round.

Late in the nineteenth century and in the early years of the twentieth, however, with the creation of the Reserve and the construction of the Tamarack Club and cottages and the large, elegantly outfitted wilderness camps like Dr. Cole's Rangeview on the Second Lake, the visitors no longer boarded in the homes of the residents. Instead, they hired the local people as caretakers, cooks, and cleaners, used them as waiters and gardeners and golf caddies at the club, so that the near equality of summer visitor and year-round resident began to disappear. A mutual parasitism based on a rigid set of class distinctions very much to the advantage of the outsiders took its place.

Then, when the stock market collapsed and the Depression took hold, one by one the small textile, shoe, and paper mills owned and managed by corporations based elsewhere shut down; and the downstate market for timber shrank and soon disappeared altogether. With the flow of outside capital gone dry, local people could no longer pay their debts. The banks downstate started calling in outstanding loans, and farms and homes, many of them heavily mortgaged, were repossessed or sold for back taxes, and land that had been in families for generations was sold off for a few dollars an acre, some of it to summer people, the rest to the Reserve. Gradually, by the mid-1930s, most of the year-round residents of the region found themselves out of necessity surviving solely as the seasonal, part-time, underpaid employees of the summer people. In two generations a class of independent yeomen and yeowomen had been turned into a servant class, with all the accompanying dependencies, resentments, insecurity, and envy.

Not Hubert St. Germain, though. The son and grandson of Adirondack guides, Hubert had no such diminished sense of himself as had his neighbors, or he never would have become the secret lover of Alicia Groves. Neither servant nor boss, the Adirondack guides were throwbacks to men of an earlier era, when the region had not yet been settled by white people—solitary, self-sufficient hunters and trappers and woodsmen who thought of themselves as living off the land, regardless of who owned title to it. They were viewed by locals and outsiders alike as independent contractors—somewhat the way the artist Jordan Groves was viewed. Thus, late one Saturday afternoon in October, when all the summer people had left the region to shift for itself once again and Jordan Groves met Hubert St. Germain for the first time at the Moose Head Inn in Sam Dent, after drinking a half-dozen bottles of beer with him and losing at arm wrestling to him—a thing that rarely happened to Jordan Groves—the famous artist felt easy about inviting the local guide home to eat with him, and the guide felt no discomfort in accepting. It was late at night by then, and the family was asleep. The men cooked steaks in a cast-iron skillet and drank whiskey and continued arm wrestling at the kitchen table until finally, at midnight, the artist was able to put the guide's arm flat to the table.

Alicia lay in bed upstairs and listened to the two men laugh and talk. Something in the voice of the stranger attracted her. It was not his north country accent. Alicia was not especially fond of the way the local people spoke; she sometimes had difficulty understanding their flattened, brisk English. But she liked listening to this man—his tone was sweet and unbroken, pitched lower than her husband's. She could not hear their words very well, even though the door to the hallway was open, but she knew that they were talking about cars, she could make out that much, comparing the virtues and limitations of Model T, A, and B Fords, agreeing that for this climate and these roads the Model A was the best vehicle. The stranger called them that, "vehicles," not cars.

She heard the stranger say that he ought to be getting home, adding with an odd wistfulness that he hated going back to his house at night now. Alicia got out of bed and put on her robe and walked to the doorway of the bedroom.

"Why's that, Hubert?" her husband asked.

The stranger said, "On account of the house being empty now. My wife got killed a year ago last November," he added in a flattened, expressionless voice, as if he were too used to speaking these words, and people's sympathy only made him feel worse and this was a way to deflect their sympathy. Even so, he felt obliged, despite his full knowledge of the inadequacy of his words, to let people know of his pain and loss, because they were real and inescapable, a part of who he was, and people who did not know of his wife's death often unintentionally said things or asked questions that squeezed his heart in an iron fist, bringing back full-blown his memories of that cold late-autumn night when the state trooper came to his door and told him that his young bride, his wife of three months, a passenger in a car driven by her older sister, had been killed. The car had hit a patch of black ice on the old Military Highway in West Tunbridge and had slid sideways off the road, gaining speed as it slid, crashing into a maple tree as thick as a man, hurling his bride from the car onto the frozen bare ground, a blow that crushed her skull and broke many of the large bones in her body. Now he got to the subject early, volunteering the information in a rehearsed, efficient, unemotional way, as if his wife had been someone else's wife.

Alicia made her way down the narrow back stairs to the kitchen and heard the stranger say to her husband, "Mostly I'm over it. But it comes back hard sometimes when I go home late like this."

Alicia's husband said, "Oh, Jesus Christ, Hubert, I'm sorry. I'm really sorry. And I apologize for bringing it up."

"You didn't bring it up. I did. You would've liked her, probably. Sally was good. A good person."

Alicia stepped into the kitchen and saw Hubert St. Germain for the first time and was startled and felt her throat tighten. She felt herself go out to him and was astonished by the speed and force of it. This had never happened to her before. There seemed to be a light in his face, as if someone in the room were shining a flashlight onto it. She couldn't tell if it emanated from her fixed gaze and was reflected back by his sun-burnished face or if his face somehow gathered light on its own. Though she had never seen him before, even at a distance or in a crowd, he seemed strangely familiar to her. She had the uncanny feeling that he could have been her long-lost brother, taken from the family before her birth and raised in the forest by peasants as their own and now suddenly, unexpectedly, placed here before her. He was a squarely built man of average height and wore a denim shirt buttoned to the throat and tan trousers and leather boots. His brown felt hat was pushed back on his head, and when Alicia Groves entered the room, he stood and removed his hat, and a shock of sandy hair fell across his forehead. His skin was smooth and fair, his eyes bright blue with pale, almost white eyebrows that gave him a look of innocent surprise. She guessed he was in his middle thirties, a few years older than she, a few younger than her husband.

"Please . . . please, sit down," she said, and he complied.

His words slightly slurred, Jordan Groves said, "Sorry we woke you. This's Hubert St. Germain. He's a guide over at the Tamarack Wilderness Reserve. Hubert, this's my wife, Alicia."

"Yes, ma'am, really sorry about waking you up," Hubert said. "And pleased to meet you, for sure. I was just leaving," he added and stood again and squared his hat.

"I overheard the last part of your conversation. I'm sorry about your wife, Mr. St. Germain. That's a terrible thing."

"Yes, ma'am, it is. Thank you."

"You should stay the night here," she said. "We have plenty of room. It's late, and you shouldn't be driving anyhow. I know you boys have been drinking. And I can understand how difficult it must be to go home to an empty house. Please," she said. "Stay."

"Yes, Hubert, spend the night here and go home in the morning," Jordan said.

"Really," Alicia said. "I want you to stay."

The guide hesitated a moment, then accepted their invitation, grateful for it. Too many nights through the hard year and a half since his wife's death he had ended up drinking late with strangers at the Moose Head until the place closed or drinking in a stranger's kitchen like this and finally having to make his way back to his cabin, driving drunkenly over narrow country roads, his Model A coupe drifting from one side of the road to the other, the headlights of oncoming vehicles doubling in his blurred vision, until at last he pulled up in front of his cabin and staggered inside, where, still fully clothed, he dropped onto his bed and, before losing consciousness, let himself be crushed by the weight of his loneliness, and wept. And then he blacked out, and the next morning remembered only the sad fact of his weeping and the feeling of his chest being pressed by a stone the size of the room itself. And with each day's waking his loneliness and sorrow were worsened by his fear that neither was due to the death of his wife, that both had been in him all along.

Alicia lay in the darkness with her husband sleeping next to her. He had come to bed only minutes earlier and was snoring already and smelled of alcohol and meat and sweat. She heard the bed in the guest room creak and imagined the guide turning in his sleep, dreaming of his lost bride. Or perhaps, she thought, lying in bed in the room next to hers, he, too, was awake and listening for some indication that she was thinking about his presence in her house, and perhaps he was as eager as she for them to talk to each other with no one else present. And though Alicia soon fell asleep, when she woke in the morning her mind was instantly filled with this thought. And when the guide woke in the Groveses' guest room bed, his loneliness and sorrow seemed mysteriously to have fled. When the artist, Jordan Groves, woke, he was mildly irritated by how late he had slept and hurriedly washed, shaved, and pulled on his clothes, so that by the time Hubert St. Germain and Alicia Groves were sitting down opposite each other at the breakfast table, the artist was already at work in his studio.

NOW THAT THE AFFAIR HAD BEEN DISCOVERED BY THAT DAMNED socialite, Alicia decided that she could not go on seeing Hubert any longer. She knew that she could have stayed hidden from the woman's sight; Hubert could have insisted on speaking to her outside, and she would have gone away; Alicia must have wanted to be seen by her, to be discovered, uncovered, revealed—not so much to the rest of the world, but to herself. She would break it off immediately and wait for the Cole girl to tell Jordan what she had seen, and Jordan would draw his own conclusions: simply, he would know at once that his wife had been lying to him all these months. She had not been playing visiting nurse at the medical center in Sam Dent at all, had she? She had been with Hubert St.

Germain those afternoons. He would bring those conclusions to Alicia, and she would have no choice but to confess everything.

But at least she could tell him that she had ended the relationship. She would say that she had ended it so that their marriage, however broken and betrayed, could continue in some form. And she would tell him that she was ashamed and remorseful, even though she was not ashamed of what she had done and was not remorseful, regardless of the damage it had done to her marriage. She would humbly accept her husband's righteous wrath and stoically endure the license he had now—license to conduct, without guilt and probably not even secrecy or discretion, an affair with Vanessa Von Heidenstamm. Alicia would be almost relieved by that, however. If he were openly having an affair, Alicia would no longer have to deal with his secrets and the lies that went with it and the rumors and gossip, which for years had afflicted the marriage, making it sullen and suspicious and sexually tepid.

When Alicia arrived home, Jordan was not there, and his new assistant, Frances, was taking care of the boys, amusing them in the studio. They were teaching her the names of the artist's tools and equipment, the girl explained brightly, so that she could make an inventory.

"Frances is very smart, Mama," Wolf said.

"And she's nice, too," Bear added, and the girl reddened.

"I'm sure she is. Where did Mr. Groves go?"

"I don't know. He said he had some business to attend to. He took his airplane. That's a swell thing to have, your own airplane that you can land on water."

"He'll take you for a ride, if you want," Wolf said. "Papa likes taking people for rides in his airplane."

"There are brownies on the kitchen counter by the stove, and milk in the icebox. Help yourself when you're ready. I'll be upstairs, so just holler if you need me," Alicia said and went into the house. She would write to Hubert now and tell him of her decision. Alicia was glad that Jordan was not at home, so that she could write the letter before she had a chance to change her mind; and she was glad that he had taken his airplane, because she could hear its engine a half mile upriver and could hide the letter before he came into the house.

Upstairs in the bedroom, sitting at the writing desk, Alicia took out a vanilla-colored envelope and a sheet of stationery, and she wrote,

Dear Hubert, this is the first and last letter I will write to you. What happened today has brought me to my senses. I will always treasure the love that we shared with each other, but we cannot continue this any longer. You are the only man other than my husband whom I have ever loved or ever will love. I am grateful to have had that. Before I knew you I was content and, though I did not know it, unhappy. You made me very happy, but with it came a terrible discontent. It cannot go on. The costs to my children and to my marriage are too great. When that woman came to your house today, I was forced to look at myself through her eyes, and I realized that I have been swept up in a kind of madness. Please forgive me for allowing it to happen. Forgive me for loving you.

And signed it, *Always, A.*

She folded the letter, sealed it in the envelope, and wrote Hubert's full name on the envelope and put it into her purse. Tomorrow she would drive to town and stop at the turnoff by the Clarkson farm where Hubert's mailbox was located, and she would leave the letter in the box.

No, she would do it now, she decided, before Jordan returned. Before she understood fully what she was giving up. Before she could change her mind.

JORDAN GROVES FLEW HIS AIRPLANE FROM THE SECOND LAKE south over the headwaters of the Tamarack River into the wilderness and then around to the west and across the Great Range, the same way he had come in, so as not to be seen by anyone fishing the First Lake or hiking in from the clubhouse. Shortly, he was on the other side of the Great Range, beyond the Reserve and flying high above the broad valley. He was on his usual route now, following the river home, headed downstream from the outskirts of the village, flying over the scattered roadside farms and the green meadows and cornfields and the clusters of maple and oak and elm trees. There were crosswinds in the valley at this altitude, churning the air slightly, and rather than climb out of the turbulence, he dropped down until, at about twelve hundred feet, cupped by the surrounding mountains, the air smoothed, and he was able to see the freshly oiled road that ran like a scorched ribbon alongside the widening river, and he could even make out individual cows in the fields and people working in their gardens and yards. Only a few vehicles were visible—a dump truck trundling into town, then Darby Shay's delivery van carting the week's groceries over to the poor farm in Sam Dent, and then, headed in the opposite direction, he saw the tan Packard sedan that he recognized as Vanessa Von Heidenstamm's and, following close behind, the modified Model A Ford coupe that he knew belonged to the guide Hubert St. Germain.

Seeing the two of them in the same frame made Jordan Groves freshly ashamed of his mad pursuit of Vanessa Von Heidenstamm. Though he had not seen much of the guide since that autumn night when he'd first met him, he liked the man. The artist admired the guide for his honesty and stoicism and independence. He had been impressed by the straightforward, tough-minded way the man handled the death of his wife. Hubert St. Germain, the longtime caretaker for the Coles, would do without complaint whatever Vanessa asked him to do, but no more or less than that. Hubert St. Germain had the calm good sense and moral clarity not to indulge in elaborate fantasies about the woman, no matter how seductive a game she played. Hubert St. Germain would never find himself out there at the Second Lake, uninvited, unexpected, hoping to step into the living room and take the woman into his arms and make love to her. The guide was a man another man could admire, a man another man could try to emulate.

The situation was new, but his emotions were familiar to him. He saw that this was fast becoming one of those times when, to clear his mind of weakness and confusion and to regain the meaning of his life, Jordan Groves periodically left home and family and journeyed alone to a far place. It had been nearly two years since his August '34 trip to Greenland, four years since the winter in the Andes when he climbed Chimborazo, Cotopaxi, and Aconcagua and hacked his way through the jungle to Machu Picchu and lived for a month in a hut by the shores of Titicaca. On each of these journeys he had made a daily written record of his thoughts and observations and his sometimes reckless and dangerous experiences, exact and truthful and unsparing, and he had made drawings of the people he met and the places he visited. Each time, on his return, he had published a revised, lightly edited version of his journal as a book, along with many of the drawings. He hadn't been able to finish the Greenland book yet because he'd been so taken by the natives and their hardy yet delicate ways and their persistent good cheer that he'd filled his sketchbooks and journals with drawings of human beings and had neglected to make pictures of the glaciers that surrounded them. It was the huge white glaciers, those vast mountains of ancient ice, he realized later, that had made the people seem simultaneously strong and vulnerable. To make sense, to be faithful to his perceptions of the Greenlanders, his book needed the glaciers. For that he would have to return to Greenland.

Though not best-sellers, his books had been very well received, partially because of the drawings, but also because the artist was a clever writer with a knack for storytelling. Mostly, however, his readers enjoyed the explicit nature and apparent honesty of his descriptions of his sexual encounters with the women native to those places. To his wife and friends and even to journalists interviewing him, he claimed that those episodes were mostly "tall tales," fictionalized autobiography, and no one pressed him on the point. But the drawings, made from life, confirmed the claims made by the words, for Jordan Groves, like the American expatriate writer Henry Miller, seemed to hold nothing back, recording in both pictures and words his misadventures alongside his adventures, his happy ease in succumbing to temptation and his occasional principled resistance to it, his delight in the life of his body as much as his compulsion to muse philosophically on subjects great and small. He himself made no claims for the books as literature—he referred to them as his "travel books"— but critics and reviewers admired them, albeit with a certain condescension, invariably noting that, for an artist, Jordan Groves was a remarkably good writer.

Flying along the river, he glanced ahead and saw the Clarkson farm coming up on his right, and then he saw what appeared to be his own car stopped at the lane that led up Beede Mountain to where Hubert St. Germain had built his cabin. He banked hard to the right and circled back over the mountain and the guide's log cabin and down, and, yes, it was his own black '34 Ford sedan all right, and there was Alicia standing beside the mailbox posted at the side of the road, and she turned and gazed up at him as he flew low and passed overhead. He banked left, crossing over the river, and circled back a second time, dropping the airplane down to just under a thousand feet, and when he flew over Alicia, who stood by the car now with the driver's door open, he leaned from the cockpit and waved to her, and Alicia, looking sad and lonely even from this distance, slowly, almost hesitantly, as if she wasn't sure who he was, waved back.

And then he was gone, homeward bound, thinking, No, not this time. No more journeys. No more months away from Alicia and the boys, traveling to exotic, far-flung lands, living like the natives among the natives in order to reinvent himself and coming back to tell the world how he had done it and whom he had done it with and what it was like there. The Greenland book would have to remain unfinished, and any future books would be about his life in the Adirondacks in the bosom of his family. From now on he would find his inspiration at home. And any solitary reinventing he did would be done in daylight, inside his studio.

A few moments of following the Tamarack River, and then he was above the fork where it joined the Bouquet River and doubled its width and depth, and he had entered the township of Petersburg and could see among the distant trees the chimneys and the black-shingled roof of his house. He began his descent, and for the first time in nearly a week he thought again about the war in Spain and the fight to save the republic from the Fascists, for that week the republic had begun issuing arms to civilians in Madrid, and when the airplane touched down and the pontoons sprayed high fantails of water behind it, Jordan Groves brought back to his mind the American men who were signing up for the Lincoln Brigade, many of them his friends and longtime political allies, and for a few seconds, as he taxied along the riverbank and brought the airplane up to the hangar ramp, he envied those men. But when he looked over to the side yard where the girl, Frances Jacques, was pushing Bear on the tire swing that hung from a high branch of the big oak, while Wolf at her side patiently waited his turn, the artist all at once ceased to envy the men who were enlisting to fight Fascism in Spain, and he concentrated instead on the promises he would make to his wife tonight. This time he would change his life right here at home. The war in Spain would have to be fought without him.

In town, Hubert St. Germain slowed and parked in front of Shay's General Store and watched Vanessa Cole's Packard continue on, speeding past the roadside lines of towering elms, headed for the clubhouse, where she would leave her car and walk the mile-long trail into the First Lake. It was a simple but somewhat arduous way to get from what passed for civilization to what passed for wilderness. You needed to be fit enough to make the hike into the boathouse at the First Lake, row a mile and a half across it to the Carry, where you took a different guide boat and rowed two more miles to the camp. In his shirt pocket Hubert had the list of supplies that Vanessa had written out for him at his cabin. It will take two trips, he thought, studying the list. Maybe three. He'd try to lug half the supplies in this afternoon, mostly the food, and bring in the rest tomorrow.

It looked from the list that she was planning to stay awhile, at least two weeks. Or even longer, she had implied, telling him to check at the clubhouse on the first of August, where, if she decided to stay on, she would leave a new list with Mr. Kendall. Hubert was not to come out to the camp unless she arranged for it beforehand. She wanted to be alone with her mother to share their grief over the tragic loss of her father at Rangeview, the one spot on earth that was sacred to him. Although Hubert did not think that the death of Dr. Cole was particularly tragic—Dr. Cole had enjoyed a good long life, after all, and his heart attack had killed him quickly—he was just as happy to stay away from the two women, so long as they didn't need him for anything specific, because otherwise they tended to turn him into a generalized servant, a rustic houseboy, expecting him to stay out there at the camp and do for them all sorts of things that they could easily do themselves, without adding anything to the monthly retainer they paid him.

Dr. Cole had always been more respectful of the guide than his wife and daughter were, more aware that the guides and caretakers were specialists whose wilderness skills and knowledge, handed down over generations, had taken many years to acquire. In some ways, Dr. Cole was like Alicia, Hubert thought. They both enjoyed having him teach them as much as he could of what he knew and they did not—the names of the native flowers and plants and insects and the habits of the animals and the fish and the birds. They both wanted him to tell them who in town was related to whom and how. They even wanted to learn the histories of the houses and farms of Tunbridge and who had once owned the land. Dr. Cole had treated Hubert St. Germain as an equal, when, of course, in the eyes of the world he was not the doctor's equal. No, the death of Dr. Cole by heart attack was not tragic. But Hubert would miss him nonetheless. Especially since from now on he would have to deal directly with the wife and the daughter.

It was not clear to him what Vanessa Cole had concluded back there at the cabin, but it was enough that she suspected he and Alicia were lovers. They would have to keep from seeing each other for at least as long as Vanessa Cole stayed at the camp. When she left the Reserve and returned to the city, he and Alicia could take the measure of any damage done and decide what to do then. But he knew they could not be together again the way they had been before.

In any event, he decided, until Vanessa Cole was gone from the Reserve, they would not be able to meet as they had. He was unsure of how to communicate this decision to Alicia. He did not want to write her a letter. He and Alicia had communicated only in person, never in writing. From the beginning, he had simply counted on her appearing at the door of his cabin three after-noons a week, except for when he was up at the lakes. All spring and into the summer, over and over again, she had knocked softly on his door and entered his life, making it seem suddenly large to him and precious and exciting. Before then it had felt small, nearly worthless, dull. And sorrowful. And lonely. Which was how it would have to be now, for a month, perhaps longer, possibly for-ever—depending on what Vanessa Cole did with her suspicions.

That's all they were, though—suspicions. What could Vanessa Cole care if her hired guide and caretaker was having a love affair with a woman who happened to be the wife of a man she barely knew? The artist Jordan Groves wasn't part of the Coles' circle; he wasn't even allowed on the Reserve or at the clubhouse, not since he'd landed his airplane at the lake and had that fight with Kendall. Also, Hubert had heard that Vanessa Cole was angry with the artist for flying her up to Bream Pond on the Fourth of July, the same night her father died, and leaving her there to walk back alone. If she was still angry with him, then she'd probably enjoy suspecting that the artist's wife was sleeping with her family's hired guide and caretaker. She'd like that. She wouldn't want to do anything that helped end the affair. She'd want to keep her suspicions to herself.

Hubert walked up and down the aisles of the store, followed by Kenny Shay, the owner's son, who carried the items the guide selected back to the counter and stacked them there—tinned beef, bacon, eggs, cheese, oatmeal, spaghetti, bread, butter, canned vegetables and fruit, sugar, and condensed milk, and hard goods, too, like candles and kerosene and soap—a long list of supplies that Hubert would lug into the lakes on his back and take across to the camp in his guide boat, where he knew Vanessa and her mother would need him to cut enough firewood to last them two weeks or longer. No doubt he would have to make some small repairs on the place as well, and, depending on their mood, he might have to go back to the clubhouse and bring in fifty pounds of ice from the icehouse and before dark catch them a pack basket full of trout and clean the fish for them, cooking a half dozen tonight and putting the rest on ice. He would not get home until late. But it was work for which he would be fairly paid, according to his old agreement with Dr. Cole, and there was no other paying work anywhere in the region for him right now, not without taking away the job of one of the other guides. Still, he was not looking forward to doing it.

As Vanessa neared the camp, the pace of her rowing picked up. She glanced over her shoulder at the shore, looking to avoid the rocky outcrop that extended into the water on either side of the landing, then scanned the deck and grounds, hoping for a few seconds that somehow she had hallucinated this or dreamed it, all of it, and she would see her mother and maybe even her father standing on the deck, dressed for dinner, cocktails in hand, anxiously awaiting her return. Ever since the meeting in New York at the lawyer's office, Vanessa had felt that she was having one of those frightening dreams with no beginning or end, where you know you're dreaming—you must be, because everything is out of control and unpredictable, and you feel guilty of some dark, unnamed crime—but you're unable to wake from it.

She prayed that she would wake from this dream. And then she did. Her mother sat gracefully on the hull of an overturned guide boat, her barefoot legs crossed at the ankles. She sipped champagne from a crystal flute. She wore a simple gold bracelet on her wrist. From her distance, Vanessa admired her mother's gentle, slightly dreamy poise, the way she looked down at the rocky shoreline as if she were remembering something privately amusing, and Vanessa decided that it was the dress that made her look so lovely, a cream-colored, low-necked, beltless frock by Muriel King that hung straight from the shoulders. It was the dress, but even more it was the unselfconscious privacy of her thoughts. What a beautiful woman, Vanessa said to herself. I will look that beautiful someday. I will know how to dress like that someday. I will know how to have thoughts like that someday. Then she saw her father. He was standing on the deck. He was dressed for dinner. His hands were clasped behind his back, and he was rocking ever so slightly on his heels, looking with pride and good-natured satisfaction at his wife down at the shore, as if he had created her, a painting or a photograph he had made. There was nothing impatient about him, nothing distracted—he had taken a moment to stop and look fondly and with profound appreciation at his wife without her knowing or posing or worrying about pleasing him.

But the deck was deserted, there was no one at the shore,

there was not even a guide boat, and there was no one walking among the tall pines that surrounded the camp. She had not been dreaming. Her father was dead. And she had indeed committed a dark, unnameable crime. For the first time since forcing her mother to Rangeview and imprisoning her there, Vanessa was truly terrified of what she had done.

Up to this moment, whenever she saw what she had done, she had justified it to herself, rationalizing her rash acts, telling herself that she had no choice, none, they had trapped her, Mother and the lawyers and the doctors, and now they wanted to put her in a cage and keep her there for the rest of her life. Or worse. Those were facts. Everything else was speculation or memory, febrile and unreliable. Since childhood, Vanessa had felt trapped by her parents, as if they were predators and she their intended prey—trapped and then put in a cage for later, when they would have the time and occasion to devour her properly. As a small child, Vanessa could not listen to those old fairy tales being read to her without crying and begging whoever was reading to stop, stop. Those old stories of children put into ovens by stepmothers and wicked witches. Children climbing sky-high bean stalks to the giant's lair. Children being led by a piper into a mountain cave, never to be seen again. They terrified Vanessa. She could not bear to say or even hear nursery rhymes without feeling her chest tighten and her legs go all watery, making her cry to her nanny Hilda or to the child reciting the rhyme, *"Stop! Stop saying that! I hate that! It's nasty and scary. You're only doing it to scare me!"*

People—her nanny Hilda and the babysitters, other children and their parents, and her own parents and their friends—were impressed by Vanessa's exquisite sensitivity and smiled down at her and praised it, as if she were the most delicate flower of all and therefore the most precious. But she knew, even as a very young girl of five and six, that her inability to listen to the fairy tales and nursery rhymes that other children loved had its origin someplace else, because the tales and verses made her feel the way she felt when she almost remembered being naked and lifted high in the air by a big man and placed up on the fireplace mantel with a scary hot fire burning below, the big man turning into her father, who disappeared suddenly behind his camera box, covering himself with a black hood, when something made a whooshing sound and a flash of light so bright that for a few seconds she couldn't see anything and only knew that she was being lifted again by a big man and carried to a sofa that was hard and scratchy on her bare bottom and back, where she was placed just so, her naked legs and arms arranged just so, her head turned just so. She remembered the diamond shapes in the carpet on the floor, dark red against a field of green. And then another whooshing sound and flash of light that made her close her eyes tight, and she kept them closed tight, clenching them like fists, wrinkling up her nose and crinkling her forehead, making herself ugly, until her father carried her to her crib, where he put her nightie back on her and kissed her on the cheek. And then her mother, led to the crib by her father, leaned down and stroked Vanessa's hair slowly, dreamily, with eyes half closed, smiling, as if she'd never felt anything so soft and lovely before.

At her father's funeral at St. James Episcopal Church, when it was Vanessa's turn to speak, she started to talk about what her father was like as a young man, before he went off to war, when she was the very little girl that Dr. and Mrs. Cole had recently adopted, but somehow she got away from what she'd planned to say. She had meant to describe him as heroic and wise and all-knowing, the way little girls are supposed to remember their fathers, but instead she found herself describing him the way she actually remembered him. She said that he was cold and detached and that he saw people, including his own daughter, as objects to be examined and cut open and repaired, as a thing to be photographed and privately exhibited for his exclusive, secret pleasure. What began as a loving daughter's eulogy ended as a turgid, blurred accusation that so upset everyone that afterward no one would speak to her. Until the morning two weeks later when her mother announced that she had scheduled a meeting for that afternoon with Whitney Brodhead to discuss her father's will. When they entered the lawyer's conference room and Vanessa saw Mr. Brodhead seated at the head of the long table with a sheaf of papers spread before him and Dr. Reichold standing at the rain-sopped window looking down at the street, Vanessa knew that she was just as trapped now as she had been all those years ago, lifted into the air by a big man and placed naked up on the mantel with the fire burning somewhere below, and her father, behind the camera box and hidden under his black cloak, saying, *"Humpty Dumpty sat on a wall. Humpty Dumpty had a great fall, and all the king's horses and all the king's men couldn't put Humpty together again. . . ."*

Vanessa dragged the guide boat from the waterline at the rocky shore up to the knoll beyond, rolled it over onto the gunnels to dry, and walked quickly to the house. She had been gone longer than she expected and knew that her mother would be thirsty and hungry and would need to use the toilet. The water system for the camp was primitive, but effective—a pipe that ran downhill from a spring behind the cookshack fed a wood-fired water heater in the kitchen of the main building and the several bathrooms. There was an outhouse for the help, of course, but no bathing facilities for them except the lake.

She unlocked and opened the door to her parents' bedroom and entered. Her mother was seated on a straight-backed chair by the dressing table, just as Vanessa had left her hours earlier, her hands and ankles bound and tied to the chair. The silk scarf had slipped from her mother's mouth to her chin, and her mouth gaped open. Her head lolled to one side, eyes closed, and her breathing sounded labored and raspy, as if she had climbed a steep hill.

Vanessa hurried to her side and untied her hands and ankles and removed the scarf. "Mother? I'm sorry I took so long, Mother. Are you all right?"

Evelyn Cole's head wobbled, and she turned, opened her eyes, and looked at Vanessa with a puzzled expression, as if not quite recognizing her daughter. Half lifting the woman from the chair, Vanessa guided her mother with one arm around her waist from the chair across the room to the bed and gently lay her down and covered her with a Hudson's Bay blanket from the chest at the foot of the bed. "Oh, Mother, I'm so sorry," she said. "Please, please, please, be all right."

Evelyn said, "Water. Give. Me. Water. Vanessa."

Vanessa ran into the bathroom and filled a glass, thinking, Please don't die. This isn't what I wanted. All I wanted was not to be trapped by you and Daddy. Then she heard the bedroom door open and close behind her. Rushing from the bathroom, she heard the click of the lock in the door. The blanket lay in a white, black, and red heap on the floor beside the bed.

Vanessa yanked on the door latch and shrieked, "*Mother!* Open this door! I'll *kill* you for this!" She ran to the window, shoved it open, and unhooked the screen. In seconds, she was out the window and racing around to the front of the building, where she saw her mother already at the shore struggling to turn the guide boat off its back, unable to do it.

Vanessa approached her mother methodically, calmly. "It's too heavy for you."

Evelyn Cole let go of the boat and looked out at the lake as if seeking help. There was no one there. The sun was halfway between the meridian and the far side of the lake, and the water glittered like hammered brass. Her daughter was insane. Her daughter was going to kill her, Evelyn knew it now. She said, "Vanessa, please. Let me go. I promise, I'll do anything you want."

"It's too late, Mother. I don't believe you."

"Please, Vanessa. Please don't kill me. I'm your mother, Vanessa."

"No, you're not." They stood facing each other across the upturned boat. "I don't want to kill you, for heaven's sake. I just want . . . ," she began and left the sentence hanging.

A few seconds of silence passed. "What do you want from me, Vanessa?"

Vanessa took a deep breath. "I want . . . I want you to be a good girl. That's all. While I figure out what to do with you."

Vanessa took her mother firmly by the elbow and guided her slowly back up to the house. When they reached the deck, Evelyn said, "I'll be good. I promise. I'll do whatever you ask."

"Hubert St. Germain is coming soon with supplies. I'm going to have to keep you locked up and quiet while he's here." Vanessa glanced back and checked the glimmering horizon for Hubert's boat. No sign of him yet.

"Please don't tie me up again. I swear, I'll stay out of sight and will be quiet as a mouse. Please, Vanessa." The ropes had burned Evelyn Cole's wrists and bare ankles, and the scarf over her mouth had made her feel as if she was suffocating. She meant it, she would do exactly as Vanessa wished. She would stay in the bedroom with the door closed while Hubert was at the camp, and she would not call for help. Vanessa would have to come to her senses eventually. She couldn't be mad. She couldn't be capable of killing her own mother. "Vanessa," she said, and waited until Vanessa's gaze came back to her. "I am your mother."

"Stop saying that!" They stood at the closed door of the bedroom side by side. "Come," she said and held out her hand. "Let's go in now." With her free hand Vanessa turned the key and pushed the door open.

"You don't understand. You're my child, Vanessa. I'm your mother."

"Stop saying that! I've got to think. I've got to think about what's next."

"I'm afraid, Vanessa. I'm afraid of what you're going to do next. Please, remember, you're my child."

"Don't say that again."

"Vanessa, you are."

"What are you trying to say?"

"I'm trying to tell you the truth."

"Right. If you want to tell me the truth," Vanessa said, drawing her mother into the room and leading her to the chair, "you can tell me who my real mother was. And my real father. Not that it matters much now."

"I'm your real mother," Evelyn said simply.

Vanessa turned and looked closely at her. She looked away again. "No. No, you're not. My real mother never . . . a real mother wouldn't treat her daughter the way you've treated me," she said. She put her hands on Evelyn's shoulders and pushed her down into the chair and gathered the strands of rope from the floor. "A real mother wouldn't steal her daughter's inheritance and try to have her locked up in a mental hospital. A real mother would fight tooth and nail against anyone who'd try to do that. A real mother would protect her daughter."

"It's true, Vanessa. You are my child."

"Oh, no, I'm not. Because a real mother wouldn't lie about it for thirty years. She wouldn't tell her daughter she was adopted if she wasn't."

"Daddy didn't want you to know. Because he was ashamed of me, and angry. For a long time he was very angry. And I was scared. Scared that, if you did know the truth, other people would find out."

"I don't know what you're talking about. What . . . what is the truth?"

Evelyn looked up at her daughter's anxious face and sighed. This was a conversation that she had longed for and had imagined having a thousand times, but now that it was actually taking place she was very frightened, and for a few seconds she wanted to end it, wanted to say, No, you are not the child I bore before your father and I were married. You're some other woman's child. You are not the baby all grown up that I conceived one drunken spring night at a Williams College mixer. She wanted to say, You're not the child whose father I could not name, a college boy whose face I could not remember the next morning, when I stumbled still drunk down the stairs of the fraternity house and out the door into bright sunlight, my party dress stained and half buttoned. You are not the baby I bore in North Carolina that fall at the home for girls like me, girls whose parents could afford to send them into hiding for six months and claim they'd gone abroad for a semester to study French or Italian or music appreciation, returning to college and proper society in the spring, slim and fresh faced and all but virginal again. Evelyn Cole did not want to tell her daughter that her parents had paid to keep the baby, their grandchild, in the home, which was in fact a posh private orphanage in Asheville, North Carolina, while Evelyn finished her junior and senior years at Smith, where she was courted by the very promising Carter Cole, a Yale man from a distinguished old New England family, a well-born man bound for medical school and inherited wealth, a man who, to the delight and relief of her parents, did indeed marry her. And one night a year later, when he was interrogating his bride about her past sexual experiences, as he often did that first year of their marriage, demanding to hear every last detail, wanting to peer into her sexual past as if it were a set of pornographic photographs, she broke down and finally told him everything she could remember about that terrible party at the fraternity house at Williams College. He had known that his bride had not come to him a virgin—she couldn't lie about that, he was training to be a doctor, after all—but now he learned that her past, and thus his own, was further tainted by the birth of a child, a little girl who was three years old, a child never put up for adoption and old enough now to be aware of a little of her own mysterious and illegitimate origins, thanks to the sentimental indiscretions of Evelyn's parents, who had made semiannual visits to the home to visit the child and make sure that she was receiving adequate care, who had indulged themselves by staying with the child alone for hours each time they visited.

"I have no memory of that," Vanessa declared. "None."

"Daddy was always afraid that you did. You were so precocious a child, so intelligent, that he kept waiting for it to come out. He was afraid that somehow you knew I was your real mother, and it would become known to other people. And he didn't want that."

"But I *didn't* know! I have no memories of any visits from Grandma and Grandpa way back then. All I remember of the orphanage are the big lawns and my room there. I remember the bars of my crib and the lawns outside. Nothing else. No people. Not even other children. Except for my crib and the endless lawns, all my earliest memories are of you and Daddy and the house in Tuxedo Park and the apartment in the city and the Reserve. Were there other children?"

"At the home? There were only a few, maybe two or three. Little babies waiting to be adopted. It was very exclusive," Evelyn said. "Vanessa, I really am thirsty. May I please have a glass of water?"

"As long as you stay in the chair where I can see you," Vanessa said and went into the bathroom where, watching her mother in the mirror, she filled a glass at the sink and returned with it. She handed the glass to her mother, who drank it down and asked for another. When she came back with the second glass, Vanessa said, "But I don't understand. Why didn't Grandma and Grandpa let me be adopted when I was a little baby? Was there something wrong with me? Something that made it so nobody wanted me?"

"Lots of people wanted you. You were beautiful and intelligent and charming. They wouldn't sign the papers."

"Who? The people who ran the home?"

"Your grandparents. My mother and father. They would come back from North Carolina and tell me how beautiful you were, as if to punish me. Over and over. And how they were just waiting for the right people to come along and adopt and raise you. I think they meant that. Your grandparents were proud. Proud of their bloodlines. As you know. And even though no one knew for sure who your real father was, they knew he was at least a Williams boy. Which was something, I suppose. They wanted to be able to choose who would adopt you. So they just paid to keep you there and never signed the papers. I don't know what they were thinking, what they were hoping would happen, because nothing *could* happen. Except that you would grow older and eventually grow up there."

"What about you? You could have signed the adoption papers."

"No. I was only twenty when you were born, and I didn't dare go against my parents. And then later, by the time I was of legal age, I was engaged to marry Daddy. By then I was so used to keeping it a secret that I didn't want to think about it."

" 'It.' You mean *me*. So why did you and Daddy finally decide to adopt me? I mean, I was safely out of sight way down there in North Carolina, out of sight and, at least in your case, out of mind. You could've left me there to rot, if you'd wanted to."

"It was your father's idea. Well, no, it was my idea. Under his conditions. Once we realized that we weren't going to have any children together, I begged him to let me take you from that place and raise you as our child. He agreed, but only if I promised to say that you were adopted and never revealed to anyone, not even to you, that I was your real mother. My parents were happy to go along with it. And so were the people who ran the home. In the end, everyone got what they wanted. Which was to save face. Everyone got to save face. Even me."

"Even you. *Why* weren't you going to have children together, you and Daddy? Was there something wrong with you?"

"No, not with me."

"With Daddy, then. I never heard anything about that."

"It wasn't a physical thing with him. Not really. Your father was . . . a difficult man. Sexually, I mean. He didn't . . . he didn't like to make love. Also, he was very old-fashioned, and when he found out that I wasn't a virgin . . ." She trailed off.

Vanessa said, "Keep talking, Mother."

"Oh, I hate telling you all this!"

"It's too late to stop now. Tell me the rest."

"In the very beginning, when we first tried to make love, it went . . . badly, let's say. The fact is, on our honeymoon he found out that I wasn't a virgin, and he rejected me for a time. Later on, months later, when we tried to make love, he couldn't. And then . . . well, then he wouldn't. We were both pretty shy about it, about sex, and it was just simpler not to do it at all, and he never complained about it, and neither did I. Although it made me very lonely for a long, long time."

"My *Christ!*" Vanessa said. "This is mad. I don't know if I can take it all in. Or even believe it! It's all so fruity and weak and pathetic. You disgust me, Mother. Truly. You amaze and disgust me. Both you and Daddy. And Grandma and Grandpa, too. But especially you!"

"Vanessa, please don't be angry with us. We did the best we could."

"Well, they're all dead, Daddy and Grandma and Grandpa. So I can't get back at them for what they did. But you're not dead. And look at you, you're trying to put me out of the way again, like you did when I was born. Like Grandma and Grandpa did when I was a baby." Vanessa took the glass from her mother, set it on the dressing table, and pulled her arms behind the chair and tied her wrists. "Where are all those photographs Daddy took of me when I was a little girl?" she suddenly demanded. "You know the ones."

"I don't . . . I don't know." Her mother looked up, wide-eyed and frightened, at Vanessa. "Those photographs? What photographs? They're in Daddy's albums, I suppose," she said. "In the library here, where he kept them stored. And on the walls, framed. And at home."

"No. You know what I'm talking about, so don't play dumb. Photographs of me. Naked. I want them."

"Naked! What do you mean? He took hundreds of photographs

of you back then. He loved photographing you. He had his own darkroom and everything, where he developed and printed them. But I never saw any pictures of you naked. What are you talking about? Please don't put the scarf over my mouth, Vanessa. It makes me feel like I'm suffocating."

"From before the war. From when I was four or five. Or maybe I was only three and recently 'adopted.' You were there, Mother. You knew! You knew he was taking those pictures."

"No. Daddy was very shy about that. He didn't like to see you naked, ever."

"If you don't tell me the truth, I'm going to tie the scarf over your mouth. I don't want to listen to your lies anymore."

"Vanessa, it is the truth! Daddy always made me or Hilda make sure you were properly covered before he went into your room, and he never bathed you or even saw you being bathed. Some things I don't remember from those years before the war, you know, because of my bad nerves back then. And the medicines. But I do remember that."

Vanessa sighed heavily. "Oh, God, Mother, you're still lying to me. Or else you're lying to yourself and believing it. Either way, it's a lie. Because you were there, and you know where those pictures are. Daddy was very orderly and never threw anything away. I'm sure you've gone through all his files since he died and know exactly where those pictures are. You said you remember being present when he took them."

"No, no! He wasn't like that, Vanessa. He wasn't."

"I'll bet I'm not the only naked little girl he took photographs of. *Wasn't* the only naked little girl, I mean."

"Your father wasn't the kind of man who—"

Vanessa cut her off with the silk scarf, tying it tightly this time so it wouldn't slip down. "No more lies, Mother. No more lies," she said, walking to the open window, which she shut and locked. Then she pulled down the shade, dropping the room into darkness. "I'll come back for you after Hubert's been here and gone. Maybe then you and I will go through those albums in the library together. Won't that be nice? Just the two of us. What fun. Mother and daughter leafing through the family albums. Maybe then you'll tell me everything."

She locked the bedroom door behind her and walked from the living room to the porch. From the deck she saw a guide boat a half mile out on the lake. It was Hubert St. Germain—smoothly, expertly, his oar blades barely making a ripple in the water—rowing toward the camp.

The doctor shook the young woman's hand and said, Good-bye, Vanessa, and bon voyage. Your luggage will be in your stateroom, he added, and she nodded as if agreeing. He turned her toward the other passengers, and she followed them onto the bus. When the bus had departed, the doctor walked into the hotel bar and ordered a schnapps and filled his pipe with tobacco and lighted it. A half hour later, in a soft, drizzling rain, the passengers arrived at the airfield and were taken inside a cavernous hangar, where they were inspected a second time for matches, lighters, and batteries. Beyond the hangar, tethered by its nose to a mooring mast, the enormous zeppelin floated in the air, ten feet from the ground. The silver ship was nearly a sixth of a mile long, shaped like a gigantic whale. An open staircase extended from its gleaming belly to the ground. One by one, the passengers climbed the stairs and entered the leviathan. A steward escorted the American woman to her room on Level B and left her alone there. She removed her hat and veil, exposing a single red spot above each eyebrow, tiny circular wounds recently healed. After a few moments, she stepped to the large rectangular window and looked down at the crowd of well-wishers and officers on the ground. A uniformed brass band played "Muss I Denn?" and a choir of Nazi youth sang the "Horst Wessel Song" and "Deutschland Über Alles." Gradually, the crowd below—the brass band, the Nazi youth contingent, the Zeppelin officials and groundsmen, and the government officials and SS officers—began to diminish in size. Without a ripple of felt movement, the airship was silently rising. At about three hundred feet the muffled sound of the diesel engines penetrated the silence of the stateroom, and the great zeppelin slowly turned northwest and in the gathering dusk headed toward the lights of Koblenz, following the Rhine to the sea.

"You needn't carry it to the house," Vanessa Cole said to the guide and smiled winningly. "Just unload everything here by the shore." She placed her hand lightly, like a fallen leaf, on his thick shoulder and continued to hold the smile. She was the same height as he, Hubert noticed for the first time, tall for a woman, but not as tall as Alicia. It had somehow pleased him from the start that Alicia was taller than he, as if there were a rightness to it, a legitimacy. It was an observation that he had never carried to its logical conclusion: that if she had been shorter than he it would have been somehow wrong, illegitimate. He did notice now, however, that it also seemed right to him that Vanessa Cole was tall, even if not as tall as Alicia, and for a second he wondered if people from away, especially the women, ran taller than local people.

"You sure? I don't mind lugging it up to the house, Miss Cole. Most of it goes to the pantry anyhow," he said.

She said she was grateful to him for coming out on such short notice and didn't want to keep him at the camp any longer than necessary. Besides, her mother was napping on the living room sofa, and Vanessa didn't want to disturb her. She glanced down at the four cardboard boxes of food and other supplies the guide had unloaded from the boat and saw that certain items were missing. "I guess you'll be making a second trip out anyhow. Can you do that today?"

"Probably not. This here's mostly the food. It's getting a little on, so I figured to bring the rest tomorrow and maybe use what's left of today to cut you some wood and tend to whatever else needs tending to." Hubert grabbed a box and hefted it to his shoulder. "I'll take it into the pantry the back way, real quiet. So's not to disturb Mrs. Cole."

"No! Here, let me have that." She took the box from him and set it back on the ground. "I . . . I'm sorry. Is there any way you can make that second trip this afternoon? You could just bring it out and drop it here on the shore for me. Don't worry about the wood or anything. I can do that myself. I . . . I just need you to bring the rest of the supplies and leave them here on the shore. Please?"

Hubert looked closely at the woman's face. She was strangely agitated, he thought, more than usual, that's for sure. She was almost always wound a little tight, but in a fluttery, flirtatious way that put him off, like she was playing him for a rube or something. This was different, as if she was scared of having him go up to the house. Or somehow scared of him on a more personal level, like she thought he might be going to hit her or try to seduce her against her will, both of which were the furthest things from his mind. He liked her better this way than the other, however. He stepped back and looked at her face directly, and she lifted her chin slightly and stared back. For the first time he saw how truly beautiful she was and understood what all the fuss was about. For years he'd heard the rumors and the gossip—the high-society marriages and divorces, the love affairs with rich, famous men and even with local men not so famous and not in the slightest rich and with married members of the Tamarack Reserve and Club, at least one every summer and sometimes more than one. No man, young or old, could resist her, that was the word locally. But up to now Hubert had not understood why. Up to now, however, her full gaze had never really fallen on him. He had never felt *seen* by her and thus had never experienced the intense, diamond-hard clarity of her need before. It was not sexual need strictly, but a little like that. This was something beyond desire. It was an urgent need to be seen by *him*, to be made real by *his* gaze. And along with it came a silent but clearly felt declaration that he, Hubert St. Germain, was the only person on the planet who could do the job, the only person who was capable of truly seeing her and thus the only person who could make her existence a reality.

He asked her if she was all right.

She shook her head like a horse tossing its mane from side to side and gave him that sorrowful, scared, needy look again. "I'm not . . . ," she began, and then said, "Yes, I'm okay. I think I'm okay. You're kind to ask."

"I imagine it's been hard on you, losing your father like that. So suddenly and all. And being here. Where he died, I mean. I remember when my father died it was a long time before I could go back to where it happened, to where they found the body." This was more than he had ever said to her at once, and it surprised him, and surprised him even more when he continued. "I guess it was because he died unexpectedly, sort of by accident. It was different with my mother, because she was sick for a long time first. And with Sally, my wife, it was different then, too, because I never had to go back to where she had died. Although I remember the first time I drove past where the car crashed, I got all weak in the knees and couldn't look at the tree she'd hit. It wasn't so bad the second time, because by then the road department had come out and cut the tree down, in case somebody else might go off the road and hit it the same as Sally's sister did."

"Yes, I heard about that. I'm sorry for that, Hubert. For your loss. It must have been awful."

"For a spell it was. We weren't married long, but we'd been together a long time. High school sweethearts, sort of."

For a few seconds they were silent. Then she said, "What about you, Hubert? Are you all right? I mean now, today."

"Well . . . no, not exactly." He surprised himself by answering honestly.

"What do you mean?" She reached out and touched his sleeve lightly, holding it between thumb and forefinger, reinforcing her plea to go ahead, Hubert, tell the truth.

"I guess . . . yes, I am kind of upset. Actually, I'm kind of worried about you coming to my place. When Alicia, Mrs. Groves, was there. In case you got the wrong idea," he added, preparing to lie, knowing he would not be believed anyhow, and hating it, the lying, regardless of whether she believed him. He was a man with secrets, perhaps, but he did not lie.

"There was no wrong idea to get, Hubert. I mean, your private life is your own. It's no business of mine. I don't know Mrs. Groves, anyhow. Not personally. But she seems like a good person. And I do know you're a good person."

"This is sort of a strange conversation for us to be having. Isn't it?"

"Yes, I guess it is." She was still holding his sleeve. "I wish . . . I wish you could be the one to help me. I need someone to help me." Her eyes opened wide and turned dark.

He heard himself say that he would help her. She wasn't going to make him lie about Alicia, she was changing the subject for his sake, so maybe he was in her debt for that. "What do you need me for?"

Vanessa said, "I've done something . . . something wrong.

Wrong, and very rash. And I don't know what to do about it, Hubert. I'm confused, and I'm in trouble. A lot of trouble." She let go of his sleeve and pressed the flat of her hand against the side of his upper arm. It was a friendly, trusting, comforting gesture, as if he and not she were the one asking for help and were receiving it from her touch. "Oh, God, I don't know why I'm telling you this."

"What have you done?" Their faces were drawn close together now, their eyes locked, and he could smell her hair. It was like fresh-cut grass. Or maybe tea leaves, he thought. A woody, clean smell.

"You must promise to tell no one. It has to be a secret. No one else must know."

"You can trust me."

"You can't tell anyone. Promise me."

"All right. I won't tell anyone," he said, and meant it.

"I've done . . . I've done something bad to my mother."

"Your mother? Mrs. Cole? What do you mean, 'something bad'? I don't understand."

"It's hard to explain. It's just, I got trapped in . . . a situation, trapped by her, and to escape it I did something very . . . rash. And now I don't know what to do about it. I can't undo it. And I can't keep doing it, either. Because . . . well, because she's my mother. And it's wrong."

"Tell me what you've done. It can't be but so bad. I'll help you," he said again. "Have you accidentally hurt her or something?" Maybe they had a quarrel that turned violent, he thought. It happens sometimes in families, even families like the Coles. It had happened in his.

"No, I haven't hurt her, not physically."

"Well, it can't be so bad, then."

"Oh, yes, it's bad, Hubert." She took her hand away from his arm and held his hand in hers and told him to come with her to the house. "I shouldn't be doing this, involving you, but I don't know what else to do. I don't have anyone to turn to, Hubert."

"It's okay, Miss Cole. You can trust me."

Vanessa turned and walked quickly toward the house, Hubert following a few feet behind. They crossed the wide deck, passed through the screened porch, and entered the living room. He checked the sofa—Mrs. Cole wasn't there, asleep or awake. He looked around the room and said to himself, So she lied about that. He wondered what else she'd lied about. Maybe everything. Maybe he shouldn't have agreed to help her. She was capable of tricking him into behaving in a way that he'd be sorry for later, sorry and humiliated. Something ugly was going on. Maybe a thing has been done here that only rich people do, he thought, and he wished that he were not here in this house alone with this woman, wished that he were by himself in the deep woods tracking a deer instead of following this nervous, frightened woman who lied all the time. If he could not be alone in the woods, he wished he were with Alicia in the mountain meadow up behind his cabin, showing her the new-blooming pasture roses, the black-eyed Susans, and the pink yarrow. Alone in the deep woods; and with Alicia: they were the only times he had been happy in years. Maybe since he was a small child. Maybe always. Even with Sally, his wife—whom he believed he had loved, at least until he met Alicia—even with Sally he had not been happy and had preferred being alone. Secretly, he knew that his grief over his wife's death had been eased and tempered by the sudden solitude that had followed it.

Hubert said, "Your mother's not here, I guess."

"No. She's . . . she's in her bedroom."

"Maybe I should take a look at her," he said. "Make sure she's okay."

"No! She's all right. She's fine. It's just . . . she's indisposed."

"I believe I need to see her, Miss Cole. You said some things outside that make me think I need to see her. Just to make sure she's okay."

"Yes, I guess I did," she said and sighed. "All right. You can see her. But you mustn't talk to her. You mustn't. And you can't tell anyone that she's here. You said I could trust you. And you said you'd help me, remember?"

"I did," he said, but he did not promise her anything more. He was a man who tried not to make promises that he might not be able to keep; yes, he had told Vanessa that she could trust him and he'd help her; those were promises he could keep. But he was not sure that he would not talk to Vanessa Cole's mother or tell someone she was here at Rangeview. Not until he had seen the woman first with his own eyes and had determined what Vanessa had done to her. For that was what she'd said, wasn't it? That she had done something bad to her mother.

Vanessa unlocked and opened the door to her parents' bedroom. She stepped aside, and motioned for him to enter. He walked to the doorway. Looking past Vanessa into the bedroom, he saw the woman. It was Mrs. Cole. Her name was Evelyn, he remembered, but he had always called her Mrs. Cole. Dr. Cole had long ago told Hubert to call him Carter. The guide had liked that. The woman's hands and ankles were bound, and there was some kind of cloth over her mouth, and Hubert did not know what to think. Whatever he had expected to see, it was not this.

Mrs. Cole looked over at Hubert St. Germain, the family's longtime guide and caretaker, standing by the door, his hands hanging empty at his sides, Vanessa beside him, and the woman seemed to recoil from him, as if he had come to do something to her that Vanessa couldn't bring herself to do alone. Mrs. Cole's eyes widened in fear, and she shook her head wildly no, as if pleading with him not to do it.

Barely two seconds passed, and Vanessa grabbed Hubert by the hand and pulled him away from the room and slammed the door shut on her mother and locked it.

"Let me back in there, Miss Cole!"

"No. I can't," she said and stood with her back to the door.

"I got to help her!"

"No!" She cried, "Help *me,* Hubert! Please, *I'm* the one who needs you."

"*How?* What's going on here? Why is she like that, all tied up and gagged like that?"

"I can't explain. But you have to trust me, Hubert."

"Then you got to tell me the reason she's like that."

"I can't."

"Then I'll have to untie her and let her tell me."

Vanessa looked steadily at him for a moment, her lips pursed, as if she were taking the measure of the man. Finally, she said, "It's not my mother who's trapped. Believe me. It's not my mother who's a prisoner, Hubert. It's me."

"What do you mean?"

"My mother . . . my mother wants to lock me away in a mental hospital. Where they'll drug me. Or worse. Where they'll give me a lobotomy or something. She's taken my inheritance away from me. My mother wants me dead, or as good as dead!"

"She can't want you dead. She's your *mother.*"

"And that only makes it worse, Hubert. Don't you see? When your own flesh and blood wants you locked away so she can take your money or wants you mindless or even dead, it's so terrible that you don't know what to do! I panicked, Hubert. I don't know what I was thinking. I wasn't thinking, I was simply reacting. I just wanted to make it so she couldn't put me into a looney bin for the rest of my life, or worse. I felt like a caged animal. I still do! She planned to ship me off to a hospital in Europe, where I was before. So I forced her to come here, to the Reserve. But I've only made it worse. If I let her go now, she'll make me go into the hospital like she planned, the papers are all drawn up and signed, but now, to punish me for doing this, for forcing her to come to the Reserve and keeping her here against her will like this, she'll let them give me a lobotomy. I know it. I just know it. Do you know what that is, Hubert? A lobotomy?"

"I heard of it, yes." He'd read about the new form of brain surgery that doctors were performing on mentally ill people nowadays. It was in all the news, and because Dr. Carter Cole, a distinguished summer resident of the Reserve, was one of the men who had invented the procedure, even the local papers had covered it. It was being called a miracle cure. Hubert didn't think it was the sort of thing that should be done to Vanessa Cole, though. She was strange, yes, and eccentric, and by his lights maybe even a little weird, but Vanessa Cole wasn't what you'd call mentally ill. Mostly, she was rich and spoiled was all. Which weren't crimes, he knew, and didn't necessarily make you crazy. Certainly not crazy enough to warrant a lobotomy.

"So now that I've got control of her, I'm stuck with her. I can't let her leave." She laughed suddenly, a cold, mocking laugh. "If it weren't so damned awful and she weren't suffering, it'd be ridiculous. If the consequences for me weren't so final, it'd be almost funny."

Hubert was silent for a moment. "I don't know what to say. I don't see how I can help you, neither. Maybe the consequences aren't so final," he said, more a question than a statement.

"Oh, Hubert, please! Don't be naive! I know what's waiting for me over there. If I let her go now, my life will be over. It's as simple as that. I'll never see the light of day again. I'll be locked up and brain damaged for the rest of my life."

The guide tried to grasp the situation, get it clear in his mind. He was a problem solver, especially of other people's problems. He knew he had to take a step back and take the thing apart as if it were a broken machine, lay all the parts out on the table, find the faulty gear or broken belt, replace it with a new one, and put the machine back together again.

The two said nothing while Hubert pondered the situation. He asked if she minded if he smoked, and she said no, and he pulled out his pack of Luckies and lighted one and smoked. Vanessa took his pack from him and lighted one for herself. Finally he said, "Maybe the first thing is to make it so she isn't suffering like that, all tied up and gagged and all."

"No! You'll help her escape, and she'll come back with the sheriff, and they'll haul me off in a straitjacket!"

Hubert promised Vanessa that he would not help her mother escape. He just didn't want the woman to suffer unnecessarily. Also, he pointed out, if Vanessa released her mother temporarily, so to speak, and in exchange got her to cooperate in her own confinement here at the camp, they might have a chance to make her understand why Vanessa had done this, and her mother might change her mind then about the mental hospital and the inheritance and so forth. At worst, it would buy Vanessa a little time to come up with some idea of what to do with her. "If you keep her hog-tied like that, she's going to believe you actually are crazy. And you're right, she's going to want revenge." He wasn't urging her to free Mrs. Cole completely, he said. Just enough so the three of them could sit down and talk to one another about the situation and why Vanessa had reacted the way she had. Maybe that way a solution would come to them, he told her. "But in the process we shouldn't hurt her in any way," he said. "No need to keep her tied up and all. We can just keep her locked in the bedroom and bring her food there. I'll shutter the windows so she can't climb out." He told her that if Vanessa wanted, since he wasn't at the moment working for anyone else, he would bring the second load of supplies back before dark and stay here at Rangeview tonight, so they could take turns guarding her mother, while all three of them tried to come up with a resolution to this. "There's got to be a way out of this that works for both of you."

"You promise?" Vanessa asked.

"Yes," he said. "I don't lie, Miss Cole. And I don't make promises I can't keep. I think that together we can work this thing out."

She sank down on the sofa and with her head resting in her hands stared straight ahead at the dead fireplace. "All right, then. Go ahead and untie her," she said without looking at him. "And, please, call me Vanessa."

Returning to the bedroom, Hubert knelt beside Mrs. Cole and undid the scarf covering her mouth. In as soothing a voice as he could manage, he said to her, "Now don't be afraid. I'm not going to hurt you, Mrs. Cole. I'm just trying to find a way to fix this mess. You understand, Mrs. Cole?"

She nodded and, lips trembling, asked him for water. The glass Vanessa had filled earlier was on the dresser, and Hubert retrieved it and gave it to her. She drank quickly. "Vanessa . . . my daughter wants to kill me, Hubert! My own daughter! She wants to kill me."

"No, she doesn't."

"What does she want, then?" Her voice was dry as sandpaper.

"Well, that's what we're going to find out," Hubert said, helping the woman to her feet. She staggered when he let go of her. He steadied her for a few seconds, then helped her from the chaise to the bed. He sounded and looked like a calm, rational man, but he was confused and turbulent and scared. I'm in way over my head here, he thought. I wish I could talk this thing out with Alicia. Alicia would know what I should do. She would know if what I am doing is wrong or just plain dumb. Or both. I need to think about what Alicia would do in my place, he said to himself, and then concluded that she would do exactly as he was doing, and immediately he felt better about it and plunged ahead.

WHEN ALICIA GROVES RETURNED HOME, SHE WENT STRAIGHT inside the house. Passing through the dining room on her way to the kitchen, she glanced out the French doors to the terrace with the big cleft rock in the center and beyond to the grassy bluff above the wide bend in the river. In the shade of the tall oak tree her husband was pushing Bear on the tire swing in long, swooping arcs while talking to Wolf, who stood at his side, smiling. A few feet away the two red dogs lay asleep in splotches of sunlight.

Alicia stopped by the window and lay both hands on the sill, as if to steady herself. She was sure that Vanessa Cole had already told Jordan that she had seen his wife at Hubert St. Germain's cabin, when she was supposed to have been at the medical center in Sam Dent, probably adding a few lurid details in the telling. Had she buttoned her blouse correctly when she came out of the cabin to the deck? Had she smoothed her skirt? Alicia couldn't remember. When you lie you forget the truth. Alicia knew that she had been seen by Jordan from the air. He had been out looking for her, obviously, flying over Hubert St. Germain's cabin in search of his straying, lying wife, and he had found her exactly where Vanessa told him he would. And now, while he seemed to be playing contentedly with his sons, he was merely awaiting the return of his wayward wife and more lies and denials. She couldn't put herself through that, not anymore. Regardless of the consequences, she decided, she would no longer lie to her husband.

Throughout the remainder of the afternoon, and later, while she prepared supper for the four of them and Jordan in his studio studied his new assistant's inventory, and all through the evening meal and afterward, as she washed the dishes and got the boys through their baths and into bed, Alicia anxiously watched her husband and waited for him to confront her.

But he said and did nothing out of the ordinary. If anything, he was more affable and relaxed than usual. He seemed downright affectionate toward her, and at one point, passing behind where she stood at the kitchen sink washing the supper dishes, he placed one big hand on her left shoulder and the other on her right buttock and slid it down along her thigh like a promise. It was a thing he had not done in months. Involuntarily, she stepped away from his hand, and he moved on.

Finally, when the boys were in their beds and slipping into sleep, Alicia went looking for her husband. She found him in the room they called the library, but which over time had become the artist's office, for no one other than he ever used the room. It was where he wrote letters, paid bills, kept all his files and archives, and where late at night he read and listened to his beloved jazz records and smoked cigars and sometimes drank old whiskeys neat.

He was typing out a letter to the writer John Dos Passos, whom he had befriended during the trial of Sacco and Vanzetti way back in 1922. Dos had been writing about the trial, and Jordan had made a limited-edition wood engraving to help raise money for the defense fund. Later, after the executions of Sacco and Vanzetti, Dos and his wife, Katie, on several occasions had visited the artist and his family in Petersburg. They had worked together in '31 and '32 to help free the Scottsboro boys, and recently the two men had become collaborators in the effort to raise money for medical supplies for the republicans in Spain. Dos had been urging Jordan to join him in Spain and make a series of pictures based on Goya's famous engravings of the Napoleonic War. Until now, Jordan had not turned him down. But tonight he wrote, *Too much work to do here, too many commitments, too many family obligations keeping me here. . . .*

Alicia sat on the leather sofa and smoked a cigarette while her husband typed at the desk. When he finished, he folded the letter and put it into an envelope, addressed and stamped the envelope, and swiveled around in his chair to face her.

"I've just told Dos to forget about the Spanish thing," he said and smiled. "I'm not going over."

Alicia nodded somberly. "That's good, if it's what you want. To stay here instead, I mean."

"It's exactly what I want. From here on out, I'm a homebody," he said and paused. "And I'm not going to Greenland, either."

"Oh. Well, I guess that's good, too. If it's what you want."

"Alicia, listen. There's something I need to talk about with you. Something serious. About us."

"Yes. I know."

"You know?"

"Before you say anything more, Jordan, I have to tell you that it's over."

"What is?"

"I ended it," she blurted.

"Ended what?" He leaned forward in his chair, as if he hadn't heard her correctly.

"What happened . . . between Hubert and me."

"Between you and Hubert? Hubert St. Germain?"

"It's in the past now. I wrote him today and told him that it's over. When you saw me out there this afternoon I was putting the letter in his mailbox. By now he's read it, so he, too, knows that it's finished."

"Hubert? Hubert St. Germain? What the Christ are you talking about, Alicia?"

"You *know* what I'm talking about. Don't make me say it. Please, Jordan. I'm so sorry it happened, and so ashamed. I don't know what I was thinking, I must have been crazy. But I promise you, it's in the past now. And I swear, I'm profoundly sorry."

"You're sorry."

"Yes. Please, forgive me, Jordan."

They remained silent for a moment, Jordan staring at his wife, who looked down and away, shamefaced. He took out his tobacco and papers and slowly rolled a cigarette and lighted it. Finally, he said, "Are you telling me that you're having an affair with Hubert St. Germain?"

"Yes. *No!* I'm telling you that it's over. I've ended the affair. I won't see him again, ever. And I'm asking you to forgive me. I know it won't be easy, and I don't deserve it. Please, Jordan."

Jordan's face had clouded over and darkened. This had never happened to him before. In every married couple, he believed, one was a liar and the other a truth teller. Alicia had always been the truth teller. Now, suddenly, the poles were reversed, a circumstance that shocked and confused him even more than what Alicia was actually confessing. As long as he knew that he was the one who lied, the one who kept secrets and generated elaborate deceptions, then he knew who he was and how that man behaved. And as long as he believed that Alicia never lied or kept secrets or deceived him, he knew who she was and how she behaved.

But forgive her? *He* was the one who had always needed forgiveness. He had never been asked to forgive her for anything before. He wasn't sure he knew how. What did it feel like, anyhow, to forgive someone? Jordan Groves bore grudges; he had enemies and knew who they were and enjoyed keeping them identified as such: Jordan Groves was a son of a bitch who didn't mind the reputation, because it kept at bay people who were capable of hurting him. But he had never found it necessary to forgive anyone. Not even his parents. Forgive and forget might be how it went for most people, but not for Jordan Groves. Thanks to his optimistic egoism and self-confidence, Jordan had little trouble forgetting; it was easy for him; but once a lie or a deception was forgotten, what was the need for forgiveness? If you truly forgot the offense, how was forgiveness even *possible?* Had he been raised Catholic like Alicia, he might have been able to conflate the two, but his parents had been strict Presbyterians, and Jordan Groves's atheism was founded on that immovable Protestant rock. Thus, while he knew that deep down, like all human beings, he was an irredeemable sinner, he was hard-hearted.

"Well now. So you've been fucking my friend Hubert St. Germain."

"Yes."

"How long?"

"Since mid-March. But not—"

"No 'buts,'" he said, cutting her off. "And no greasy details. Right now all I want is to know the facts."

"All right."

"Where?"

"At . . . at his cabin. Nowhere else."

"How often?"

"Only sometimes. Not often. Oh, Jordan, don't do this, please!"

"How often? Twice? Twenty times? Since mid-March, it must be hundreds of times."

"We met a few times a week, sometimes once. Sometimes not at all."

"Who else knows about this?"

"No one, Jordan. I swear it. Except for that woman . . . Vanessa Von . . . whatever. Vanessa Cole."

"Vanessa? How the hell does *she* know?"

Suddenly Alicia understood her mistake. She felt herself blush with shame. She realized that she could have lied. She *should* have lied. But it was too late now. She had no choice but to go on telling the truth. "Oh, God. I . . . I'm so stupid. She came to Hubert's cabin today, and she saw me there. I thought . . . I assumed that she knew, and that she told you. And when you flew over the cabin and saw me stopped at Hubert's mailbox, I guess I assumed that you had seen her. Or she had telephoned you. Or something. Oh, God!" she cried.

Jordan shook his head sadly. "You certainly have been a fool. But not as much a fool as *I've* been. Are you in love with him?"

She hesitated before answering. "I . . . I thought I was. I was unhappy, Jordan. For a long time I was very unhappy."

"I don't care about causes! There are a thousand reasons why a woman commits adultery. And a thousand and one why a man does it. Right now all I care about is getting the material facts. I don't even care if it was good sex or bad sex or anything in between. That's your private business and will only disgust me anyway. I want the facts. So I can . . . so I can know what to do next." He studied his hands and saw they were shaking, and he was silent for a moment. Then he asked, "Are you in love with Hubert St. Germain? Are you still in love with the son of a bitch?"

She hesitated. "Yes," she said. "But I have closed my heart to him."

"Oh. You're in love with him, but you've closed your heart to him. Whatever that means. Does it mean you're no longer in love with me?"

"No, it does not, Jordan. I will always be in love with you."

"You will, eh? Well, that's a little hard for me to grasp. Here's a fact. Except for you, I have never been in love with anyone. Only you. Period. So I don't know what the hell you mean when you say you're in love with Hubert, despite having 'closed your heart to him,' and that you will also always be in love with me." He rubbed out his cigarette in the ashtray. "I don't know how you can be in love with both of us."

"It's not like that. Being in love, I mean. It's more complicated and confusing than that."

"Not to me. For me, with every woman the love switch is either off or it's on. And it's always been on with you, Alicia. With everyone else, off."

"I've never doubted your love for me," she said quietly. "But all those women, the women you've slept with, you never loved any of them?"

"No. Absolutely not. You know that, you've always known that. Cold comfort, maybe, but we're not talking about me here, are we? Oh, I know I might be partly to blame for driving you into the eager arms of the noble Adirondack woodsman Hubert St. Germain. It's obvious even to me that I'm hard to live with and have not been a faithful husband and have left you alone here with the boys for weeks and months at a time. And I know in some people's eyes ol' Hubert's a charmer, even if a somewhat mournful and inarticulate one. And I know that after nearly ten years of marriage any woman gets restless and maybe a little curious about what it might be like to fuck someone other than her husband. So there are all kinds of causes ready to hand. So many that there's no point in discussing them. What I have to know is, what exactly has happened, Alicia? What has happened? So that I can decide what I am to do now. My next move."

"What do you mean?"

"I mean, do I divorce you? Or do I fall down on my knees and promise to be a better husband? Do I fly into a rage and knock you down and bust all the furniture? Or do I weep in sorrow and self-pity for having lost the love of my life? What the hell am I supposed to do? I don't know the answer to that. Do I drive over to Hubert's cabin and drag him out of his filthy adulterous bed and beat the shit out of him? Or do I sit down with him over a bottle of whiskey and talk about the perfidy of unhappily married women? Oh, for Christ's sake, Alicia," he cried, and his voice broke. "What am I supposed to *do*? What am I supposed to feel?" He spread his arms wide and opened his body and face to her.

She came forward and got down on her knees in front of him and put her head against his chest and wrapped her arms around his waist. Weeping now, she said, "All of it, Jordan. Do all of it. If you ask for a divorce, I'll give it to you. If you promise to be a better husband, I'll believe you. If you beat up Hubert, I'll understand. Though Lord knows it's not his fault. None of it is. It's all my fault. If you sit down and get drunk with him and talk about what an awful woman I've been, I'll understand. Do all of it, Jordan. Do *anything*. Do everything. Just please, in the end, please forgive me, Jordan."

Tears streamed down his broad cheeks. "Not possible, Alicia. It's not possible. I can't forgive you because I can't forget what you've done. Not as long as I can picture the two of you crawling all over each other naked in bed. And what you've said. That you still love the man. It's not fair, I know, I don't have any right to feel the way I do. I know that. Because I've had my share, more than my share, of dalliances or liaisons or whatever you want to call them. But there's a difference, Alicia. I never loved any of those women! They were just flashes of light in the dark. Fireflies. I never shared my secrets with them. Only with you, Alicia. I never let them know me. Only you."

They stayed silent for several moments, Alicia with her head against his chest and Jordan with his arms around her, holding her close. She heard his heart pound, and he felt her back shudder as she wept. In all their years together, they had never both wept at the same time. She had wept, because of his sins against her, or he had wept out of guilt, but separately.

Finally, he let go of her and told her to go upstairs to bed and leave him alone. "I need to be alone. I need to think. I need to know what's really happened here, and I don't believe you can help me with that." He pulled his handkerchief from his back pocket and wiped his face dry and gave it to her to do the same, which she did.

Then, awkwardly, she stood up, and when she turned to leave she saw that the dogs had come into the room and were sitting alertly by the door, watching Alicia and Jordan with worried expressions on their long faces.

Alicia said, "They know."

"What do they know? They're dogs."

"They know that something terrible has happened to us."

"Has it? I don't know yet what has happened to us. I need time to think. Go to bed, Alicia. I'll be up later. Or maybe I won't."

She left the room, and the dogs followed, still worried. When Jordan heard Alicia's footsteps overhead, he turned back to his desk and picked up his letter to Dos Passos. He held it to the light and studied it for a moment as if trying to read it through the envelope. Then he tore the letter in half and half again and dropped the pieces into the wastebasket.

The three newcomers learned at breakfast that they were listed for two missions today, a morning flight and an afternoon, their first flights over enemy territory. It was not great weather for flying. The early morning rain had stopped, but a blanket of low clouds remained. They had been waiting for a week for their airplanes to arrive from Bilbao and had been given Breguets, not the Russian Polikarpov monoplanes they had requested. The Breguets had been fitted out with two machine guns and bomb racks that held four twenty-five-pound bombs. Their mission was to bomb a pair of gunpowder factories deep in enemy territory, just beyond the Jarama River, fifteen miles from Madrid. To get the job done with the Breguets they would have to do it twice. All nine of the foreign pilots in the squadron stood by their planes until they saw the starting signal, a white flare shot from the field house. As soon as they were in the air, the planes moved into a V of V formation, in which each of the three-man patrols was in a V and the three patrols themselves were in a V. The American named Groves flew on the right wing of the first patrol, which was led by the Englishman Fairhead. Chang flew on Fairhead's left wing. The ceiling had settled at three thousand feet, making it easy to cross into enemy territory unseen in the clouds. When they had passed over the target factories and flown a few miles beyond, Fairhead swung the formation back toward home territory. The right-wing patrol crossed over the top of Fairhead's lead patrol, and the left slid under, the three together making as quick and tight a 180-degree turn as a single patrol alone could make. When they were almost on top of the factories Fairhead gave the signal to attack, and all nine planes dove, still in a V of V formation. Fairhead's lead patrol was to take out the antiaircraft battery located between the two factories. The two wing patrols were led by the veterans, Papps, the Englishman, and Brenner, the American, who had Whitey on his wing. They went for the factories. The pilots lined up their bomb sights and released the bombs, continuing the dive, machine-gunning people, mostly civilians madly racing away from the factory yards. At three hundred feet they flattened out their dive and sped across the Jarama River and until they got into friendly territory kept their aircraft as close to the ground as possible, following the narrow valleys and draws to keep the enemy from seeing where they'd gotten to. Later that same afternoon they made the return trip, all nine of them, to bomb the same factories. There was much more antiaircraft fire this time, little puffs of white smoke here and there, like small detached cumulus clouds, growing more numerous as the airplanes approached the factories. They dropped their bombs, finishing off the factories and, as they had before, machine-gunned anyone foolish enough to be caught in the open. This time, on their return to base Fairhead led them down along miles of enemy trenches, and following his example the pilots fired their Vickers .303 machine guns at infantrymen helplessly firing back with small-bore rifles and revolvers. After their first pass, the American named Groves, the one called Rembrandt, ceased firing. It was April 4, 1937. The American had suddenly remembered that it was an anniversary. Twenty years ago on this day he had shot down two German Fokker Dr. Is over France. He held formation, but his guns went silent, while the others kept firing their machine guns until they finally ran out of ammunition and headed back to the base.

A DENSE, LAYERED, ROSE-TINTED MIST HOVERED ABOVE THE
lake as Jordan Groves came over the Great Range and began his
descent. From above, the mist obscured the pilot's view of the
black surface of the water. There was no wind. He cut his speed
as close to a stall as he dared and brought the biplane in gently, like laying a newborn baby into its downy crib. He felt the
lake before he saw it, and when he knew the pontoons had settled squarely into the glass-smooth water he brought the engine
speed back up a notch and headed for the hidden cove south of
Rangeview, where he had anchored the day before. From a distance of a hundred yards he could make out the shoreline easily
enough, but little else, nothing higher up on the shore, not the
clear blue sky above the mist or the towering pines and not the
Coles's camp buildings. Just the mossy rocks and the low pucker
bushes at the edge of the lake and the graveled spills where the
brooks and streams tumbled from the heights into the lake.

He pulled into the cove and quickly anchored the airplane and
strode ashore. It was not yet six in the morning. He had slept
barely two hours the night before, half of it on the leather sofa
in his office, the other half in his easy chair. His mouth was sour
and dry from whiskey and tobacco. All night long he had struggled to make up his mind about something, anything, but had
been unable to do it. His entire life felt like a swirl of irresolu-

tion, until just before dawn when he made up his mind to fly out to the Second Lake and speak with Vanessa Von Heidenstamm. He had no idea what he would ask or tell her. But she had been a witness to his betrayal, perhaps the only witness—other than Hubert St. Germain, of course, and Alicia herself, and there was no way he could expect to be comforted or enlightened by talking with either of them. Not now. They could only bring him more pain, more irresolution. Vanessa, however, might somehow help him capture the calm objectivity that he needed in order to regain his sense of himself as a man, a man of action. He could not bear thinking of himself in any other way.

Rather than sneak furtively through the brush and forest the way he'd done the day before, Jordan approached the camp forthrightly, from the shore. He had no fear today of being seen, no shame at being here, no guilty fantasies to hide from himself or anyone else. All he wanted was to tell Vanessa what his wife had confessed to him and ask her what she had seen at Hubert St. Germain's cabin. From those two points of contact, plus his remembered long history of his marriage and his own crimes against it, he could begin to triangulate and locate his exact position in the shifting present. And once he knew that much, he would know how to navigate the future. Until then, he would thrash about like a child lost in the woods, abandoned and alone, with no idea of how to get home.

He stepped onto the deck and pushed open the screened door to the porch, and there on the wicker couch lay Hubert St. Germain, startled awake by the sound of the door closing and astonished by the sight of Alicia's husband standing before him. Hubert may well have been dreaming about the artist, he couldn't remember, but for a few seconds he thought he was still dreaming about him, and somehow in the dream the artist had found out that his wife had been sleeping with Hubert and that she and he were in love with each other, and now the artist had come to kill him.

The man did not seem angry, though. He stood over Hubert as large and sad as a bear. Slowly, Hubert sat up and pushed the blanket away. Fully clothed, he put his stockinged feet into his boots, and leaned forward and carefully tied the laces. Then he sat back and looked up at Jordan Groves and waited for something bad to happen.

For several moments neither man spoke. The artist reached behind him and drew up a large wicker chair and sat down heavily in it, facing the guide. Neither man had taken his eyes off the other's face. "All right, then. So tell me, Hubert," Jordan finally said. "Tell me why you did it."

The guide held his breath and then slowly exhaled, as if in relief. So it was over. Over and done with. "I guess she must've told you . . . about us."

"If I understood you, if I knew why you were willing to take my wife away from me, I'd probably want to be you. Her I understand. Me I understand. But not you. She has all kinds of reasons for falling in love with someone other than me. I can accept that. But you, Hubert, you I do not get."

"I don't know what you mean, if you understood me you'd want to be me."

"Because then I'd be a real romantic. Like you. But I'm not. Y'know, Hubert, I've fucked other men's wives. It's true. Just like you. But I never wanted to take them away from their husbands. I only wanted to fuck them. Was it like that for you, Hubert? You just wanted to fuck Alicia? Maybe you're like me after all."

"I never meant that," he said. "She's not like that. And neither am I."

Jordan nodded. He agreed, Alicia was not like that, and neither was Hubert. "That's the thing I don't understand, why you'd want to steal another man's wife," he said. "I don't get it. It's outside my mentality." He looked around him as if registering for the first time where he was located: the Tamarack Mountain Reserve; the Second Lake; Rangeview. "What are you doing out here, anyhow? Fucking Vanessa Von Heidenstamm, too? Maybe I'm wrong about you. Maybe you're not a romantic. Have you been servicing both of them all along? You're quite a stud, Hubert. I'd never have figured you for that."

Hubert said no, there was nothing between him and Miss Cole, and said nothing more. What could he say to Jordan Groves? The guide was not a man of many words. He tried to be truthful and accurate about everything, but too many things, especially when it came to human beings, and even more especially when it came to men and women, were too complicated to speak about honestly or accurately. He had never spoken of the puzzling, conflicted mix of elation and apprehension he had felt when he married his high school sweetheart, Sally Lawrence. Not even to Alicia. And he'd never even tried to speak of the shameful mix of sorrow and relief he had felt when she died. He had told no one of the beatings he had endured at his father's hands when he was a boy and his mother's inability—or was it her unwillingness?—to protect him and his three brothers from the drunken man they called, with a sneer, the Old Man. Hubert, the youngest, had been abandoned by his brothers one by one as soon as each was able to leave home, the first for Alaska, the next for Colorado, the third for Montana—loners all, guides, hunters, trappers, woodsmen, each safely protected by his own personal wilderness, except for Hubert, the youngest, who, after the Old Man died drunk in a snowbank when Hubert was seventeen, had stayed on in the Reserve, the Old Man's wilderness, doing the job his father had done before him.

He never spoke of any of this, not even in painless, smooth generalities. There were no words to describe the feelings that since childhood had warred in his large, wounded heart, and he had almost given up on ever finding them, until he met Alicia, whom he came quickly to believe was willing and able to give him those words and listen to his use of them with sympathy and understanding. That was why he had begun to steal her from her husband. It hadn't been his intention or desire. It surely was not merely to make love to her, although their lovemaking, tender and trusting and passionate, had brought him closer to speaking of these things and revealing his secret self than he had ever been before.

There was no way he could tell this to the sad, angry, bewildered man before him. So he simply shook his head and said no. No to the man's accusation that he was fucking Vanessa Von Heidenstamm. No to his charge that he had wanted to steal the man's wife. Hubert had wanted only to be wholly known and understood by another human being, and because she was a woman, a beautiful, loving woman, he knew of no means of obtaining that understanding other than by making love to her, and afterward, talking in the dark of what's right and what's wrong, sorting out the conflicted welter of feelings that each had endured in the past and were fast creating anew, and later, walking in the high meadows, naming the flowers blooming there and naming the birds in the trees from their songs. Until the moment yesterday when Vanessa Von Heidenstamm knocked on his cabin door, it was their lovemaking and its accompaniments that had brought him to the point where he could at last begin to speak directly from his divided heart. And now he saw that he had no choice but once again to silence his heart, to return to being the man of few words, the simple, solitary man of the lakes and woods and mountains, the much admired and sometimes envied Adirondack guide.

"So what the hell are you doing out here this early in the morning, sleeping on the porch, instead of out back in the cookshack or the lean-to?" Jordan asked him, thinking that the guide had a better right and reason to ask him what *he* was doing out here this early in the morning. He had no idea of what he would give him for an answer. How do you tell a man like Hubert St. Germain that you don't know why you are where you are? That you're looking for some solid ground to stand on, and you think this strangely incandescent woman can somehow give it to you? How can you tell the man who has been sleeping with your wife that, because of him, you no longer know who your wife is and therefore no longer know who you are, either?

Hubert said, "I'm helping Miss Cole out with her mother."

"Her mother, eh? Why? Is she ill or something?"

"No." Hubert sucked thoughtfully on his lips for a few seconds, then said, "It's not something I can talk about."

"What the Christ does that mean?"

"You better get Miss Cole to explain. It's complicated."

"I guess to hell it must be," Jordan said and stood up. "You and I, Hubert, we have more to discuss. A lot more."

"I expect so."

"Where is she, Vanessa? Is she up yet?"

"Can't say."

Damn the man, Jordan thought. What the hell did he and Alicia ever talk about? It must have been completely sexual between them, he thought, at least on her part, and he felt himself shudder with anxious jealousy, something he could not remember ever feeling before, not with Alicia, certainly, and not with Anne, his first wife, whom he had met and married right after returning from the war. He'd come home an American innocent made cynical by what he'd seen and done in the skies over France and had been brought briefly back to his innocence by marrying a slim, sweetly smiling, blond girl from his Ohio hometown. But her own innocence and naiveté, cut with his new cynicism, had left him exhausted and empty of affection for Anne within a year, so that when he left Canton for Greenwich Village in 1920 to study with Charles Henri, he refused to take her with him. Anne Zayre, his war bride, as he referred to her, had been incapable of making him jealous or sexually insecure, although before his departure for New York she had tried to hold him by deliberately conducting several flagrant love affairs, which had not upset him in the slightest. They had merely eased his guilt for abandoning her and her world and his familial past for a life in art.

Alicia, a much greater sexual threat, due to her physical beauty and Viennese charm and smooth intelligence, had up to now so flattered him by word and deed for his sexual prowess that it simply had never occurred to Jordan that another man could satisfy his wife as completely as he—until this man, Hubert St. Germain, came along, this melancholy widower of the woods, this man of a few well-chosen words who had never been farther from his traplines and hunting grounds than Albany and Schenectady, if he'd even been that far. It made no sense, Jordan thought. None.

Except for the old perennial sexual attraction of the bourgeois woman for the proletarian male. That must be it. It was an attractiveness that Jordan Groves, no matter how radical his politics, was unable to generate for himself, except among aristocratic women. Aristocratic women, he believed, had the same weakness for men like him as Alicia had for men like Hubert. That's the explanation, he thought, it's all about class, and felt a little better, his jealousy no longer quite so tainted by sexual insecurity. He was merely angry and confused again.

He was about to knock on the door to the living room and go inside, when the door opened as if of its own accord, and there was Vanessa, in tan slacks and one of her father's flannel shirts untucked and open at the throat, her hair pulled back and tied with a black ribbon. She was barefoot and carried a small round tray with two mugs of steaming coffee.

Startled to see Jordan Groves, but evidently pleased, she gave him an open smile and leaned forward and kissed him on his unshaven cheek as if greeting a family friend. "Why, Jordan, I didn't expect to see *you* out here this morning. And so early!" She brushed past him and set the tray on a table by the couch where Hubert sat and quickly disappeared inside again, returning with a third mug of coffee. "Isn't this a beautiful morning?" she said and raised her cup to the lake and the pinking mist and, on the far side of the lake, the mountaintops floating above the mist.

Jordan picked up one of the mugs and sipped at the strong black coffee, closing his eyes for a moment as if to gather his thoughts. Vanessa took the seat he had vacated earlier and looked first at Hubert, then at Jordan standing beside her. Both Hubert and Vanessa seemed to be waiting for Jordan to speak.

"It's all very strange," Jordan finally said.

"What is?" she asked.

"The three of us out here together, politely drinking coffee by the lake, as if nothing's happened."

"But nothing has happened, Jordan," Vanessa said, and she meant it, because in her mind nothing had happened that could not be explained away. At least nothing between her and her mother that Jordan could possibly know of, and nothing between her and Hubert, and so far nothing between her and Jordan. And since she had said not a word to anyone other than Hubert about seeing Alicia at Hubert's cabin yesterday and drawing the obvious conclusion, she thought nothing had happened between the two men, either. Everything, for the moment, was neatly separated into discrete compartments that did not communicate with one another. Vanessa was still able to track all the lies and keep the contradictions and inconsistencies between them from revealing the larger, comprehensive truth. She believed that she alone knew that truth, of which Hubert knew a small part, and Jordan a lesser part, and his wife, Alicia, an even lesser part. Vanessa's mother, Evelyn, knew her part of the truth—that her daughter had kidnapped and imprisoned her here in the middle of the vast wilderness of the Reserve and had somehow convinced the family's longtime guide and caretaker to assist her in carrying out this crime. Thanks to Hubert St. Germain, Evelyn Cole was free now to move about the camp and was no longer tied to a chair and gagged, as long as she stayed inside the main building and out of sight. If she did not try to escape, Hubert had said, he wouldn't tie her up, while behind him Vanessa had nodded threateningly over his shoulder. Hubert had tried to explain to Evelyn Cole, as if it were a perfectly reasonable thing, why her daughter was doing this to her.

Evelyn Cole was no longer afraid that Vanessa was going to kill her. Not as long as Hubert was present. But the man was inarticulate and not very bright and was obviously smitten with Vanessa and in her thrall. He didn't know the half of it, anyhow, Evelyn believed—that Vanessa's rage and insane need to punish her mother had little to do with her fear of being sent to a mental hospital in Zurich or of being cut out of her inheritance from her grandparents and father. No, it was rooted somehow in the distant past, in the darkness of her early childhood and the sordid things she imagined had occurred there. Most of Evelyn Cole's own memories of those years were cloudy and indistinct, blighted by a pervasive, unaccountable, nameless shame. But, really, she was sure that nothing terrible had happened in Vanessa's childhood. Certainly nothing at the hands of her father. There were no naked photographs of Vanessa that she knew of, although she had not gone through her late husband's files, as Vanessa thought, or his albums. Somehow she had been afraid to examine them.

The guide had made several halfhearted attempts to explain to Evelyn Cole why Vanessa was doing this to her and had asked her to reconsider her decision to send Vanessa to Zurich and agree to turn her daughter's inheritance over to her and, as he put it, "let bygones be bygones." And if Evelyn agreed, the man said, he would take her back to the Tamarack Club tomorrow and would even be willing to drive her home to Tuxedo Park in her car. "Miss Cole can stay here at the lake, if she wants, and I'll come back up on the train," he said, adding that he'd need a few dollars' advance for the fare.

Evelyn had agreed at once, but Vanessa read her mind and told the guide that her mother was lying, that as soon as she got back to the city she would take out a fresh set of commitment papers and would send the sheriff here to carry her out of the Reserve in a straitjacket, tossing her in a paddy wagon and driving her to some upstate insane asylum, where she'd be confined with the lunatics for the rest of her life. It would be worse than sending her to the hospital in Zurich, she had said to Hubert. And the man had believed her, and when the three of them had finished eating supper, he had locked Evelyn in the bedroom again. "I'm sorry to have to do this, Mrs. Cole," he had said to her. "Maybe in the morning you two will see more eye to eye." Then he had gone outside and closed and hooked the winter shutters over the bedroom and bathroom windows, plunging both rooms into darkness.

Out on the porch, Jordan Groves said to Vanessa, "Look, I came out here this morning to talk to you. I don't need ol' Hubert here to hang around while I'm doing it. I don't know what you two have going on between you, but I've got enough reasons of my own to want to drive the man into the ground with a hammer. So if you value his physical well-bring, you'll tell him to disappear for a while, until I'm gone from here. Then you can resume whatever it is you two were doing before I interrupted. All right?"

"All right," she said. "But, believe me, there's nothing going on between us. Hubert, do you mind?"

He said no, he didn't mind and got up and left the porch for the deck outside, disappearing in the direction of the outbuildings among the trees in back—the guesthouse, the toolshed, cookshack and woodshed, the outhouse, and the open lean-to where the help slept.

Afraid that her mother, still locked inside the bedroom, might hear the artist's voice and cry out for help, Vanessa needed to get Jordan Groves away from the main building. "Let's walk down by the lake," she suggested, and the two left the porch and made their way across the sloping, rust-colored blanket of pine needles down to the rocky shore. She needed to keep the two men apart, too. Hubert, his resolve somewhat softened by her mother's pleas last night, was not an altogether reliable ally in this and might take it into his mind to confide in Jordan or ask for his help, and she had no idea whose side Jordan would take in this, once he knew the truth.

He pulled his leather jacket off and spread it across the hull of Hubert's overturned guide boat, against the dew. They leaned back on the boat and held the mugs of coffee close to their mouths, warming their faces and hands, and gazed at the rising mist and the smooth, black surface of the lake. A pair of loons cruised low over the lake from north to south and dropped into the water with a quiet splash. Every few seconds the water was puckered by feeding trout and then was still again.

"I keep looking along the shore for Daddy's ashes," she said. "Or do you think when they hit the water they just sank?"

"The ash dissolved right away, probably. He's part of the lake now. It's what he wanted, right?"

"What about the bigger bits and pieces? There were some. I looked."

"On the bottom, I expect. Or in the belly of a lake trout. Watch what you catch and eat," he said.

"Jordan, really!" she said and smiled. "Where's your airplane? How'd you get out here?" she asked.

"Anchored in a cove up a ways. No sense in advertising its presence."

"I didn't hear it come in," she said and wondered if her mother had.

"I cut the engine back pretty far. Practically glided it in." He turned to Vanessa then and said, "I know you saw my wife over at Hubert's place yesterday."

"Yes. I did."

"And what did you make of it?"

"Make of it? Why, nothing. I went there to hire Hubert to bring in supplies to Rangeview. I had business with him. I assume she did, too. That's all. Why, was there more to it than that?"

"A lot more. What's he doing here now?"

"You're changing the subject, Jordan. And it's not really any of your business anyhow," she said. "But if you must know, he rowed out with the second load of supplies after dark, so I suggested he sleep on the porch and go back in daylight."

"Well, that's not what he told me. Anyhow, what he's doing out here *is* my business. The man's been sleeping with my wife. She's in love with him, she says. So if he's sleeping with you, too, I'd like to know it. It's got nothing to do with you. You're free to sleep with anyone you damn well please."

"Thank you very much." She laughed lightly and lay the palm of her hand against his cheek. "No, Jordan dear, I'm not sleeping with Hubert. He's very pretty, and sexy in a stolid sort of way. But there's nothing between us. I'm curious, though. What *did* Hubert tell you?"

"About why he's out here? He said he was helping you with your mother. Didn't make sense, so I didn't believe him. I don't believe you, either. The fact is, I'm reasonably sure my wife's in love with a man who's screwing at least one other woman. You. And probably a couple more for good measure. I'm going to see that she knows it, and I'm going to take the bastard down for it."

"For what?"

"For deceiving her. And me. And deceiving you. Though I don't expect you're in love with him, too. Are you?"

Vanessa laughed again. "Oh, if I'm in love with anyone, Jordan Groves, it's probably you," she said. Smiling, she put her mug down on the boat and kissed him, sweetly, sincerely, not quite passionately, but capable of becoming passionate in a matter of seconds, he could tell. Reluctantly, he removed her hands from his face and pushed her away, and her expression suddenly darkened, and she said, "Oh, dear."

He followed her gaze and saw what she saw—Hubert St. Germain trudging slowly toward them, head down, hands at his sides, and a few feet behind him, Evelyn Cole. She walked wood-

enly, but with calm determination, her face cold and tightly knotted. And she held a double-barreled shotgun aimed at his back.

"What the hell is *this*?" Jordan said.

"Oh, Christ, she's got one of Daddy's guns," Vanessa whispered.

They drew near, and in a trembling voice Evelyn Cole told
Hubert to stop right there. "Mr. Groves, I need you to take me
out of here in your airplane," she said.

Hubert said, "I went to check on her, and she was waiting
with the gun. It was in the closet. We forgot." He looked glum,
as required by his lines, but also oddly relieved, and Jordan wondered if this were an event somehow rehearsed and staged for his
benefit, some kind of weird, amateurish piece of theater.

"He doesn't *have* his airplane, Mother! Please, put the gun
down. You don't need the gun!"

"No, I do have it. I have my airplane," Jordan said. "But somebody tell me what the hell this is all about."

"They've gone crazy, Mr. Groves! Crazy! Both of them. They
won't let me leave. You have to take me out in your airplane!
Where is it?"

"He doesn't have it here, Mother. He came by boat. Hubert
brought him in, didn't you, Hubert?" Vanessa looked at the guide
and then at Jordan Groves with pleading eyes, *Lie for me, please.
Both of you, goddamnit, lie for me!* Neither man's eyes answered
one way or the other.

Jordan took several steps to his right, separating himself from
Vanessa and the others. Evelyn Cole watched him warily, but kept
the shotgun trained on Hubert's back. The end of the barrel wobbled a little, Jordan noticed, as if it had grown heavy to her. He said,
"I don't know what's going on, but it can't be worth someone's getting
shot. Whyn't you let me have that gun, Mrs. Cole? I'll fly you out, if
you'll give me the gun." He extended his hands, palms up.

"No, you can't!" Vanessa cried. "You don't have your airplane! Don't believe him, Mother. He's lying. He came over in Hubert's boat. See? It's right here," Vanessa said and patted the hull of the guide boat.

"Put the gun down, Mrs. Cole. We don't need anybody getting hurt. We can all discuss whatever's going on. Whyn't you give the gun to me?" Jordan said and with both hands extended took a step closer to her.

"I heard the airplane," Evelyn Cole said. "I was awake, and I heard the airplane. They've kept me prisoner, Mr. Groves. My daughter's lost her mind, and this one, he's helping her."

Hubert slowly turned around, saw the over and under barrels of the shotgun a few inches from his chest, and inhaled sharply at the sight. He wasn't sure the woman had ever fired a gun. Dr. Cole was the hunter. A good shot, too. But he'd never seen the wife with a gun in her hand. He looked along the length of the under barrel and saw that the safety was off and knew that the shotgun was hair triggered and remembered the box of shells stored in the drawer of the gun rack in the doctor's clothes closet. He concluded that both barrels of the shotgun were loaded. The woman was having trouble holding the gun, he could tell. The barrel was ninety centimeters long and in her weakened condition was too heavy for her. If she doesn't fire it first, Hubert decided, she will have to lower it. The moment for her to fire the gun has almost passed, he thought.

Mrs. Cole took her eyes off the guide to glance at Jordan Groves's large open hands, then his eyes. She saw that he was a kind man, a worried man, and that, unlike the guide, he was not caught up in Vanessa's insanity. "Please, Mr. Groves," she said to him. "Please help me."

"Vanessa," he said. "For God's sake, let me take her out of here, before something really bad happens."

"It already has," she said. Suddenly Hubert grabbed the barrels of the gun and wrenched the weapon to his left, with both hands pushing it away from Jordan and Vanessa so that if it went off it would fire harmlessly into the air. Evelyn Cole tugged fiercely back, surprising Hubert with her strength, causing him to yank hard on the barrels. The woman pulled back, but then lost her grip on the stock, and suddenly the barrels of the gun in Hubert's hands felt like twinned snakes. He let go of the barrels and the shotgun flipped 180 degrees in the air, end over end. In precise, unforgettable detail Hubert and Jordan and Vanessa saw it happen. They watched in horror as the hair-triggered shotgun fell through the air between them and Vanessa's mother, and the stock hit the ground first, and the gun fired. Both barrels emptied almost simultaneously into the woman's chest. The force of it blew her backward the length of her small body and tossed her onto the ground in a crumpled heap, arms and legs akimbo. Her head flopped once, twice, then was still. Blood bubbled from her open mouth onto the hard ground. The dark, fist-size hole in her chest instantly turned scarlet and filled and overflowed. Her blue eyes stayed open, as if in permanent surprise.

No one uttered a word. The morning mist had risen above the warming lake and had dissipated. The sky was cloudless and azure colored, and on the far side of the lake the mountains of the Great Range glowed in bright sunlight. Jordan looked across the glassy water, and each individual tree—one and one and one— leaped from the bright greenery, sharp to the eye, even from this distance. A perfect Adirondack day. The sound of the shotgun blast echoed back once from the high gray cliffs. The two black loons broke free of the water and flew low to the northern end of the lake and disappeared above the trees.

Vanessa said, "Oh, my God. Oh, my God. She's dead, isn't she?"

Hubert knelt down beside the woman and touched her throat. "Yes."

"You're sure?" Jordan said. "She's really dead?"

"Yes," Hubert said. "She took both barrels." He stood up and looked off at the mountains on the far side of the lake.

Vanessa turned and started walking toward the house.

"Where are you going?" Jordan called.

"To get a shovel!"

"What the hell for?"

She stopped and looked back at him, her fists on her hips, and studied him for a second. "To bury her, Jordan," she said and hurried on.

"To *bury* her! My Christ! Will you tell me what on earth has been going on here?" Jordan said to the guide.

Hubert stood and looked at his hands. His guilty hands. This was an accident that shouldn't have happened. If he hadn't tried to take the shotgun away from her, the woman would have had to put it down of her own accord. Or she would have handed it over to the artist. Maybe the artist would have flown her out of here then. And maybe Vanessa Cole would have agreed to do what her mother originally wanted, ship her off to that hospital in Europe. Only first they'd make the mother promise no brain surgery, no lobotomy that can turn you into a vegetable, that would be the deal, and maybe in a few months or a year Vanessa would come out cured of whatever mental sickness she had, and she would return to America, and her mother would have forgiven her by then for all this. For being kidnapped and imprisoned here at the camp by her own daughter. And someday Vanessa Cole would get her inheritance and enjoy the kind of life she was supposed to have.

"Hubert, for Christ's sake, answer me! The woman has just

been killed! This is goddamned serious. And Vanessa just wants to bury her and forget it? Are you two both crazy, like the old woman said?"

"No. What she told me made sense. Sort of. Oh, hell, at least yesterday it did."

"Who? Who made sense?"

"Miss Cole. Vanessa. She told me that her mother signed her into a mental hospital in Europe and took away all her inheritance money from her father and her grandparents. It was extreme, maybe, what the mother did, and Vanessa was really scared of going into the hospital. What she did was maybe more extreme than what the mother did, but it was understandable, I guess. Because she was scared of having brain surgery. You know, a lobotomy. I was trying to get them to find some kind of agreement is all. It was wrong, what Vanessa did, tying up her mother and keeping her here against her will. It was wrong what the mother was doing, too. But it was an accident, Jordan, the gun going off."

"Yeah, it was an accident. I know that. You know that. But it won't look like an accident if we let Vanessa bury her out here," Jordan said. He tossed his jacket on the ground, turned the guide boat over and slid it on its keel toward the water and in. "You've got to take the body out and report what happened. I'm not supposed to be here, especially with the airplane, so it's up to you, Hubert. If we load the woman's body into the boat now," he said, "before Vanessa comes back with the damned shovel, you can row it across the lake to the Carry." From there the guide could get the body of the woman over to the First Lake on the cart the guides used for hauling supplies between the two lakes, row across to the boathouse, leave the woman's body, and walk in and report what had happened. "And by the way, Hubert, nobody needs to know I was out here this morning. It'll only complicate things. So c'mon," he said, "give me a hand with her before Vanessa tries to stop us."

The guide didn't move, except to pick up the fallen shotgun. He broke it open, removed and automatically pocketed the empty shells, and looked down the barrels. "This's going to hurt me, you know," he said. "Accident or not. People talk." He snapped the shotgun shut and hefted it in his hands, noting its balance. It was a custom-made Belgian .28 gauge. Worth at least a thousand dollars, Hubert thought. He said to Jordan, "Word'll get out. People will know that the wife of one of my best clients got herself killed by her own gun in my presence. In my care. Guides are supposed to make sure things like this don't happen."

"We don't have a choice. Anyhow, it'll blow over eventually. People talk, but they forget, too."

"I'm a guide, Jordan. Word'll get out. Someone in my care got herself shot, and it might even look like I shot her myself. Wouldn't matter that it was an accident. Look, this is a serious problem for me. You don't understand, Jordan, it's the only living I got," he said, then added, almost as an afterthought, "Vanessa says nobody knows her mother is even up here. Except me. And now you. And you, you're setting up to say you weren't even here this morning."

"What about Kendall? He must know."

"Yes, but he thinks it was of her own free will that she came in to the camp. He wouldn't check on whether she's still here or left already for New York City. Vanessa could drive off and say she took her mother with her, and nobody'd be the wiser."

Jordan held the boat by the gunnel and looked back at the man. Was he serious? Was he really going along with her? Had that been their plan all along? It slowly dawned on Jordan that

Vanessa and Hubert might have been working together from the beginning, and not only had they been sleeping together, they had also been trying to scare Mrs. Cole into releasing Vanessa's inheritance—and when she agreed to that, they would murder the woman. Maybe they planned to make it look as if she'd died of natural causes, smother her with a pillow or something, or drown her in the lake and just say she went swimming and never came back. Vanessa probably promised Hubert more money than he'd ever imagined making in a lifetime. The artist's unexpected arrival this morning had stymied their plan, or at least complicated it. And then Mrs. Cole found her husband's shotgun. And now she was dead, but not of natural causes. Explainable, though. An accidental shooting.

Jordan looked up the slope toward the house and saw Vanessa coming from the tool-shed carrying a long-handled spade and a pickax. "C'mon, Hubert," the artist said, "help me put the body in the boat and shove off. For Christ's sake, hurry!"

"No. We can't do that. Not without Vanessa's permission. It's her mother."

"I don't know what kind of spell she's put on you, man, but I'm not waiting for her permission." Jordan let the boat float a few feet from shore. Moving fast, he got his arms under the woman's body and lifted it and carried it to the boat and gently laid it in the bow. He put the oars into the boat and looked down and saw blood smeared across the front of his shirt. "Damn!" he said.

He grabbed the guide by the shoulder and shoved him in the direction of the boat. The man didn't move. "Hubert, get in the goddamned boat, and start rowing!" Again Jordan shoved him, but Hubert stood rooted to the ground, still holding the shotgun loosely in one hand.

From fifty yards off, Vanessa saw the boat bobbing in the

water and her mother's body in the boat, saw the bloodstains on Jordan's white shirt and Hubert with the gun, and started to run toward them. "Stop! You can't take her, Jordan! You can't!" she cried. Dropping the tools at the shore, she ran knee deep into the water. She pushed Jordan aside, grabbed the boat, and drew it halfway back onto dry land.

Jordan said, "Let Hubert take her in and report it. It was an accident, Vanessa. That's all. You've got to report it, Vanessa."

"No! No one will believe me! Don't you understand? People will think I did it! The police, everyone, they'll all blame me. Because of . . . because of what she was doing to me. And what I've done to her." Vanessa was panting, her eyes darting from one man to the other. "She was sending me away, back to that mental hospital, Jordan. And my grandparents' trust and my inheritance from Daddy, she took them, Jordan. So not only am I certified crazy, I've got a motive. Motive, opportunity, and means, Jordan. Plus crazy."

"No one has to know about that," he said.

"It's all documented, Jordan. They made me sign the papers, my mother and her lawyer."

"I meant, what you were doing to her. Out here. No one has to know that. It takes away motive, at least. And craziness."

"We can swear it was an accident," Hubert said. "Because it's the truth. We'll swear we were here and we saw it."

Jordan turned to him in surprise. "You can say *you* were here and you saw it. Not me. As soon as I can, I'm flying out of here. You and Vanessa can claim it happened any damned way you want."

Vanessa looked at the two men as if they were boys and simply did not understand the ways of adults. "If they don't believe me, and they won't, what makes you think they'll believe you,

Hubert? Or you, Jordan? If I have to, to protect myself, I'll say you both were witnesses. But it won't matter, no one will believe you, either. They'll just think you're both covering for me. The famously philandering artist and the lonely widower of the woods, they'll think you're both in love with me. Or at least were sleeping with me. They'll say I worked my wiles on you. Oh, and will you tell the sheriff why Mother had the gun in the first place, Hubert? Will you say she got the drop on you when you went to make sure she was still safely locked away in the bedroom? You could go to jail for that alone, you know. Aiding and abetting a kidnapper. Or maybe I'll just claim you did it, Hubert. All on your own. You shot her because you're so in love with me, you big hunk of a man, and in your own love-struck way were only trying to free me from my mother's nefarious intention of tossing me in the loony bin and spending all my money. Which would be better spent on you, right? I mean, look, your fingerprints are all over Daddy's gun! And poor little me, I don't even know how to shoot a gun. Or maybe I'll say you two were out here early in the morning, fighting, because Hubert's been sleeping with your sweet wife, Jordan, and Mother tried to stop you—"

"Jesus, Vanessa," Jordan said. "Stop."

"Oh, don't worry, I wouldn't do it." She smiled wanly at Hubert, then at Jordan. "But seriously, whatever you say or I say happened, no one's going to believe us. Unless I confess that, yes, I shot my mother, and you're only covering up for me. People will believe that story easily enough. But no matter what story they believe, someone's going to jail for this mess. Me, for sure. But maybe you, too, Hubert St. Germain. Possibly even you, Jordan Groves. Because no one's going to believe it was an accident. And in a way, it wasn't, was it?" She looked down at her mother's body in the boat. "Oh, God, she's really dead, isn't she? This isn't a dream, is it?"

"No," Jordan said. "It's real, Vanessa. That's why we can't lie about it. Regardless of the consequences."

Vanessa said, "You don't mind lying about your being out here, though. Do you?"

"That's . . . that's different."

"The main difference being you can get away with it."

"I'm thinking maybe we should take the body in and report it," Hubert said. "I'm thinking maybe Jordan's right."

"You're not listening to me," Vanessa said. "Either of you. If you take my mother's body in and report her death, no matter how you tell it, I am definitely going to jail for a long, long time. Or I'll spend the rest of my life in a mental hospital. There's no way around it. Please, you two, help me with this. I need you both. Please help me. We can bury her in the woods, and then you both can leave, and tonight after it gets dark I'll take the guide boat and go back to the Club and drive away. No one will see me leave. That'll be the end of it. Nothing will happen to either of you. Nothing will happen to me."

"How will you explain her disappearance?" Jordan asked.

"I won't."

"What do you mean?"

"I'll just say she was fine when I dropped her off in Tuxedo Park after our trip to the Adirondacks with Daddy's ashes."

"There'll be a search. Up here, especially. Where she was last seen alive."

"The only people who'll know where to look will be you two. And me. And I'll never tell anyone. If you never tell anyone, Mother's disappearance will remain a mystery, pure and simple. Of course, I'll stay under suspicion for years, maybe forever. But I can live with that. I've lived with worse."

Hubert said, "No one would think to ask Jordan about it, probably. Nobody knows he's been here. Me, though, they would ask. Since it's known I brought supplies in yesterday."

"You'd have to lie, then. You'd have to say she was fine when you last saw her," Vanessa said.

"I don't like lying. I'm not much good at it."

Jordan gave a short, hard laugh. "I'd say you're damned good at it."

The three stood with their backs to the lake and the boat and Vanessa's mother, and were silent for a long moment. Jordan put his jacket on, took his tobacco and papers from the pocket and rolled a cigarette and lighted it and smoked.

Finally, Hubert sighed and said, "She wouldn't be the first person who's buried in these woods and nobody knows it."

"I expect not," Jordan said.

"There's always been stories about hunters going into the Reserve alone and not coming out and no body ever found."

"That right?"

"Yes. Some of it might've been funny business, some of it not. When it's local people, of course, everybody pretty much knows what's what."

"But you wouldn't call Mrs. Cole local people."

"No. Not really."

"She'd have to be buried deep, with rocks on her," Jordan said. "To keep the animals from digging her up. You understand I'm just speculating here."

Vanessa looked at the ground and was silent.

Hubert said, "You'd need someplace high, where there's no brook or stream. Snowmelt moves the banks around a lot in spring and washes out any low places."

Jordan said, "You'd have to replace the sod, make it look natural again. No tracks."

"Yes," Hubert said. "You would."

For a long moment neither man said anything.

"You know the land hereabouts," Jordan said to Hubert. "Any good ground high up that's not covered with trees, where there's rocks close by?"

Again, neither man spoke. Then, as if he'd had the spot in mind for a long time, Hubert said, "There's a bluff about a quarter mile east of the house."

The three of them looked from one to the other, each to each. Jordan picked up the shovel and pickax and passed the shovel to Hubert. With the shotgun in one hand, the shovel in the other, Hubert led Jordan and Vanessa up the slope toward the tall pines and into the woods beyond. Behind them, the guide boat, half in the water, half out, rocked gently on its keel, and Evelyn Cole's cold dry eyes stared at the morning sun.

The American woman sat alone in the dining saloon on Level A of the airship. She was dressed in the same brown tweed jacket and skirt as when she'd first boarded, except that the wide-brimmed hat and veil had been replaced by a green chenille head scarf knotted in back and worn low on the forehead, like a flapper of a decade ago. Not having eaten dinner the night before, she was evidently hungry and ordered a full breakfast off the menu. She looked with mild interest at the silk-covered wall opposite her. Twenty-one panels were painted with scenes illustrating last year's flights of the Graf Zeppelin, the Hindenburg's sister ship, to South America. She looked at the pictures in sequence from left to right, one at a time, as if they were sections of a mural, instead of a collection of individual pictures. During the night the Hindenburg had passed over England, and at a nearby table three middle-aged men in business suits and an elderly, silver-haired lady, Americans, were discussing the coronation next week of George VI. One of the men had gotten the news of the day early this morning from the airship's radio operator. They agreed that the abdicated king's forthcoming marriage to Mrs. Simpson, whose divorce from her previous husband had been granted a day ago, was scandalous. Imagine an American president behaving like that, said the lady with the silver hair. She spoke with a crisp Connecticut accent. Seated at a banquette in the corner of the dining room, a German woman with two small blond boys waited to be served. The younger boy got down on the carpeted floor to play with his windup toy, a tin car driven by Mickey Mouse. He wound the key and set the car on the floor. It ran under the table and came out the other side, making a whirring noise and giving off metallic sparks. Quickly, the steward crossed the room, grabbed the toy, and stopped the wheels from spinning. In German he said to the mother, I'm sorry, Frau Imhoff, but I must confiscate this. We take no chances with sparks. The Americans, meanwhile, continued to discuss the news of the day. Franco's advance against the republic is going swimmingly, said the man who had visited the ship's radio operator. His air force destroyed a Basque town called Guernica, near Bilbao. The man next to him said, That's only thanks to the Germans, of course. Who the heck do you think was flying those airplanes? Certainly not Spaniards or Italians. The third man said, In the future the main use of airplanes will be in war. As airborne artillery. And all the casualties of war will be civilians. Mark my words, it won't be like the last one. The lady from Connecticut said, Oh, dear, I do hope you're wrong. This is so depressing a subject. Can't we talk about something else? She turned then and smiled at the young woman seated alone by the window. Would you like to join us? she asked. Do you speak English? I'm afraid none of us speaks German. Before the woman could answer, the waiter arrived with her breakfast. He set the plate before her, and she began to eat at once. For a few seconds the silver-haired lady and her three com-panions watched her, waiting for a response. Finally, they turned away. The lady raised her eyebrows and pursed her lips. No speaka da English, one of the men said, and the others smiled uneasily and quickly resumed their discussion of the news of the day.

THE SITE WAS A FLATTENED PATCH OF AN ANCIENT GLACIAL esker where tall red pines grew straight as masts and there wasn't much ground cover, other than a warm, fragrant bed of pine needles. A spill of boulders from a shifted brook lay close by, and while the men dug the hole, Vanessa busied herself lugging rocks and piling them at what she felt was the foot of her mother's grave. Then she sat down on the ground a few feet away to watch, her arms across her knees, her chin resting on her arms. Jordan, in shirtsleeves, his leather jacket on the ground nearby, swung the pick and loosened the gravelly soil, and Hubert shoveled the dirt into a neat, conical pile. Vanessa was silent and dreamy seeming. While they worked the men spoke to each other in low voices, as if to keep from waking her.

"You ever do this before?" Jordan asked.

"What? Bury somebody in the Reserve?"

"No. But, yeah, that, too. I meant, you ever dig a grave before?"

"Not in the Reserve. But yes, a couple times I've had to dig a grave."

"Who for?"

"For the family," Hubert said. "My family. In the old family plot off Hitchcock Road."

"Who'd you bury?"

"My old man. Then my mother."

"What about your wife?"

Hubert was silent for a moment. "She's in the town cemetery."

"You ever shoot anybody before?"

"I didn't shoot her, Jordan. The answer is no."

"What about in the war?"

"I was only seventeen, and I had to take care of my mother. So I stayed out. My brothers went over."

"Oh. Too bad. You would've been a good soldier," Jordan said.

"Why do you say that?"

"You've got all the necessary skills. You'd have made a good sniper. And you don't rattle easily when someone gets shot."

"Go to hell, Jordan. I didn't shoot her."

"She didn't shoot herself."

"What about you? You ever shoot anybody in the war?"

"I was a flyer. I shot at other airplanes, not people."

"There must've been people in those planes, though."

"True enough, Hubie. True enough."

"Did you shoot any of those airplanes down?"

"Two. I made two kills, both on the same day. April 4, 1918."

"So you shot people, then. You killed people."

"Yes. Germans. But I didn't have to bury them."

The moldering, sunlit bed of fallen needles quilted the ground. The view of the lake and mountains was blocked by trees, Vanessa noted, but it wasn't a bad place to be buried, she thought. Daddy might even have preferred having his ashes up here instead of in the lake. A light wind slipped delicately through the tall pines above, and sunlight fell in patches between the feathered branches of the trees and warmed the ground where she sat. She wondered if she could trust the two men equally. She decided that, under pressure, Hubert would crack before Jordan. Hubert

St. Germain was a local, however, and a guide, a man more trusted by the authorities than Jordan Groves, the Red, the artist from away. They'd probably go easy on Hubert, take whatever he said at face value and search for Vanessa's mother elsewhere. They'd check her bank records, interview the cook and housekeeper and gardener in Tuxedo Park and the doorman and housekeeper in Manhattan, they'd call all her known friends and ask them if they'd heard from Mrs. Cole in the weeks since she was last seen by Russell Kendall at the Tamarack Club going in to the Cole family camp at the Reserve with her daughter. Jordan Groves, the artist from Petersburg, they'd have no reason to question, so he'd not have to lie or cover up. Unless, of course, someone heard or saw him fly in this morning or sees or hears him flying out later today. But she wasn't worried about Jordan. He was used to lying, despite the fact that he claimed to tell the unvarnished truth, regardless of the consequences, in those travel books of his. They were probably mostly lies, too.

Hubert was a different sort of man, however. It wasn't that he so much loved telling the truth as that he hated lying. Keeping silent, saying no more than necessary, that was his way of avoiding both. The sheriff, or maybe a police inspector from missing persons in Manhattan, would ask him when he last saw Mrs. Cole, and he'd say the date. Where? they'd ask. Out at the Cole place. Did he see her leave the camp? No. Did he see the daughter there? Yes. Did he see the daughter leave the camp? No. Were they both still at the camp when he left? Yes. Thank you very much, Mr. St. Germain.

Vanessa doubted they'd even bother to go to the trouble of rowing out to inspect the place. Russell Kendall might send someone from his staff to Rangeview to check around for signs of anything suspicious; but he'd probably send Hubert St. Germain, since the guide knew the place so much better than anyone else and had keys to all the doors.

When the hole was nearly five feet deep and difficult to dig any deeper without needing a ladder to climb out of it, the three returned to the lake for the body. Again, Vanessa stood off a ways and watched as the men worked. They wrapped the body in the white, red, and black Hudson Bay blanket from the bedroom where Evelyn Cole had been imprisoned, making a shroud of it by tying the blanket at the ends and the middle with rope—the same pieces of clothesline Vanessa had used to bind her mother's ankles and wrists when she was still alive. Then Hubert and Jordan grabbed on to the ropes and carried the body of Evelyn Cole, like a log, up the slope behind the compound to the grave, for it was that to them now, a grave, not a hole in the ground. They walked slowly and stayed silent, as if the two men were pallbearers and the woman coming along behind were a priest or minister.

With the body wrapped in the blanket, they could no longer see the dead woman's face and the ugly wound in her chest and the blood, distancing them somewhat from the violence of her death and bringing them closer to the inescapable fact of her death, its finality.

That would be the hardest thing for Jordan and Hubert to lie about, Vanessa realized. The actual fact of her mother's death. It would be far easier to lie about *how* she died.

Vanessa herself would have no difficulty claiming that her mother had simply disappeared, that's all. There is no explanation for it, she'd say. The woman has vanished. One can speculate about why or how for as long as one wants; but the fact, the only fact that counts, is that the woman is gone. Vanessa would have no trouble forgetting all other facts and concentrating on that one alone, until it became the only fact that mattered. Absent a sure sense of the necessary and essential nature of the truth in all things known and unknown, it's actually difficult to lie. It may even be impossible. In that sense, Vanessa was not a liar. She knew the meanings of the words *true* and *false* and was adept at distinguishing between a person who was a liar and one who was honest—Jordan was the first, Hubert the second—but she herself was neither. Her understanding of the truth of a given event was less of a concrete thing existing in the world—whether revealed or concealed, known or not—than of an incidental attribute. For her, the truth was more a coloration of reality than the organizing principle of its underlying structure. For her, it was utterly, and merely, contingent. Thus the truth was somewhat transient and changeable, one minute here, the next gone. It was something one could assert and a moment later turn around and deny, with no sense of there being any contradiction. Merely a correction. For Vanessa, the truth was like a bird that flies from tree to tree, so that the statement, *The tree has a bird perched in it*, referred to this nearby tree, then that, as the bird flew to the next tree, then that, and on through the entire forest of trees, and from there to the next forest, until the bird had flown around the globe, tree to tree, forest to forest, and had come full circle and could perch all over again in this tree nearby. By then, however, people had lost interest in the bird and its location.

The men solemnly lowered the body into the grave with two pieces of rope and when it was down dropped the ropes onto it.

"Do you want to say anything over her?" Jordan asked Vanessa.

She stood at the edge of the open grave and looked down into the darkness. "Don't make me talk, or I'll start crying. I don't want to cry over her. Or Daddy either. Not yet," she said and stepped away.

"But you will?"

"What?"

"Cry over them."

"Yes."

"What about you, Hubert? You want to say a few words over her?"

"I can't tell if you're joking or not," Hubert said.

"I'm serious enough. I'm not religious myself, but I thought maybe one or both of you might be."

"I guess I'm not especially religious, either. Not in a churchy way, anyhow. But it seems a shame to just bury her like this. Like she was a dog that got put down or something."

"That was my thought," Jordan said, and it was. He hadn't been joking.

Vanessa said, "Will you two stop! Just put the rocks into the hole, and shovel the dirt back in."

"Hubert? You want to say the words?" Jordan asked.

I really ought to do it, the guide thought. Of the three, he was the one most responsible for her death. But he shook his head and said, "No. You say the words, Jordan. You're better at talking."

Jordan nodded and stood at the foot of the open grave and addressed the dead woman. "Mrs. Cole, Evelyn, Mother. This is not easy. I speak for all of us. We are truly sorry. We're sorry that, for reasons no one could have anticipated, we were unable to prevent your accidental death this morning. No one of us wished you dead, especially by such violent means. We're also sorry that we were unable to provide you with a proper funeral and that we cannot comfort your many friends and acquaintances from all—"

"Jordan! For God's sake, stop it!" Vanessa shouted. "You're making a mockery of her!"

Hubert said, "No, he isn't. He's just saying the truth. Except he's not saying that I might have prevented her death, if I hadn't tried to take the gun out of her hands. He should say that, too. Go ahead, Jordan, and finish."

"We're sorry, yes. We're sorry that we can't comfort your many friends and acquaintances, because we have promised to protect your daughter, Vanessa, from being charged with kidnapping and confining you against your will and possibly even charged with your murder. Although we all know that your death was an accident. It's not her fault that a family quarrel got out of hand and ended tragically like this. It's not my or Hubert's fault, either, that we found ourselves witnesses to your unfortunate demise."

"You see, Hubert? He is mocking her. And us, too. You and me. Are you through, Jordan?"

"Yes, I'm through. We can bury her now," Jordan said.

When they finished filling the grave with large rocks and had shoveled back all the dirt they had taken out of it, they tamped down the low mound and scattered a thick layer of pine needles over it. They took dead branches from the trees nearby and raked over their tracks, and when they were done it was midafternoon and the forest had been restored to its former condition.

At the shore of the lake they tossed the bloodstained rocks and clumps of moss and sod into the water. Jordan wondered about the gun. He told Vanessa that Dr. Cole's shotgun should disappear, too.

"Take it with you when you leave in your airplane. Drop it in the lake."

"Sorry. I've committed all the crimes I'm going to commit today."

"Do you want it?" Vanessa asked Hubert. "I know you admire

it," she said, thinking that possession of the gun would tie him even more closely to the shooting, making him a more trusted ally in this—trusted to lie about the whereabouts of Evelyn Cole and how she came to be there.

"It's a good weapon. But I'd have to explain how I came by it."

"You can say I gave it to you. As a remembrance of my father and in gratitude for all the years you worked for him as a guide and hunting companion. I would have given it to you yesterday, if I'd thought of it. If I'd known it was there."

"Too bad you didn't," Jordan said. He stripped off his blood-stained shirt and squatted at the water's edge to rinse it clean.

Vanessa glared at his bare back for a second, then smiled, because his back was pretty and because he was right and was bold enough to say it. She liked that about him—his willingness to say out loud whatever he thought was the case.

"This isn't working," he said and stood and shook out the shirt. "I'll have to burn these clothes when I get back to my studio."

Hubert scanned the lake and saw a guide boat putting out at the Carry, a pair of fishermen in it. "We got company," he said.

Quickly, Jordan ducked behind a ledge a few yards from the shore, well out of sight of the fishermen. "This means I'm stuck here till they go in," he said, more to himself than to the others. Jordan was not eager to go home and face Alicia again. For a few hours he had succeeded in not thinking about her, in spite of Hubert's presence, which had briefly released him from the dark, painful grip of his busted marriage. At the same time, however, he wanted to leave this place and put this particular mess behind him. Also, he believed that as soon as Hubert was gone and he and Vanessa were alone, she would begin to weep over the death of her mother—he suspected she was saving her tears for the occasion—and he would have to comfort her.

One of the things that had most attracted him to her from the beginning and especially today was her refusal to be comforted, and he didn't want that to come to an end. Being swept up by a woman's unfocused anger was new to him and had a fresh, erotic charge to it. Jordan Groves was used to responding to the sadness of women, not their anger, and in recent years that had grown old and tired.

"I don't think they saw you, Jordan," Hubert said. "But if we can see them," he said to Vanessa, "they must be seeing me and you standing here like dummies."

"That's all right. It'll only corroborate that you were at the camp and Mother and I were here together. So go ahead," she said. "Leave now. Don't forget the gun."

Hubert said, "All right, I'll keep the doctor's shotgun and say you gave it to me as a remembrance."

"It's the truth. Daddy would have wanted you to have it."

He pushed the boat into the water and saw the pool of blood in the bottom. Without comment he rocked the boat and dipped the near gunnel into the lake, letting a few inches of water in. Then he drew the boat back onto land, turned it over and emptied it. Gently, he wrapped the shotgun in his jacket and lay it and the oars in the boat and pushed the boat into the lake again. He seated himself in the stern and took up the oars. "Against the rules, you know, for a guide to be carrying a shotgun or rifle in the Reserve. Only the clients. Handgun's all right, though."

"Don't hurt yourself thinking about it too much, Hubie," Jordan said. "Just remember, you don't have to lie. All you've got to do is leave a few things out. Like the fact that you saw me out here."

"There's a few other facts I got to leave out."

Vanessa said, "Can you see who that is?" She shaded her eyes with the palm of her hand and gazed at the fishermen, now in the middle of the lake.

"I think it's Ambassador Smith and his guide, Sam LaCoy. They'll probably fish till five or so and then head back to the clubhouse, so as to get there before dark. Ambassador Smith, he always stays at one of the clubhouse cottages."

"Tommy's a friend of my parents. When you pass near, tell him that Mother and I want to be alone, okay?"

Hubert nodded and without saying good-bye commenced to rowing across the lake, toward the Carry. He kept the boat on a line that would bring him close enough to the other boat to be heard, close enough to give Ambassador Smith and Sam LaCoy the message from Miss Cole, who was staying at Rangeview with her mother to mourn the death of Dr. Cole in the place he loved best. As he rowed, Hubert began gradually to feel that he was no longer a partner in crime with Jordan Groves and Vanessa Cole; he was a loyal Adirondack guide again, a man with a known role in life and fixed protocol, and was relieved by it. He thought about the hand-tooled Belgian shotgun wrapped in his wool jacket in the bottom of the boat. A beautiful weapon, he said to himself, almost calling it a beautiful animal. To him, guns were living creatures, and he was going to enjoy keeping company with this one, admiring it with his eyes, holding it in his hands, walking in the woods with it, using it to hunt down and kill other living creatures.

ALICIA KNEW JORDAN WASN'T IN THE HOUSE—HE HADN'T COME up to bed, and she'd heard his airplane take off at dawn—and did not know when he might return or what he would say or do then. She did not yet believe that their marriage had ended. Because of the boys, he would not ask for a divorce, she was sure of that much. Jordan would never leave their upbringing to her and was incapable of raising them alone. And he was not in love with anyone else. He wouldn't leave Alicia for another woman. Not even that Von Heidenstamm woman. And because Jordan was a sexually confident man, sure of his power to attract all types of women, he was not likely to be threatened by the fact that his wife had slept with Hubert St. Germain, who was not a sexually confident man. She did not think Jordan would become violent, even though he was known for his occasional outbursts of violence. There were men whom she might have slept with, she thought, men who might have made him lash out physically against them and against her as well—famous artists, rich men, politically committed men of the left, like Dos, who actually had once suggested to her that they become lovers. But, no, now that she thought about it, not even the rich and famous author John Dos Passos had made Jordan Groves jealous. She had told Jordan that Dos had invited her to meet him secretly for the purpose of making love—waiting before she told him until after Dos and Katie had gone back to New York, explaining that Dos had been drunk and probably would have propositioned any halfway attractive woman in the room that evening. Jordan had found it funny and faintly ridiculous. "Dos? The little rascal," he'd said. "I didn't think he had it in him."

Jordan competed with every man he met, whether in arm wrestling, making art, politics, money, or gathering the attention of women, but he seemed jealous of no man. Jealousy was close to envy, however, and Alicia knew that there were certain men her husband envied. But as types rather than as individuals. That may be the difference between the two emotions, she thought: one felt jealous of individuals, but one envied types. And she knew, as only a wife can, that her husband secretly envied, not men like

John Dos Passos, but the poor. Especially the poor working-class men and women of his town. Her husband wished that he could be the famous artist Jordan Groves and yet also be one of them, one of those he perceived as the oppressed, the downtrodden victims of the rich and powerful. And it wasn't just the poor, out-of-work, white Americans of his town, but also the Eskimos he'd lived among for months in Greenland and the Inuits of Alaska, the Negro field hands he'd drawn and painted in Louisiana, the Cuban sugarcane cutters, the Indians in the Andes silver mines, and most recently the peasants and workers fighting against the Fascists in Spain. He wanted to be one of them. He envied their powerlessness. To him, their powerlessness signified an innocence that he had abandoned long ago, when, after he'd come home from the war, he'd refused to work alongside his father, the carpenter, and had left his war bride and gone east to New York to become an artist.

Though Hubert St. Germain was an Adirondack guide, a type of man much admired in the region by the locals as well as by the wealthy visitors who hired him, Alicia knew that nonetheless he was in fact little more than a servant to those wealthy visitors. He was a man whose only power in the world came from his intimate knowledge of his immediate environment and from his quiet, dignified acceptance of his powerlessness. In that sense, Hubert, as a type, was like those Inuits and cane cutters and the Spanish peasants. She could imagine Hubert joining one of the Communist or anarchist brigades of workers and farmers, marching off to wage war against Franco and the Fascists. Well, not Hubert himself, exactly, but as a type of man. The type of man her husband envied. The type of man she had fallen in love with, she suddenly realized, and to whom, for nearly five months, once and twice a week and more, she had given her body and all its secrets.

She went through her day as she normally would, tending to the boys and her gardens and the house, to all appearances the calm, competent, organized wife and mother she had been for over a decade now—ever since her one most self-defining act of defiance, when she'd disobeyed her parents by dropping out of Pratt to elope with the artist, her professor, the suddenly celebrated Jordan Groves. She was filled today with the same fear and uncertainty she had felt those long years ago. Her parents had forgiven her—once she was pregnant—and had reluctantly come to accept their daughter and son-in-law's bohemianism, as they saw it, and leftist politics and atheism. At least she hadn't gone to America and run off with a Jew or a Negro. The artist could always change his way of life as he grew older and wiser, unlike a Jew and a Negro, who could never change who they were, and besides, he was financially successful and famous and interestingly eccentric in a very American way. Alicia's Viennese parents liked and admired self-made Americans for their energy and confidence almost as much as they liked and admired their Prussian neighbors to the north.

All day Alicia's stomach felt tight and light, like a helium-filled balloon, and her arms and legs were weak and watery. Her hands trembled, as if she'd drunk too much coffee. Standing on the threshold of a life whose shape and details she could not imagine terrified her. Whatever happened or did not happen over the next few days or weeks, she knew that her life would never again be the same as it had been. By nature, Alicia did not like surprises. It was one of the reasons she had so easily adapted to her husband's willful and impulsive nature. He was free to go and come, to make all the big decisions regarding the overall shape of their life together, so long as from one day to the next, year after year, she was allowed to play the unwobbling pivot. She was free neither to act nor react, and while other people, especially women, felt sorry for her and wondered why she so placidly accepted her husband's outrageous public behavior (he wrote about it in his books, for heaven's sake, for all the world to read), she had not felt sorry for herself. Lonely, perhaps. But there had been a useful and satisfying trade-off: her stability and commonsensical maintenance of the everyday and her tolerance of her husband's waywardness had endowed her with a capacity for making him feel guilty. And now she had lost that capacity, perhaps for the duration.

A little after three o'clock, Hubert St. Germain knocked at the kitchen door. Alicia hadn't heard him arrive or knock. She was in the library playing Jordan's Jimmie Rodgers records on the cabinet-size Victrola, teaching Wolf and Bear to memorize and sing the songs, a gift to Jordan when—or was it if?—he came home. All three were sitting on the floor together singing "Hobo Bill's Last Ride" along with Jimmie Rodgers, when Alicia heard the dogs bark and looked out the window and saw Hubert's Model A in the driveway.

"Stay here, boys. Someone's here," she said and told them to keep practicing the songs. "But be careful handling the records. You know what they mean to Papa. No scratches or fingerprints." She went through the kitchen to the door, roiled by anxiety mingled with anger. What on earth was he thinking, coming here like this? Was this his response to her letter? Or had Jordan confronted him somehow, threatened him or even physically attacked him? Or maybe Jordan had simply told him, Go ahead, you want her, she's yours.

It didn't matter. It was too late for that now.

She hushed the dogs, opened the door, and was relieved that the guide had a downcast expression on his face, shoulders slumped. A defeated man, she thought, though his face showed no signs of having been attacked by her husband. Defeated by her letter, then.

"You read my letter, Hubert," she said. "Oh, Hubert, why did you come here?"

"No, no. What letter? I . . . I haven't been home. Not since yesterday, actually. Not since right after you left my place. I . . . I need to talk with you, Alicia."

"Jordan could come home any minute, Hubert. You shouldn't be here. He knows . . . about us. I told him last night. I didn't mean to, but I thought he'd already found out about . . . about us, and it just came out."

"Yes, he told me. I know where he is. He won't be back till after dark."

They were silent for a moment, as if registering the visible changes that had occurred in each other's face in the past twenty-four hours. They weren't the same man and woman they had been yesterday afternoon, and it showed. Their faces were drawn and tightly held. They looked years older.

Finally Alicia said, "Hubert, I wrote you a good-bye letter. I put it in your mailbox, and Jordan saw me. He flew over, and I thought he knew about us. Because of that girl, and—"

"It doesn't matter," he interrupted. "I just need to talk with you," he said again. "About us, yes. But something else."

"Not here. Not in the house. Come down by the garden," she said and led the way, the big red dogs bounding ahead, and as they walked, Hubert began telling Alicia what had happened at the Coles' camp at the Second Tamarack Lake. He told her everything.

She heard him out without stopping him and was first shocked and then dismayed, and then frightened—frightened for him and also for her husband. They sat in the shade of a large maple tree in the Westport-style Adirondack chairs Jordan had copied from one he'd first seen several years back on the porch of a Westport summer cottage on the shore of Lake Champlain. He had rented a barn and organized a crew of local unemployed carpenters to manufacture the chairs and sell them to tourists. But the tourists never materialized, and the project, like so many others, had fallen apart, leaving Jordan with a dozen of the wide-board chairs to distribute around the grounds and porches of his own house. Jordan had loved the clean, geometric simplicity of the design and their ease of construction and comfort, and couldn't understand why so few other people, especially people with the money to buy them, had the same appreciation.

"Do you realize what you and Jordan have done?"

"Well, yes," he answered. "It was illegal. But it wasn't wrong. Was it? Like hunting off-season on the Reserve, that's illegal, too. It's against the rules. But I do it. Lots of folks do it. They have to, most of them." Hubert was exhausted. He couldn't remember when he'd felt this many strong, conflicted emotions. He wanted to disappear into the woods and stay there alone for as long as it took until he and everyone else had forgotten all about Dr. Cole's widow, Evelyn Cole, who had mysteriously disappeared way back in the summer of '36, and the secret love affair he'd had those many long years ago with the wife of the artist Jordan Groves.

"Yes, it is wrong," Alicia said, her accent growing more noticeable as she spoke. Even she could hear it, but when her feelings ran high she couldn't do anything about it. "You didn't *have* to do it, you know. Bury that woman out there and make it so that now you have to lie about it, lie about how she died and what you did afterward, just to protect the daughter. How did she convince you to do it?" she asked, incredulous. "Especially Jordan. How did she talk him into going along with this scheme?"

"What do you mean, 'especially Jordan'?"

"Nothing. It's just that he's more skeptical of people than you are, I guess. Less trusting. Particularly of women. Rich women."

"You think I trust rich women?"

"You trusted me."

Hubert was silent for a moment. "What do you think I should do?"

"Oh, Lord, Hubert, I don't know."

"What will you tell Jordan?"

"Jordan? Nothing. Unless he first tells me what you and he did today. And he won't do that."

"No, I guess not. He wouldn't have any need to do that," he said. "I'm the one who needed to tell you. Is he going to leave you, Alicia? Because of us?"

"I don't think so. Not as long as we stop seeing each other, you and I. And we will stop, Hubert. This has to be the last time we can be together."

"I know." He shook his head slowly from side to side, as if saying no with great reluctance. "Everything's a damned mess, isn't it? Everything."

"Yes."

"What should I do?"

"Is that why you came here today, to ask me what you should do?"

"No, I came . . . I came because I love you. And I trust you to tell me the truth. I need to know the truth, Alicia, because it's the only way for me to tell right from wrong. For maybe the first time in my life since I was a kid, I don't know if what I've done is right or wrong."

"You know what I think, don't you?"

He was silent for a moment. "Yes, I suppose I do," he said. "I guess I knew all along what I should do. I just needed to hear it from you. You think I should go and tell Russell Kendall what happened, and show him where we buried the body."

She didn't answer him.

He stood slowly, like a tired old man. With his back to her, he said, "I should leave now."

"Oh, Hubert, I'm so sorry that it all came down to this. I wish I had known back . . . back when it first started."

"Would you have turned me away, if you'd known it was going to end like this?"

"No. I wouldn't."

"Me neither."

"Good-bye, Hubert. I loved you very much."

"I love . . . I loved you, too. Very much."

He walked alone up the stone steps to the back of the house, and when he passed by the kitchen door on his way to his car, he saw the two little boys standing there, somber and worried looking. He was a stranger to them. Alicia's sons. They were Jordan Groves's sons, too. And this was the house that Alicia and Jordan Groves had built together, the life they had made together, man and woman, husband and wife, father and mother and children, and the evidence of all their years of work together was here in front of him. It came home to him then—the foolish, deluded thing that he had done these months with Alicia, the strangely passive state of mind it had gradually induced in him, transforming him without his knowledge into a man made foolish and deluded by no one but himself. The love affair with Alicia Groves was why he had agreed to help Vanessa Cole keep her mother a prisoner. It was why he had ended up this morning struggling over the gun with the woman. It was what had caused her death. It was why he helped bury her on the Reserve.

The boys were very serious, as if they could read the guide's thoughts. The older one said, "Hi," and the younger boy tried a small smile.

"Hello," Hubert said and moved on. When he got into his car, he saw the gun lying on the passenger seat, Dr. Cole's Belgian shotgun, still wrapped in his jacket. That, too, he thought. I'll have to tell the truth about the gun, too. And how I came by it.

VANESSA'S BEDROOM, HERS SINCE CHILDHOOD, WAS IN A SEPARATE wing of the main building, with a wide view of the lake and the Great Range, and when Jordan asked to see the rest of the house she led him there in a roundabout way.

"You won't find any James Heldon paintings anywhere but in the living room. Daddy liked prominent display."

"I don't care," he said. "I'm interested in how people lay out their houses. Tells you a lot about them. It's a form of behavior, like a painting. You can learn from it. What to emulate, what to avoid."

They passed from the living room into a windowless hallway, and off the hallway to a small room with a corner fireplace and rough-cut floor-to-ceiling shelves stocked with books—complete sets of Kipling, Cooper, and Trollope, the entire Harvard Classics and the Yale Shakespeare in twenty-eight volumes—and on tables slabs of large, illustrated books on hunting and fishing. One long shelf held the entire set of Little Blue Books. Jordan pulled down two at random and leafed through them: number 562, Sophocles's *Antigone*, and number 200, Voltaire's *The Ignorant Philosophers*.

"Your father's?"

"Yes."

"Not exactly light reading."

"No. This was the nursery," she told him. "Until I was four. Then it became Daddy's library."

She spoke slowly and deliberately now, somewhat out of character, Jordan thought. He was waiting for her to crack and come apart. Any minute now what has happened will hit her, and she'll become a different person, he thought. A sad and sorrowful woman filled with guilt will replace the incandescent, tough-talking woman filled with smooth, fast-running anger. He didn't want that transformation to occur, but knew that it was inevitable and that once it did occur he would be transformed, too. He would return to his senses. Or, more accurately, he would return to being the man he had been when he'd first arrived here this morning. When she became sad, he in turn would be obliged to acknowledge that what he had helped her do today was not just illegal, it was wrong, inhuman, and probably stupid as well. And then he would be obliged to face once again the fact of his wife's adultery, weighing it against the fact of his own adulterous indulgences and infatuations, trying to balance his anger and fear against his regret and guilt. And Hubert would no longer be merely his partner in crime, but also his rival.

Jordan Groves had no philosophy for this task, no ethical system with sufficient rigor and discipline to give him a coherent, self-sustaining style. As long as Vanessa kept her cool, however, he could keep his. He tried to help her hold on to the glittering mixture of warmth and brittleness, of humor and anger, that resisted dissolving in sarcasm or superficial irony. It was sexy to him, and he liked it—two can play at that game—and now he needed it. The last thing he wanted from her was sad sincerity. He thought of those *Thin Man* movies with William Powell and Myrna Loy and *My Man Godfrey* with Powell and Carole Lombard and *The Petrified Forest* with Bogart and Bette Davis. He thought of Ernest Hemingway's stories and James M. Cain's *Double Indemnity.* That was the style he needed, and he felt that if he could keep on affecting it, he could become it, and she would become it, too.

"I assume he bought these books by the foot and had them shipped from New York. Carried in by backpack."

"More or less. But he read them. They're from the house in Tuxedo Park. After the nursery became the library. He was the one who taught me to read. Every summer until I was sixteen and had graduated from college he made a list of books in the library that I had to read and report on."

"Sweet sixteen and already a college graduate? Come on. Am I supposed to believe that?"

"Check the social register."

"Can't say I own one."

"Look in the library," she said. "Everything you need to know is in the library. Everything."

"I'll take your word for it." He ambled from the room out to the hallway, where two rows of framed photographs hung on the walls—lakes, rivers, mountains. No people or other animals. "Daddy's?"

"But of course."

"He had good equipment."

"The best. He had Alfred Stieglitz as his adviser."

"Stieglitz takes pictures of people, though."

"He only advised Daddy on technical matters," she said quickly and changed the subject. "Coming up is my bedroom, dressing room, and bath. Cinderella's Suite."

"Cinderella had sisters, as I recall. Stepsisters."

"I always thought of her as adopted. It was a screwy family, anyhow. No father, just a stepmother and a fairy godmother. And, of course, Prince Charming," she said and placed her hand on his forearm and curtsied.

"Your feet are not exactly tiny."

"I beg your pardon!" She kicked off her moccasins and extended one foot for him to observe and admire. "Long and narrow and perfectly arched. A dancer's feet," she declared and walked on ahead of him, stepping lightly, like a ballerina.

"Why'd you call it 'Cinderella's Suite'? I don't picture you sweeping the hearth."

"I didn't call it that. Daddy did. His and Mother's quarters he called Olympus. The dining room is Mead Hall. The guest quarters is the Lodge, the library is the Beinecke, the kitchen is the Scullery, and so on. The living room is Valhalla. All very mythic. All quite hilarious. In a Yale-ish way. He even had wooden signs made and hung them over the doors. Until Mother made him take them down."

"Why?"

"Actually, the only sign she objected to was 'Cinderella's Suite.' But she couldn't complain about it without having to say why. So she made him take them all down. On the grounds of hilarity."

"Hilarity?"

"She was against it. It gave her headaches."

"So why'd she object to calling your quarters Cinderella's Suite?" Jordan asked. They had stopped in front of the closed door at the end of the hallway.

"You ask too many questions, my prince," Vanessa said and opened the door and entered.

The room was large and like the rest of the house paneled with wide, carefully roughened boards sawn from first-growth spruce trees, made to look as if they'd been split off the tree trunk with a maul and a wedge. Light off the surface of the lake flooded the bedroom. A Navajo rug hung on the wall above the bed. Otherwise the room was bare of decoration and gave the impression of being an extra room, a guest room suited to anyone and everyone. It was neat and orderly, with no evidence of Vanessa's having slept there—no clothing out, no cosmetics or perfumes, no keepsakes. Just a single bed, a reading chair and table and kerosene lamp, a narrow, waist-high, pine dresser, and a wood-stove. Off the room Jordan glimpsed a small dressing room with open shelves that held neatly folded towels and blankets and extra sheets, and beyond that a bathroom. All very plain and spartan. It surprised him. He felt that she was as much a visitor here as he.

Vanessa sat on the edge of the bed and gazed out the wide window at the lake, its surface glittering like polished silver plate. The sky had turned milk white under high cirrus clouds, and the mountains were dark gray, almost black, in the distance. The two men fishing were still out there in their guide boat. Vanessa patted the bed beside her and said, "Come here and look. The fish must be biting."

Jordan sat a few inches from her and saw the fishermen on the lake and checked his watch. Three thirty-five. Another hour and a half, at least, before those two retreat to the clubhouse and I can fly out of here, he thought. He was as reluctant to go home, however, as he was anxious to leave this newly haunted house, haunted as much by the woman beside him as by the woman they had buried in the forest behind it. Vanessa was starting to spook him—her calm, slow-moving, slow-talking tour of the house, her placid deflection of his questions and barbs. He was no longer afraid that she would start to weep in grief and guilt and oblige him to comfort her. Quite the opposite now. He was afraid that she would *not* break into sobs and tears of anguished remorse, that she would simply continue this cold, playful repartee. It occurred to him that in fact she felt no grief, no remorse. No fear, even.

She turned to him and pushed his jacket open. "You're not wearing a shirt. Where is it?"

"I put it to dry on the deck railing," he said and remembered the bloodstains again and that he would have to burn the shirt or Alicia would ask him how he'd gotten it bloodied. He knew that Vanessa was not thinking of his shirt splashed by her mother's blood, but of his naked torso. The idea that, despite everything, Vanessa was thinking about his body excited him. She pushed his jacket open further and looked at his chest and partially exposed shoulders, and he felt heat travel to his face and groin.

"You will have to stay inside until nearly dark, probably," she said.

"Yes."

"You can't let anyone know that you've been here."

"No."

"Do you think they can see your airplane from out there?"

"No. It's anchored in a cove well out of sight. It's behind a tree-covered spit of land. They'd have to come right up on it in the boat to know it was there."

"That's good," she said and slipped his jacket off his shoulders altogether and pulled first one cuff, then the other, and drew the jacket away from his arms and dropped it onto the floor. "You're very beautiful," she said.

"You said something strange back there."

"What?"

He reached down and retrieved his jacket and slipped it on. "About the sign, 'Cinderella's Suite.' You said your mother objected to it, but didn't want to say why, so she had all the signs taken down."

"I said that?"

"Yes. Why did she object to it?"

"I don't know."

"Sure you do." Jordan left the bed and sat in the chair facing her, his back to the window. Her equanimity scared him a little. He knew she wanted him to make love to her, but the calm ease with which she made that evident signified something other than physical desire, something more mental than of the body, as if her body were merely following orders.

"I don't want to talk about my mother or my father. Not now," she said. "Maybe not ever," she added. Then she suddenly said, "Jordan, did you know that my father was . . . that he performed lobotomies? Do you know what a lobotomy is?"

"Sure. It's brain surgery for psychos. It was in all the papers a year or so ago."

"Daddy invented the procedure, you know."

"I thought some Portugese quack developed it. Sounds medieval to me, like a pseudoscientific surgical exorcism. I can't believe your father fell for that."

"Oh, he more than fell for it. He was working with some people at Yale doing experiments on chimpanzees and monkeys, and then he was in Portugal, where he assisted in a dozen lobotomies, and last year he got permission to do it on human beings at the clinic in Zurich, where Mother was so set on sending me."

"You expect me to believe that?"

"It doesn't matter if you believe it or not, it's the truth. He taught the doctors there how to do it, because it's not been approved here in the States. It's brain surgery, but you don't have to be a brain surgeon to do it. You just drill a couple of little holes in the front of the skull, insert this cutting instrument that Daddy invented himself. He actually showed it to me, a long, thin steel shaft with an L-shaped blade at the end. You twiddle it back and forth a few times, remove, and presto! No more demons. No more troublesome behavior. No more bad daughter."

Jordan just smiled. He didn't believe a word she was saying. But why on earth would she tell such a story? Was it to cover her disappointment that he had rejected her overtures? He hadn't really rejected her, anyhow; he had merely backed away from her first touch and changed the subject, changing it only temporarily, perhaps. In matters of seduction, Jordan Groves was passive. Never the initiator, he let the woman come to him, giving her the responsibility for the invitation to the dance, and only then, when the dance had begun, would he take the lead. That's all he was doing here, he thought—foisting on to Vanessa the obligation to declare her intent to have him make love to her, so that afterward he could tell himself that he had merely been complying with her wishes, fulfilling her needs, not his, slaking her lust, not his. Though, naturally, he well knew that he had met his wishes, too, had fulfilled his needs and slaked his lust as much as the woman's.

That it was a pattern he knew, but he had never examined the causes. In every other action in his life, he was the initiator, the prime mover, but when it came to sex, he let the woman come to him. Or rather, he *made* the woman come to him. Even his wife, Alicia—except for that first time, way back when they left the gallery party drunk on champagne and new fame and went to his studio downtown, and he asked her to marry him and she said yes, and to celebrate they took off their clothes and made stormy love the entire rest of the night, until dawn broke and gray New York winter light drifted through the high windows and skylight of the studio and fell onto the two of them lying asleep in each other's arms. From then on, though, he had waited for Alicia to come to him. For Jordan Groves, a man's sexual favors were precisely that, favors. A woman's were something else—a request, perhaps, a statement of need or of desire strong enough to require explicit expression by the woman. In a small way, it comforted his vanity and assuaged any residual guilt afterward that, in order to have sex with a woman, he had not been obliged to overcome her objections by any means fair or foul. And he never risked being rejected.

He surprised himself, therefore, when he stood up and took off his leather jacket again and crossed to the bed and sat next to Vanessa and put his bare arms around her. He kissed her on the mouth, softly, and then, as he felt his passion rise, with force this time.

Vanessa pulled away and pushed him back and said, "Wait. You don't believe me, do you? You think I'm lying."

"Lying? You mean about your father? No, not exactly."

"That means you think I'm lying."

"It means you sometimes say things that are not exactly false and not exactly true, and it's hard for me to know where they fall between the two."

"What do you mean?"

"I mean, was your father interested in lobotomies? Yeah, sure. Why not? He was a brain surgeon, after all. Did he perform them himself? Maybe he did, maybe he only wanted to, or intended to. But did he go to Europe and do it at that private clinic in Zurich and teach the doctors there how to do it? It's possible, I guess, but unlikely. I'm sure you *believe* he did. But based on what? And was your mother setting you up for a lobotomy by sending you to Zurich? Again, I'm sure you *believe* she was, but based on what evidence? She never said that to you, did she?"

"She didn't have to. But think about it, Jordan! What a publicity coup for the famous psychiatrist, Dr. Theobold, if he were able to say he miraculously cured the daughter of the equally famous American brain surgeon, Dr. Carter Cole, of an incurable mental illness by using the surgical techniques and tools invented by the late Dr. Cole himself. Rich parents and husbands from all over the world would be shipping their troubled and troublesome children and wives to Zurich. For a half-hour's surgery and with only a few days needed for recovery, he could charge whatever he wanted, ten, twenty, fifty thousand dollars a head! Remember, Jordan, I know these people, Theobold and Reichold and the others. They're Nazis, Jordan. Very ambitious and greedy Nazis. And I know my father."

"You're not suffering from an incurable mental illness."

"Of course not! I'm not even mentally ill. I'm suffering from *something,* though."

"What? Other than the sudden, unexpected loss of your parents."

For a long moment they both remained silent, gazing out the window. Finally, in a voice barely above a whisper, Vanessa said, "Secrets. Secrets kept from me, and secrets I've kept from everyone else. Secrets aren't like lies. They're more like brain surgery. They kill your soul. Lying is only a technique for keeping secrets. *One* of the techniques. Lies and silence and . . . and storytelling, which is nothing more than changing the subject in an interesting way. All those clever diversionary tactics. Like bad behavior in public. Reckless behavior in public. Or like this," she said, and she put her arms around him and drew him to her and kissed him and softly moaned. She whispered into his ear, "I want you to take me, now, here," and ran her hand down his chest and began loosening his belt. He kissed her on the mouth and throat and began unbuttoning her shirt—her father's flannel shirt, although he did not note that.

Far out on the lake, the two fishermen slowly reeled in their lines and lay their fishing rods in the boat. The man who was the guide, Sam LaCoy, dipped the oar blades into the still water and began to row the boat slowly back toward the Carry. The other man, whose name was Thomas Smith, a retired diplomat, once ambassador to the Court of St. James, turned in the bow and looked back across the lake at the Cole place, Rangeview. The log buildings glowed in the late afternoon sunlight.

"Do you know the Coles?" Smith asked the guide.

"Can't say I do. Not personally."

"Damned good people, Dr. Cole and his wife. He'll be missed around here."

"Expect so."

"I wonder what she'll do with the camp, now that he's gone. The widow. It's hard to imagine she or the daughter will want to hold on to it. Carter Cole was a lifelong Adirondacker, a real true Reservist, you know. His father was one of the original shareholders. Not the wife, though. And certainly not the daughter."

"You plan on making 'em an offer on the place?"

"It's a thought."

"Be good to have a camp of your own up here on the Second Lake. Instead of boarding all the time down to the clubhouse cottages."

"Yes. The Coles got in the Reserve early. My father was a little slow to realize the value of a camp at the Second Lake."

"The daughter, she must be third generation, then."

"Right. She's got quite a reputation, the daughter, Vanessa. You ever meet her?"

"I've seen her. From a distance," the guide said and pulled once on the oars, hard, driving the boat alongside the dock to where Ambassador Smith could step directly from the boat without wetting his boots or trouser cuffs. "Sorry about the fish not biting," the guide said.

"My fault, Sam, not yours. We'd have caught a string of trout, I'm sure, if I'd been ready early and didn't have to get back to the clubhouse before dark. Oh, look!" he said and pointed out a ways where ring-size ripples in the flat black surface of the water spread in widening circles, as if someone were dropping pebbles into the lake. "Now they're feeding."

The guide said, "If you owned that Cole place, you'd have yourself a couple more hours to catch your supper before going in."

"You're right about that," Ambassador Smith said. "I'll have to give the matter some thought."

The guide took up their gear and pack basket, and the two men headed into the woods of the Carry on to the First Lake, where another boat awaited them.

At breakfast on the morning of April 5, 1937, the big American, the one they called Rembrandt, announced to the others that today's mission would be his last. He told them he'd had enough. Tomorrow he was going to Madrid. He intended to stay at the Hotel Florida with the American journalist Matthews and the novelists Hemingway and Dos Passos and the photographer Capa. He claimed they were friends of his. He said that he wanted to make pictures of the war to help raise money back in the States. He was an artist, he said to them, not a soldier, and could do more for the anti-Fascist cause with his pictures than by machine-gunning men in trenches from the air, which he said was like shooting ducks in a barrel. Anyone could do that. They didn't need him for it. The other pilots said nothing. He told them he didn't care if he was breaking his contract with the Republic of Spain, the government could keep his back pay and whatever signing bonus they still owed him, he'd had enough and wanted to be able to sleep at night without seeing bodies exploding in the air. The others seemed not to mind. They went on eating breakfast. The big American was the least popular man in the unit and had been from the start. Finally Fairhead spoke. He said if this was to be Groves's last mission he might as well lead it himself. An hour later they were in the air in a V of V formation, with the departing American leading the point patrol. They had their Russian monoplanes now, the Polikarpov I–16s that the Spanish *called Moscas. There were heavy rain squalls and a low ceiling of about fifteen hundred feet. They crossed the line at Brihuega where the Italians had attempted to cut their way to Torija and began their bombing run against the lines of tanks parked alongside the valley road. The big American dropped his bombs on the tanks, and the rest of the pilots did the same, and they destroyed many of them. Then Fairhead, who led the right patrol, waggled the wings of his aircraft and pointed up and to their left, where there was a squadron of Fiat single-seat CR 32s, no match for the speed and armaments of the Russian monoplanes. The pilots put their Moscas into a sharp right echelon and began climbing, closing fast on the Fiats. There were seven of the Italians and then, still higher, another five. When the airplanes engaged, formation flying was no longer possible. They broke into one-on-one dogfights, making passing side shots mainly as they tried to position themselves behind their targets. The Moscas began to take advantage of their superior maneuverability and climbing speed. The big American got himself in on the tail of the lead Fiat and fired his 20-millimeter cannons for fifteen seconds straight, sending the Italian spinning downward, spilling a trail of water, gasoline, and black smoke. The American quickly dove after a second target a thousand feet below, but the Italian saw him coming and turned away and dove in the opposite direction. The American curled back in pursuit, but after a few moments the Fiat managed to elude him in the low clouds. When the American broke through the clouds at about five thousand feet, he looked up and saw five Fiats diving toward him. He plunged back down into the clouds again and with the Fiats close behind carved a sharp left vertical bank and completed a 360-degree turn, bringing him in behind his pursuers, firing both machine guns steadily and scattering all five of the Fiats in different directions. A few moments later when he emerged below the clouds again, he found himself in unfamiliar territory, moun-*

tainous, with the tops of the mountains in clouds. He was alone in the sky. He dropped down into a valley, hoping for some sign, a river or a road or a village that would help him read his map. As he moved along a rough valley cut with arroyos and narrow dry streambeds, he spotted too late an antiaircraft gun emplacement in among the trees. At that instant, before he heard the sound of the gun or saw the white puff of smoke in front of his airplane or the second off to his right, a third shell struck his airplane. It hit the left side of the fuselage behind the cockpit, and he could no longer fly the airplane. He was bleeding badly from his shattered left thigh and ankle, and then another shell hit the airplane, this time in the cowling, smashing the engine, igniting the fuel, and instantly the airplane flipped onto its back and began its spiraling plummet to the ground.

HUBERT HAD HOPED TO FIND RUSSELL KENDALL ALONE IN HIS office. But when he approached the corner room at the far end of the greeting desk, as it was called, the office door was open, and standing outside the door like a valet was the guide Sam LaCoy, looking at the floor as if lost in thought, wicker backpack at his feet, a pair of fishing rods in his hands. Hubert heard the manager's barking laugh and noted the trouser cuffs and shoes of someone seated just inside—Ambassador Smith, he assumed, joshing with the clubhouse manager. The English girl who greeted the guests coming and going and guarded the dining room and bar and other clubhouse facilities from intrusion by nonmembers stood at the desk, leaning on her elbows with a book open before her. It was always an English girl, because of the accent. She looked up from her book, a novel called *Caddie Woodlawn*, marked her place with her index finger, and studied Hubert for a second. The guides rarely came this far, unless in the company of a member.

"May I direct you to someone?"

"I need to see Mr. Kendall."

"Sorry. He's with a member."

"I can wait."

"As you wish."

Hubert nodded hello to the other guide.

"Hubert." LaCoy rubbed his knuckle across his nose and thumped the cork handles of the fishing rods on the floor in greeting. He was a thick-bodied man, built like a stump with green suspenders.

"They biting out there today?"

"Naw. They was only waiting till we left, I guess. We pretty much come up empty. You?"

"Never wet a line. Just lugging supplies for the Coles."

"Figured. So them two ladies staying out there alone awhile."

"Awhile, yes."

Ambassador Smith and Russell Kendall emerged from the office together, both smiling, their transaction satisfactorily completed. They ignored the guides and kept walking in the direction of the greeting desk, where Smith suddenly stopped, as if remembering something he'd left behind. "Don't mention *who* was inquiring, Russell. Not unless she shows genuine interest."

"Not to worry, Ambassador," the manager said. They shook hands and Smith moved on, his faithful guide following behind. The manager hoped Ambassador Smith was right, that if Mrs. Cole received a generous, timely, and discreet offer from an old-time reservist like Ambassador Thomas Smith, she would be willing to sell their camp at the Second Lake. It had to be done before the widow got over Dr. Cole's death, but not while she was still in deep mourning, or she might feel she was being taken advantage of. It was shrewd of the ambassador to make his move quickly, however, while the place was still associated in the minds of Mrs. Cole and her daughter with the death of Dr. Cole. A year from now their memory of the event will be dimmed somewhat, and by then they would have made new associations with the place, social and otherwise, and Mrs. Cole might not want to sell Rangeview.

The ambassador and his family would be easier for Kendall to deal with than the Cole women, especially the daughter, Vanessa. He liked the ambassador. Everyone did. And there would be a sizable commission in it for Kendall if he helped facilitate the sale. The ambassador was an extremely wealthy man from very old money who preferred to let others do his business for him, even in trivial matters. He often had his secretary make his clubhouse dining room reservations for him by telephone from New York City, even though he and his wife were right here in residence in one of the Club cottages, she out on the golf course, he out on the Second Lake fishing.

"Hubert's waiting to speak with you, Mr. Kendall," the English girl said, surprising Hubert. He hadn't thought she'd known his name.

Kendall turned to Hubert, eyebrows raised. "Yes?"

"In private, if that's okay."

Kendall nodded and went back into his office. Hubert followed him and stood facing the wide desk like a schoolboy, hat in his hands. Kendall leaned back in his chair and peered out the window behind him at the tennis courts. The window was open, and the soft tympani of the ball and racket and the ball and fine clay played in counterpoint in the background.

After a few seconds, Hubert cleared his throat and said, "There's something you ought to know that happened today."

"Really? What?" Kendall continued watching the tennis. A pair of tall, blond, long-jawed men in white flannel trousers and white short-sleeved shirts trotted back and forth on the near court like agitated storks.

"You mind if I sit down?" Hubert suddenly felt that if he didn't put himself into a chair and trap himself there, he'd turn around and walk out the door.

Kendall waved him toward the dark green club chair recently vacated by Ambassador Smith and resumed gazing at the tennis. "What happened today that I should know about?"

"You know Mrs. Cole, Evelyn Cole? Dr. Cole's wife. His widow, I mean."

"Yes. Of course."

"Well, this morning I was up to the Second Lake there, at their camp. And she got accidentally shot."

Kendall wheeled around in his chair. "*Shot!* By a gun? Oh, my!"

"Yes. By a gun. Shotgun. Over-and-under Belgian twenty-eight gauge that belonged to the doctor. I . . . I got it in my truck. My car. Outside."

"Oh, my!" the manager said again. "Is she . . . is she all right?"

"Well, no. She's dead. But it was an accident."

"*Dead!*" Kendall left his chair and hurried across the room and closed the door. "Oh, my. Oh, my, this is terrible."

Hubert looked down at his hands, one holding his old fedora by the brim, the other upturned in his lap, as if waiting for a coin from a passerby. What he was doing now did not feel any longer like the right thing. But it was too late to stop it, too late to go back to what he had been doing before. That had felt wrong, too. In little more than twenty-four hours—starting at the moment Vanessa Cole showed up at his cabin door—he had arrived at a place in his life where he could no longer choose between right and wrong. His life no longer felt like it belonged to him. It belonged to Vanessa Cole and Jordan Groves, and to Alicia Groves, and now it belonged to Russell Kendall, too.

"It was an accident. She . . . well, she dropped the gun, and it went off, I guess. It was hair triggered, and she had the safety off. I guess you could call it a freak accident. She didn't have much experience with guns and such."

"Oh, dear God, this is terrible! Where were you when this happened? She shouldn't have been handling the gun! That's supposed to be your job, for heaven's sake!"

"I was right there. Actually, when it happened, I was trying to take the gun away from her," Hubert said and instantly regretted it. He didn't have to volunteer that. He wouldn't lie, he couldn't now, but he decided to offer no more information than was absolutely required, no matter how dumb he sounded.

"You were there? You saw it? And you brought the gun in and put it in your car, for reasons I won't ask into just yet. What about the body, Mrs. Cole's body? Did you bring that in, too?"

"No."

"No? Where is she? Her body, I mean. At Rangeview?"

"Well, it's . . . it's back up in the woods a ways."

"And Vanessa Cole, where is she? Did she come in from the lake with you?"

"No."

"This is terrible news. Just terrible. The timing couldn't be worse. When it gets out, it'll be in all the papers. A thing like this, it's not the sort of thing the members want the Reserve associated with, you know."

"Yes."

"Who knows about this? Other than you, of course. And Vanessa Cole."

Hubert hesitated a moment. "I seen Ambassador Smith and Sam LaCoy out fishing when I come in. But I didn't tell them nothing about it. I just said Mrs. Cole and the daughter didn't want no company just yet." Hubert hated the way he was talking. He sounded like a country bumpkin, and he knew it, but couldn't stop himself. He was glad that Alicia couldn't see or hear him.

"So only you and I and Vanessa know about this accident. That's good. How's she taking it?"

"Okay, I guess."

Kendall sat back down and clasped his hands behind his head and stared at the ceiling a moment. "I'm tempted to do something indiscreet," he said. "Possibly illegal. But I'll need your cooperation, Hubert."

"How's that?"

"It's still possible to keep this whole thing just between us. You know, bring the body of Mrs. Cole out from the lake after dark tonight, and then you and Vanessa drive it someplace else. Someplace downstate, in the Catskills, maybe, and take the gun with you, and say the accident happened there."

"I don't know, Mr. Kendall. The body's not—"

The manager interrupted him. "You would be handsomely paid for the service, believe me. I have a discretionary fund available for . . . discretion. Do you think Miss Cole would agree to that?"

"Well, to tell the truth—"

"There are favors I could grant in exchange. She wanted her father's ashes placed in the Reserve. I could allow it. There might be other favors."

Hubert shook his head. "She doesn't want anybody to know what happened, all right. Just like you."

Kendall brightened. "Really?"

"For different reasons she doesn't want anybody to know what happened. But she doesn't want her mother's body brought out, neither."

"Why not, for heaven's sake? We can't leave it there. She's dead, Hubert. It's a human body." He started to say that Ambassador Thomas Smith was thinking of buying Rangeview and might change his mind if a scandal were associated with the place, but thought better of it. Kendall didn't want anyone getting between him and the ambassador in this transaction, and who knows whom Hubert might tell? If word got out, one of the other members might cut into line without relying on the manager to act as broker. There was a premium on camps in the Reserve.

"Well, for one thing, she's scared," Hubert said.

"Scared! Why? She didn't do it, did she? Shoot her mother. I thought it was an accident. Mrs. Cole dropped the gun, and it went off accidentally, you told me."

"Well, that's more or less how it happened."

"More or less?"

"Yes."

Kendall narrowed his eyes. "What *aren't* you telling me?"

"Nothing important."

"Whatever happens in the Reserve has to be reported to me. Especially when it's something . . . untoward. As this certainly appears to be."

"I know."

"Hubert, I could make it so you'd never work in the Reserve again."

"I know."

"You'd starve without the Reserve. You and half the people in this town," he added.

"I know," Hubert said, and sighed. He leaned forward in the chair and looked at the floor and without raising his eyes proceeded to tell the manager the rest. Or most of the rest. He did not tell him about Jordan Groves's being at the Second Lake, and he did not tell him that Vanessa Cole had kidnapped her mother and kept her a prisoner in the camp for days.

The manager heard him out in silence. When Hubert had finished, Kendall sat up straight in his chair and brushed invisible crumbs from his shirt and straightened papers and pencils on his desk for a few seconds. The thunk of the tennis ball and an occasional hearty male laugh drifted through the open window.

The manager inhaled sharply through his nose. "You are a fucking idiot," he declared. "You're a fucking idiot twice over! First, for going along with the Cole girl and burying the mother on the Reserve, when you should have simply come here immediately and told me about the accident. We could have handled the matter discreetly, with no one the wiser. So you're an idiot for having gone along with her, and God only knows why you did that, and second, you're an idiot for coming here now and telling me what you've done with the woman's body. And God only knows why you did *that!*"

"What should I have done, then?" Hubert asked. He genuinely wanted to know. "I'm not an idiot, Mr. Kendall." He sat back in the chair and gave the manager a hard look.

"Really?" The manager laughed without smiling and shook his head. "What you should have done is refuse to cooperate with that girl and instead come to me right away so I could do the thinking for both of us. Now I've got no choice but to play it by the book. The Reserve rule book. I'll have to call in the sheriff and tomorrow send a crew out there to dig up Mrs. Cole's body and bring it in. The county will probably want an autopsy before issuing a proper death certificate. It'll be in all the papers. Oh, they'll love it. And not just the local papers, either. Kaltenborn will have it on the radio. It'll make the newsreels. And the Cole estate, that'll be tied up for years. Or else in the hands of that crazy girl. And who knows what she'll do with the property."

"The property?"

"Yes. Rangeview. Certain parties have expressed an interest

in purchasing Rangeview from Mrs. Cole. It could have been a quiet, private transaction, handled by me. These are socially prominent people, Hubert. They don't like their names or activities or their financial affairs in the newspapers or associated with people like Vanessa Cole, who *does* want her name in the newspapers and her pretty face up on the 'March of Time' screen. I don't expect you to understand that. But I do expect you to act rationally. Or at least I *did*. And to leave the business of being discreet to me. That's supposed to be my business, Hubert. That's my special skill. It's why I have this job. Your business, your skill, is to guide and protect your clients here on the Reserve and take care of their property for them. Your employer, don't forget, is the Reserve. Your clients pay the Reserve for your services, and the Reserve pays you. Your allegiance, therefore, is first and foremost to the Reserve and only indirectly to your clients. The rules we follow here, all of us, you as well as I, are the Reserve's rules, written into law years ago, generations ago, by men like Dr. Cole's father, when they first created the Reserve as a private sanctuary for themselves and their families and friends. Remember that. And when you obeyed Vanessa Cole and helped her bury her mother on the Reserve, which is practically sacred ground to these people, especially those members like Ambassador Smith whose parents and grandparents created it, when you did that, Hubert, you broke the Reserve's rules. There shall be no grave sites anywhere in the Reserve. None. That's the rule that applies here, Hubert. While I might have bent that rule a little for Vanessa Cole regarding Dr. Cole's ashes, in exchange for her agreeing to move the site of her mother's unfortunate accident to someplace else, now, thanks to you, it's too late for that. We'll have to go up there tomorrow with a crew and dig up the body in daylight. How deep did you bury her?"

"About five feet, I guess."

"Oh, my. Five feet deep. Well, there you are. There's really no way this can be done quickly, unofficially, off the record. Discreetly." Kendall reached for the standing phone with one hand and dismissed the guide with a backhanded wave of the other. "It's too late to do anything today, it'll be dark in a few hours. Be here tomorrow morning at eight o'clock. I'll have two or three men who'll go in with you. And probably the sheriff."

Hubert nodded and pulled away from the sticky embrace of the chair. When he stood, he felt strangely tall, as if he were outside his body and looking down on it from above. The man he saw below was a small man, shrunken and frail, prematurely aged—a man who used to be an Adirondack guide.

The sun passed beyond the range, and the broad shadow of the mountains spread across the lake from west to east, and the light in Cinderella's Suite quickly faded. Jordan Groves and Vanessa Von Heidenstamm did not notice the approaching darkness. They were still immersed in their lovemaking. It had begun slowly, tenderly, face-to-face, with long, lingering looks at each other, like devoted siblings at the start of a long absence taking their last leave of each other, gathering in all the details they had neglected to notice up to now. They removed their clothes, their own and each other's, delicately, precisely, as if preparing to model for an artist, and once naked, seated side by side on the bed, they turned to face each other, and with their hands on each other's bare shoulders, they kissed—sweetly, as if in relief and gratitude for having come to the peaceful end of a painfully protracted argument. And then they embraced and with their hands caressed each other's breasts and backs and arms—her skin smooth and creamy and soft as fine silk, his alabaster white and tautly drawn over muscle and bone—and their separate bodies gradually lost their boundaries and merged into a third body, one that contained all their female and male differences and erased all their anatomical contrasts and inversions.

Their passion rose slowly. His because he had never made love like this before, delicately, teasingly, fully aware of each slow turning, and though it frightened him a little, it excited him in a fresh way. Hers rising slowly also, but with her it was because she had made love in this fashion many times before and knew very well its effect on a man who was used to having his way with a woman quickly and efficiently without being conscious of having lost awareness of his body. Men like Jordan Groves, egocentric sensualists, men whose lovemaking left them with a sense of accomplishment, were rarely truly satisfied by a woman, unless she managed to slow him in his headlong rush. He had to be brought, bit by bit, cell by cell, to complete awareness of his body, moving, as if he were a woman, from the outside in, rather than from the inside out, so that when he did lose his body, he lost everything. Men like Jordan Groves had to be braked and slowed. They were the only men capable of exciting Vanessa's passion. Slowing them almost to a stopping point gave her a power over them that she otherwise lacked. It brought her out of herself and forward toward another human being and through that other into the shuddering void beyond, and when that happened she cried out in joy. Afterward, with no memory of having cried out, she had to be told of it by her lover, as if she had been elsewhere at the time. For she had been elsewhere—she had left the locked and guarded, dark room of her body for the blinding light of self-forgetfulness, where there was no one to be courted or seduced, where there was no one to affirm her reality by means of his or her gaze, and no one to fail at it over and over again. Making love with men like Jordan Groves let Vanessa Cole believe for a few seconds in the sustained reality of her essential being, even though afterward she could not remember ever having experienced it as such. Even though afterward it was as if self-awareness had been surgically removed and all she had to go on, all she was capable of experiencing, was its phantom. But her belief in its existence, like a Christian's belief in a god she's never met, gave Vanessa strength and a small, transient portion of equanimity, and for many years that belief had kept her from annihilating herself.

It was nearly dark when they heard footsteps on the deck at the front of the house and then the squeak of the screened door of the porch opening and closing, and someone crossed the porch and knocked lightly on the living room door. Jordan reached for his clothes and rapidly began pulling them on, while Vanessa calmly rose from the bed, strolled naked to the dressing room, and emerged wrapped in a white cotton sheet. She told him to stay where he was and walked from the bedroom, closing the door firmly behind her. Jordan peered cautiously from the window along the front of the house to the porch. In the heavy shadow of the overhanging pines, even with a full moon rising in the east, it was too dark for him to see who was there, except that it was a man.

At the living room door Vanessa called, "Who is it?"

"It's me, Hubert. Hubert St. Germain, Miss Cole."

"What do you want? I'm not dressed."

"I got to talk to you, Miss Cole."

"Are you alone?"

"Yes."

She opened the door, but did not invite him inside. "What

do you want? You shouldn't be here now, you know." The cold air rushed into the room, and she shivered and pulled the sheet tightly around her. She was not fooled: the guide was bringing news that she did not want to hear.

"I know I shouldn't have come out. But I got to warn you."

"What, the British are coming?"

"No. I did something that I thought . . . that I thought was the right thing to do. The only thing I *could* do, under the circumstances. Only it didn't work out right."

"For heaven's sake, Hubert, you sound like you've been a bad boy. Stop beating around the bush and tell me," she said, although she already knew what he'd done and what would follow. She turned away and told him to come inside, then walked to her bedroom door and called to Jordan, "Come on out. It's Paul Revere. The British are coming." He's told someone, she said to herself. The bloody fool. She never should have trusted him. He was weaker than she had thought.

Returning to the living room, she strode to the bar and poured herself a half glass of rum and the same for Jordan. "You want a drink?" she asked Hubert. "Sit down and have a drink," she said. Then, "No, make a fire first, will you? It's cold in here."

"I could use a drink, I guess. H'lo, Jordan," he said as the artist entered the room, dressed, but shirtless, with his leather jacket on and zipped.

"What the hell are you doing here?" Jordan said.

"I'm afraid he's the harbinger of bad tidings. What do you want, Hubert? To drink, I mean."

"Same as you, I guess."

"You guess. Is that all you do, guess?"

"No. I know a few things. I'll have the same as you and Jordan," he said and knelt by the fireplace and crumpled newspaper into it and laid some sticks down and while the others watched in silence got the fire lit.

Jordan slumped in a large chair and looked at him. Finally he asked, "What's the bad news, Hubert? No, don't tell me, let me guess. You got back to your cabin and sat there looking at your dog and had a crisis of conscience. Right?"

Hubert stood and looked at Jordan, then at Vanessa, who handed him the drink. The burning pine sticks snapped loudly behind him. He saw that they had spent the afternoon making love, and was glad of it. So many things were fracturing and getting reconfigured that it felt somehow reassuring to see still more of it. What the hell, let it all come down, he thought. Everything that's broke is beyond repair. He was even glad that Alicia and he would not be able to see each other again, and that he might never be able to hire out his services to the Reserve again. Better that nothing will ever be the same again, rather than only some things. "Yes, you're right," he said to Jordan. "As far as it goes."

"Jesus Christ," Vanessa said. "'As far as it goes.'" She moved from table to table, lighting the kerosene lanterns, filling the large, high-ceilinged room with pale orange light. "My father's dead only a few weeks, and my mother's killed this morning by a shotgun blast, a regrettable, sad accident, as we know, and Daddy's ashes are in the lake, and Mother's body is buried in the woods, both deeds illegally done, and you're having a little *crise de conscience*? Get some perspective, Hubert. I haven't even started to properly mourn yet, because of all this goddamned mess, and meanwhile you're feeling a little guilty? Why should we care about that?"

"If that's all it was, that I talked to Alicia about . . . about what happened this morning and all, I wouldn't have come out here tonight. I would've just left it like it was."

"You did *what*?" Jordan said. "You told Alicia? Jesus!"

"Why on earth did you do that, Hubert? What were you *thinking*?"

Jordan said, "I'll tell you what he was thinking. He carried his little bag of guilt straight to his lover, my wife, because he couldn't handle it himself, and she's the only one he knows who would keep his secret, since I'm a part of it and she's married to me, the father of her children, and is therefore obliged to protect me. Besides, she's good at keeping secrets, isn't she, Hubie? So now Alicia knows about it, and you're feeling guilty about that, too. You're having a second crisis of conscience, and you've rowed all the way out here in the dark to get it off your chest. You can screw another man's wife, but you can't stand thinking badly of yourself. Better get used to it, Hubie."

"Jordan, don't call me Hubie."

"I'll call you any damn thing I want."

Hubert looked at Jordan, then at Vanessa. His partners in crime. Fellow liars. Adulterers. Everyone in it together, but only for him- or herself. He didn't know who any of them was any more, not even Alicia. Not even himself. All he knew was what they had done. He had no idea of why, however.

"Stop it, you two," Vanessa said. "Just tell us the rest, Hubert."

"Tomorrow morning Kendall's sending me and a couple of the boys from the Club out here with Dan Peters to dig up your mother's body and take it in for an autopsy and suchlike." He paused for a moment to let them absorb the information. "Peters is the Essex County sheriff," he added.

Vanessa and Jordan glanced at each other, then turned away and stared expressionless at the fire.

Hubert said, "Kendall knows what happened out here today."

"So I gather. Who told him?" Jordan asked. "Alicia? You told her what happened, and she took it to Kendall?" It was not like her to betray him that way. But it was not like her, he had once believed, to betray him by sleeping with another man and continuing to do it and lie about it for months. Falling in love with him, even. There wasn't much left in his life now that was predictable, except lies and betrayal.

"You told him yourself, didn't you, Hubert?" Vanessa said. "Because of Alicia. Because that's what she wanted you to do."

"Yes. I'm not sure that's what she wanted me to do, though. I did it on my own account."

"Oh, Hubert St. Germain, you're like a moth to flame."

"What do you mean?"

"You can't resist what can destroy you. You think you're being honest, but you're acting on some dumb blind instinct."

"I don't know what you mean. I thought I was doing what was right. Finally."

Jordan said, "Did you tell Kendall about me, that I'm involved?"

"No."

"Well, that's something, I suppose. But Alicia, she knows everything?"

"Yes."

Jordan pulled his tobacco and papers from his jacket pocket and rolled a cigarette. Vanessa sat opposite him, turning her glass and staring at it. Hubert looked at the fire and drank off his rum and placed the heavy glass on the end table next to him. Three full minutes passed in silence, except for the snap of the fire in the fireplace. Then Hubert walked to the door. He waited there for a second, as if expecting one of them to stop him, to ask where he was going, why he was leaving, why he had done what he had done. But no one asked him anything, and he was glad. He wouldn't have known how to answer. He didn't know where he was going, or why he was leaving, or why he had done what he had done. He opened the door and departed from them. Let it all come down.

Jordan left his chair and crossed to Vanessa and stood behind her and put his hands on her shoulders, naked beneath the sheet, and pushed the sheet away and felt her cool skin. Firelight flickered across her breasts, and the artist thought it would make a beautiful picture—a seated, nearly naked woman seen from above and behind like this, her light auburn hair loose and long and streaked with red and orange bands of firelight, her buttery shoulders and her full, firm breasts with the pink nipples barely visible, the white sheet collapsed across her lap; and emerging from the darkness that surrounded her, obscure shapes of furniture, ominous, impersonal forms slowly encroaching on the lit space filled by the naked woman, thoughtful and grave. The fire in the fireplace and the kerosene lanterns were outside the frame. All the light on the woman was reflected light. He removed his hands from her shoulders—he didn't want his hands in the picture, just the woman alone in the nearly dark room, naked and sad and in danger and aware of everything in the picture and beautiful to behold.

"You're looking at me, aren't you?" she said in a low monotone. She felt the heat and light from the fireplace and lamps on her face and upper body and the heat and light from the gaze of the man standing behind her, and she was filled with inexpressible joy. The warm illumination from both fire and man solidified her, gave her body and her mind three full dimensions and let her shape-shifting self, aswirl in a fixed world, stop and hold and, when she had become its still center, made the world begin to swirl instead. This must be how other people feel all the time, she thought.

Jordan could not resist touching her and placed his hands on her shoulders again. She shrugged them off. "Just look at me. Keep looking at me."

"I want to touch you."

"No touching," she said. It was a child's voice, high and thin, almost a plea.

Jordan took a step back and to the side and tried looking at her from a different angle, a three-quarter view, but it did not have the same mystery and sadness of looking at her from behind and above. It was merely a portrait now of a posed woman, a model instructed by the artist to sit naked in a large chair with a sheet draped across her lap. The woman he had seen before was gone.

"I shouldn't be here," he said. "Especially now."

"No."

"What will you do when they come tomorrow?"

"Whatever I have to."

"What will you tell them?"

"Whatever I have to."

"Will you tell them about me?" he asked. "That I was here?"

"No."

"Will you be all right? Tonight, I mean. Alone."

"I've never been anything but alone. I'll be all right."

He leaned down to kiss her, and she jerked away. "I said no touching."

VANESSA HEARD HIM CLOSE THE OUTER DOOR AND CROSS THE porch and deck. Then silence—except for the dry, whispering rattle of the fire. She turned in the chair and cupped in both hands the pale green glass bowl of the kerosene lantern on the table beside her and lifted it into the air. She stood, and the sheet fell away, and she was naked. She carried the lantern to the fireplace. The crackling fire warmed her belly and breasts and thighs, its yellow light flickering across her pale skin like fingertips. She gently set the glass bowl onto the cut-stone mantelpiece, like an offering on an altar. Turning, she picked up a second lamp from a table and crossed the living room. Planes of orange light slid and skidded over the walls and high ceiling as she walked into the darkened hallway and turned from the hallway and entered the library.

"Everything you need to know is in the library."

"Look in the library," she had said to Jordan. He had questioned her claim to have graduated from college at sixteen, and she had told him to check the social register, even though she knew that the social register would neither confirm nor deny her claim. She was performing for him, mixing lies with truths, and he, naturally, was believing nothing. "Everything you need to know is in the library. Everything," she had said to him, and a dreaded certainty, which until that moment had eluded her, came over her. Vanessa suddenly knew what to look for and where to look for it. There was no speculation or supposition about it; she knew that a thick, cardboard file folder tied with a black ribbon was located in a locked wooden cabinet built into the shelves behind her father's reading chair. It had always been there, and she had always avoided looking at it, and it had become invisible to her. She set the lantern on the floor and pulled the heavy, leather-upholstered chair away from the wall. She yanked hard on the wooden knob of the cabinet, and it broke off in her hand. Grabbing a poker from the stand next to the corner fireplace, she proceeded with a half-dozen blows to smash the thin panels of the cabinet door to pieces. Inside the cabinet, she saw what she had known would be there. She removed the brown cardboard file folder from the cabinet and sat on the floor and held it flat on her lap and was about to untie the black ribbon and open it, when it seemed suddenly to burn her bare skin with a dark heat. She pushed the folder off her lap, to the floor. Then she stood and picked up the folder again. It was cool to the touch, now that she no longer wanted to open it.

Vanessa left the library and carried the folder to the living room. There she held it against her breasts and stared at the fire for several seconds. The flames had begun to die, and she was shivering from the cold now. Kneeling, she placed the folder flat on the hearth. She reached behind her for the fallen sheet and draped it over her shoulders like a robe. On her knees, she stared at the file folder and reached one hand forward and nudged the folder a few inches toward the open fire, all the while murmuring and shaking her head from side to side as if arguing with herself. She pushed the folder another inch closer to the flames. She looked up at the mantelpiece. She could feel the heat of the flames against her face and throat. *Humpty Dumpty sat on a wall. Humpty Dumpty had a great fall, and all the king's horses and all the king's men couldn't put Humpty together again. . . .*

She stood then and slowly approached the mantelpiece, reached out and lifted the kerosene lantern off it. Holding the bowl in her two hands, she backed a few steps away from the fire. She hurled the lantern through the flaming mouth of the fireplace into the darkness beyond, and the entire room filled with a flash of hot light.

JORDAN GROVES MADE HIS WAY WITH RELATIVE EASE ALONG the rocky shore. The full moon above the lake was like a gigantic eye looking in on the earth. He pushed through brushy undergrowth and splashed across the mouths of small, rock-strewn brooks to the hidden cove a mile south of the camp, where his airplane was anchored. Stepping onto the near pontoon, he pulled the anchors free of the lake bottom and climbed into the cockpit and started the engine. He hit the rudders, and brought the airplane around to the south, facing the soft wind. A broad streak of moonlight crossed the water in front of him like a brightly lit, rippled runway, and his takeoff along it was quick and smooth and straight, a gracefully rising arc drawn from the surface of the lake into the cloudless, star-filled sky above. As he passed over the camp buildings, he kept his gaze fixed on the stars above and ahead of him and did not see the living room windows of the camp suddenly change color—dark orange flaring to bright yellow.

ALICIA MOVED SLOWLY THROUGH THE HOUSE, SHUTTING OFF the lights one by one. The boys had finally fallen asleep—all day and into the evening they had been anxious and somber, as if they knew that something was about to change their lives irrevocably, even though Alicia had made every effort to demonstrate to them that today was just another ordinary summer day in the life of the Groves family. Papa was gone someplace in his airplane but would be back in a day or two, she told them, maybe even tonight. Where has Papa gone? they wanted to know. She wasn't sure, it was business, it had come up suddenly, and he had left early before any of them was awake and didn't give her the details. They'd memorized and rehearsed singing the Jimmie Rodgers songs, and in the afternoon, after Hubert came and left, she asked the boys to keep helping Papa's new assistant learn everything she could about the studio, told them to go on teaching the girl the names and places of the different tools and materials the same way Papa had taught them, by making an inventory of all the inks and paints and pastels and pencils, all the blocks and plates and even the sheets of paper organized by weight and size, and the rolls of canvas and stretchers and the brushes, knives, chisels, gouges—reminding Wolf and Bear that Frances had never been inside a real artist's studio before yesterday and that by helping her they were helping Papa, because when he got back he would have lots of new work to do and would not have the time to train her himself.

With Frances and the boys safely ensconced in the studio, Alicia had continued to behave as if it was just another normal late July afternoon—weeding the garden, gathering the first summer squashes and cucumbers, restaking the branches of the tomato plants that were about to break under the weight of the clusters of new green tomatoes. And later she'd taken Wolf and Bear to swim in the river, and the dogs, as anxious and somber as the boys, for the first time refused to go into the water. They stood on the sandy shore and watched, as if protecting the boys, who dutifully practiced their strokes a short ways beyond, and when the boys came out of the water and Alicia toweled them down, the dogs lay on the warm sand of the short beach and continued their watching, as if something strange was happening, when, in fact, everything was normal, life as usual, just another afternoon and evening at the Groveses'.

But it was not life as usual, and they all knew it, even Frances, Jordan's new assistant, who at the end of the day came to Alicia and asked if maybe she should stay home tomorrow and wait for Mr. Groves to telephone before she came back to work. Alicia said yes, that was a good idea, since she wasn't sure exactly when he would be back, and there was no point in her hanging around in the studio when he wasn't here to tell her what to do. Unless, of course, she needed more time to familiarize herself with the artist's tools and materials. The girl said no, the boys had taught her real good, she said. She said they were amazing, the boys. So smart and helpful and well behaved. Alicia thanked her and gave her some money for her two days' work and sent her on her way, believing that she would not see this girl again, at least not here. She'd bump into her in town, maybe, see her by accident at the grocery store, and the girl would ask after the boys, politely avoiding any mention of Mr. Groves or her brief employment as his studio assistant. For he would no longer be there, working in his studio, managing his household, raising his sons, sharing his life with his wife. Alicia did not yet know where in fact he would be or what he'd be doing there or whom he would be sharing his life with, but from the moment she woke at dawn to the sound down by the river of his airplane engine starting up and heard the plane take off and fly over the house and up the valley, gone, she had known that he would return only to organize his permanent absence from this house and from her, and from now on his sons would at best be mere visitors in his life, his unhappy guests on holidays and school vacations.

So she was not surprised, as she walked through the house shutting off the lights, dropping the house room by room into darkness, that she did not, as usual, leave a light burning at the kitchen door for him. She passed through the library, where barely twenty-four hours ago, she and Jordan had last held each other and wept over the damage they had done alone and together to their marriage, and she stood a moment beside his desk as if he were still seated there and she were waiting for him to turn to her and say *All is forgiven*, and *All our lies and betrayals belong to the past now*. Her glance fell on the wicker basket beside the desk, and she saw in it a sealed and stamped letter torn in half and half again, Jordan's cream-colored personal stationery with his familiar logo for the return address and letterhead—a river, the River Jordan, he had once explained to her, represented by three parallel, waved lines rippling below a grove of three pines. It was his mark, his stamp, his signature. She reached into the basket and picked up the four pieces of the torn letter and envelope and saw that it was addressed to John Dos Passos. She knew then where her husband would go when he left her. She did not read what he had written to Dos. She didn't have to—he had written it before learning of her betrayal and the months of deception. He had written it when he thought he knew who she was. Everything was different now. And then she heard the high, nasal hum of the airplane in the distance, its tone dropping and volume steadily increasing as it followed the river north toward home.

The young American woman stood alone at the wide window on the promenade of Level A, ignored now by the other passengers, for they had given up trying to engage her in conversation. Shortly after two o'clock in the afternoon, the steward announced that it would soon be possible to see the coast of Newfoundland. Below, the warm waters of the Gulf Stream merged with the cold North Atlantic Drift. For the first time since leaving Frankfurt, the sky had cleared, and the passengers on the promenade peered down from the Hindenburg and watched its long shadow cross the turquoise water. In the distance, looking like tiny sailboats, icebergs cast off by the glaciers of Greenland floated southeast on the Labrador Current. Soon the airship passed close enough to one of the icebergs for the passengers to take its measure. It was a mountain of ice gleaming in the sunlight, its enormous pale green base visible below the surface of the sea. A double rainbow circled the white peak. There was a sudden noise, a rumble and then a loud crack that could be heard inside the airship, and the mountain of ice seemed to break apart. A third of it split away and slid slowly into the sea. Calving, they call it, said a man standing beside the young woman. She turned quickly. It was the short man whose Dresden doll, his gift for his daughter, had been inspected at the hotel in Frankfurt. The man smiled. It's the mother iceberg giving birth to the baby iceberg, he added. Cute, eh? She said, Yes. Will your daughter be meeting you *when we arrive tomorrow? she asked. He said that he hoped so, and the woman closed her eyes for a second and smiled warmly, as if picturing in her mind the happy reunion of father and daughter. She said, Your daughter will love the doll that you're bringing to her. He said again that he hoped so, and she said, Oh, I'm certain of it. She turned back to the window, and the shadow of the gigantic airship crossed over the iceberg below—now two icebergs, a mother and a daughter—dissolving the double rainbow and dimming the white glare of the ice to gray.*

OVERNIGHT THE WIND GREW STRONGER, A WIND OUT OF THE north that blew the smoke south in the Reserve, away from the village of Tunbridge and the Tamarack Club, driving smoke deeper into the forested valleys and slopes of the Reserve and up the steep sides of the southern tier of the Great Range, across the peaks there and on to the rolling farmlands and villages, where the smoke dissipated finally into a haze, then rose into the dark sky, undetected by humans anywhere, within the Reserve or without, making it the private knowledge only of the animals and birds residing in the Reserve, the deer and bears and coyotes, the bobcats and fisher cats, the foxes, martins, and mink, the hawks and eagles and ravens on the rock-topped peaks, and, on the lakes below and in the cold streams tumbling into the lakes, the beavers and the loons and the lingering Canada geese, and, standing in the muskegs and shallows of the headwaters of the Tamarack River, the herons and cranes, and the owls returning from their nocturnal hunts to roost in the high branches of the spruce and pine trees, where, still higher and in among the crags, the solitary cougar lifted its heavy head from sleep and smelled the smoke drifting downwind from the Second Lake, and the great cat moved off the rocky ledge and made its way down through the conifers to the open birch forest below and loped still farther down to the bands of oak, hickory, maple, and poplar that crossed the lower valleys that lay between the mountain ranges of the Reserve: all the animals and birds in steady, uniform migration from north to south, an instinctual response to the smell of smoke, a felt command registering in their collective brain to track the smoke, not to its source, as humans do, but to where it grew faint and they could no longer see or smell it, even though obedience to the command drove them from the safety of the wilderness toward villages and farms beyond the southern boundaries of the Reserve, to where humans lived, where the forests had been cut and roads laid down and life for the wild animals and birds of the Reserve was a dangerous enterprise and food was scant and often protected by loud, barking dogs and men and boys with guns.

Consequently, it was nearly dawn, an hour before daybreak, with the wind shifting from the north around to the south and building to ten knots and steady, that the first early rising residents of Tunbridge, the village nearest the Reserve, woke and stepped outside to let their dogs run or trundled to the barn to feed the livestock and milk the cow or went to the henhouse to fetch the breakfast eggs, and they smelled wood-burning smoke floating down the Tamarack Valley from somewhere inside the Reserve. At the Tamarack clubhouse, Tim Rooney, the lone night watchman, a tall, sharp-shouldered man who people said looked like a young Abe Lincoln, made his last round along the long, dimly lit hallways of all three floors of the building and passed through the dark, cavernous dining room, where the stuffed moose head hung from the wall above the six-foot-high brook-stone fireplace, and checked the several members' lounges and cocktail bar, the library and game room, the kitchens, the nursery, strolled past the locked door of the manager's office and the greeting desk, and stepped out the main entrance of the clubhouse onto the open porch carrying two folded flags, the red, white, and blue American flag with its forty-eight stars and thirteen stripes and the green Tamarack Wilderness Reserve flag with the interlocking white TWR.

The watchman stood on the porch for a few seconds and studied the slowly graying eastern sky and observed that it might rain later in the day. He wrinkled his nose and inhaled and smelled wood smoke and wondered why on a late July dawn one of the members residing in the cottages attached to the Club would want a fire in his fireplace. An evening fire was nice, regardless of the season, to take the chill off and cheer the company, but an early morning fire in July, the hottest July on record, was more trouble than it was worth, a waste of good wood. He looked down the line of bungalows facing the golf course to see which chimney was giving off smoke, but it was still not quite light enough for him to see clearly, so he took a stroll along the lane and studied each of the six cottages close up with his flashlight beam. All the chimneys were cold, and all the windows were dark; the members and their families and guests were still asleep.

Puzzled, he walked back to the flagpole and hooked the American flag to the line and hoisted it and followed with the TWR flag and stood back a ways and watched them flutter prettily in the steady south wind. It was a morning ritual, the watchman's last act before signing out and walking to his house in Tunbridge three miles north of the clubhouse. It was a way for him to check the direction of the coming weather. Last night, under a full moon, when he took the flags down, the light wind had been out of the north, driving clouds down from Canada. Sometime during the night the clouds had erased the moon, and now this morning's wind was coming from the south, promising change—lower temperatures, and rain, probably, which Tim

Rooney hoped would not fall before he got home to eat his break-fast with his wife and children and sleep for an hour and return here by noon to commence his day job tending the greens at the golf course. He felt lucky to have two jobs, even though they were only seasonal. Most people he knew barely had one.

He smelled that smoke again and caught sight of two of the women from town who worked in the kitchen, Florence Pease and Katie Henson, walking up the long hill from the road to the clubhouse. He waited for them out behind the clubhouse at the service entrance to the kitchen, and when they arrived there he said good morning and asked them if they smelled smoke or was he imagining it? Both women assured him that he wasn't imagining it, they had smelled it all the way from town. But it wasn't coming from anywhere in town or from the clubhouse grounds, it seemed to be coming from someplace inside the Reserve, they said. He asked if anyone had rung the fire bell. Like most able-bodied men and older boys in Tunbridge, the watchman was a member of the volunteer fire department, and if the big cast-iron bell on top of the firehouse had been rung, he'd be obliged to get back to the fire-house in town as fast as he could, catch breakfast where and when he could, and forget about his morning nap.

But the women said no, no fire bell, not while they were in hearing range.

If the fire was inside the Reserve, the watchman told the women, and it evidently was, then someone would have to climb a moun-tain, Goliath or Sentinel, for a look-see. They agreed. But they had work to do, they had to prepare breakfast for over a hundred members and their families and guests staying in the cottages and clubhouse bedrooms and suites, so maybe he should be the one to scoot up Goliath or Sentinel, where a view of the whole forty thou-sand acres of the Reserve could be easily obtained.

Goliath, seven hundred feet higher than Sentinel, provided the better view—there was talk of the CCC building a fire tower on the summit next year—and Tim Rooney, who was strong and young and fit, managed to reach the top of the mountain in less than an hour. By then the sky was covered by a rippled white blanket of high clouds from Canada, and the Tamarack Valley and village of Tunbridge north of the mountain and the entire broad expanse of the Reserve south of it sprawled below in full daylight. The watchman peered from his perch on top of the bare gray peak and traced the Tamarack River back upstream from the village, over the meadows of the outlying farms and into the woods that surrounded the clubhouse grounds and golf course, and saw no smoke. He looked through the woods, past waterfalls and gorges along the narrow lane that led from the clubhouse to the First Lake, across the First Lake to the Carry, and over the Carry to the Second Lake, where the half-dozen much-prized, privately built lakeside camps were situated on lakeside land leased from the Tamarack Wilderness Reserve, and saw no smoke. Then, halfway down the eastern shore of the Second Lake, the watchman located the source of the smoke. One of the camps was burning, or it had already burned to the ground, he couldn't tell from this distance; and the fire was no doubt going to spread to the nearby forest, or it had already spread into the forest and was burning its way up the wooded slopes behind the camp. It was too far for him to see with his naked eye, but there was the strong likelihood of a forest fire, if not the reality of one.

Descending as rapidly as he could, the watchman ran to the clubhouse and found the manager in the dining room eating breakfast alone at a corner table, anxious and puzzled by the faint burning smell that had greeted him when he'd left his cottage a half hour earlier. The manager received the watchman's news from the mountaintop with sober equanimity, almost as if he'd expected it, although it was only the *sort* of thing he'd been expecting since his little talk the evening before with Hubert St. Germain. He folded his napkin and sighed audibly and told the man to drive to town in the Club's one vehicle, a wood-sided International Harvester truck that had been fitted out with bench seats for up to ten members and their luggage. Raise the alarm, he instructed the watchman, if it hasn't already been done, and call out the volunteer firemen. He himself would ring the club-house dinner bell and rouse as many of the members and guests as were willing to help fight the fire and he would outfit them with shovels and buckets and lead them into the Second Lake.

The manager had no doubt as to which camp up there was burning. Rushing from the dining room to ring the bell, he glanced at his watch—a quarter to eight—and nearly bumped into the guide Hubert St. Germain, coming in. The guide quietly told him what he already knew, that there was a fire at the Second Lake, and added that fire bells were ringing all over the county, calling out the volunteers. They needed permission from the manager to drive the fire trucks and other vehicles onto clubhouse grounds in order to get into the First Lake. They also needed permission to use the guide boats there for transporting the firefighters over the lake to the Carry and on. The manager nodded his approval and told Tim Rooney, the watchman, to ring the dinner bell out on the porch steadily until he had everyone who was willing and able to help fight the fire out of bed and gathered here on the porch. He said to give them as many shovels and buckets as he could find in the gardeners' sheds and carry them in the truck up to the First Lake boathouse, where he would meet them and lead them the rest of the way in. There were guide boats in the boat-house for no more than fifty firefighters, the manager said, and the volunteers from town had first claim on them, so the members and guests would have to be prepared to hike the whole way in to the Second Lake by way of the East Shoreline Trail, which was seldom used and thus was much overgrown with brush and blowdown.

By now fire trucks from Tunbridge and the nearby villages of Sam Dent, Mascoma, and Petersburg were arriving full speed at the clubhouse, along with cars and pickup trucks filled with volunteer firemen in their fire helmets and knee-length waxed coats. One by one, the long line of vehicles drove quickly past the clubhouse and into the Reserve.

No one knew yet what the firefighters would find when they finally got up to the Second Lake. It would be nearly midmorning by then. They might find a single camp or outbuilding partially or wholly destroyed by a fire that could be easily contained and extinguished by a bucket brigade hauling water from the lake; or they might find the beginnings of a forest fire, which they could capture and control with trenches and limited burns until it burned itself out; or they might come out of the Carry and look across the lake and see half the eastern forest in flames, in which case they could only pray for rain.

Hubert St. Germain was among the first group of firefighters, the Tunbridge Volunteers, to cross the Carry. Coming along right behind the Tunbridge contingent were the Petersburg men and boys. Though he was a member of the Petersburg Volunteers, Jordan Groves was not among them. The distant tolling of the bell had penetrated his dream-tossed sleep and had accompanied his dream for a long while, and when at last he woke, it took him several minutes to clear his head of the dream and determine where he was and what he was actually hearing.

He was in his studio, where late last night, after finishing off half a bottle of Cuban rum, he had fallen asleep in his chair. He telephoned the firehouse and learned that the fire was in the Reserve, at the Second Lake, and the Petersburg trucks had already left. If he wanted to join them, he could drive his own car to the clubhouse and go in from there, or he could fly his airplane in. The artist pointed out that there were rules against landing a seaplane in the Reserve lakes. The dispatcher at the firehouse told him to forget the rules, they might need the airplane up there today.

Like Russell Kendall, Jordan Groves had no doubt as to where exactly the fire was located, and he put his plane down on the lake a short ways out from the Cole camp at about the same time as the boats arrived carrying the rest of the Petersburg firefighters and Hubert St. Germain and the men and boys from Tunbridge. Among them were Ben Kernhold and Darby Shay and his son Kenny and a batch of Kenny's teenage friends—they'd joined the Tunbridge Volunteers with the hope of getting to fight a forest fire while school was in session, but not like this, when school was out—and Buddy Eastman and Rob Whitney and Carl James. Sheriff Dan Peters and three of his deputies from Mascoma, the county seat, were there, along with thirty or thirty-five more men and boys, even including the reclusive artist James Heldon, who owned a house and studio in the village of Sam Dent. He, like Jordan Groves, spent a great deal of time in New York City and elsewhere, advancing his art, and thus was only a part-time member of the Sam Dent Volunteers. Finally, making their way slowly through the tangled brush and cumbersome rocks of the eastern shore—led by the intrepid manager of the Tamarack Club, Russell Kendall, and his lieutenant, the night watchman, Tim Rooney—came the members and guests of the Club who had volunteered to fight the fire, ten or twelve of them, including Dr.

Cole's old friends from Yale, Red Ralston and Harry Armstrong, and Ambassador Thomas Smith, all of them determined to save their ancient, beloved Tamarack Wilderness Reserve.

ACCORDING TO LATER REPORTS, PUBLISHED AND UNPUBLISHED, but generally conceded to be accurate by those who were present, by the time the firefighters arrived at the site, the main building of the camp called Rangeview had burned nearly to the ground, with only the large brook-stone fireplace chimney left standing. The nationally known artist James Heldon managed to retrieve from the wreckage of the house one of what he claimed were twelve high-priced paintings that he had placed on loan to the late Dr. Cole. The artist was confident that the appraised value of the eleven destroyed paintings would be covered by the late doctor's fire insurance. However, most of the rest of the furniture, household goods, and personal possessions were destroyed or so badly damaged by smoke and by water tossed onto the dying fire by the bucket brigade as to be unsalvageable. The firefighters with great effort managed to confine the fire to the nearby grounds and, with the exception of several large pine trees located next to the main building, saved the surrounding trees and outbuildings and kept the fire from spreading to the adjacent forest. They were aided in this by the heavy rain that began to fall within minutes of their arrival at the site.

On the basis of pale green pieces of shattered glass found in the fireplace and certain other evidence, Essex County sheriff Dan Peters stated that the fire appeared to have been started by a kerosene lantern either thrown or, much less likely, accidentally dropped into an already lit fire in the fireplace. It was assumed by all that the person who threw—or dropped—the lamp was Vanessa Cole. Vanessa's mother, Evelyn Cole, was at first thought to have been in residence at Rangeview at the time of the fire. But the region's other well-known artist, Jordan Groves, said that he had flown Mrs. Cole from the Second Lake over to Westport on Lake Champlain the previous evening. Presumably, she had made her way to the Westport rail station and later returned by train to her home in Tuxedo Park, New York. It therefore appeared that at the time of the fire Vanessa Cole was alone at Rangeview. Russell Kendall, the manager at the Tamarack Wilderness Reserve Club, and the guide Hubert St. Germain confirmed this.

When the firefighters first arrived at the camp, Vanessa Cole was nowhere to be found, and it was feared that she had perished in the fire. The firefighters, once they had succeeded in keeping the fire from spreading to nearby trees and the outbuildings, searched in vain through the still smouldering rubble for the remains of the woman. Meanwhile, the artist Jordan Groves, guided by intuition and a more thorough and intimate knowledge of Vanessa Cole's mind than that available to the others present, left the group and bushwhacked his way uphill through the dense woods behind the camp and discovered the poor woman in a clearing about a quarter mile away. As he did not bring Vanessa in until sometime later, many of those present did not learn firsthand what had happened to her or even that she had been found by Jordan Groves. It was raining very heavily by then, and many of the firefighters and most of the volunteers from the clubhouse had started making their way back, either along the shoreline trail or across the lake by guide boat to the Carry and from there on to the First Tamarack Lake, where a second flotilla of guide boats awaited the brave, exhausted men and boys of the Adirondacks and the loyal members and guests of the Tamarack Wilderness Reserve.

JORDAN GROVES STRODE QUICKLY UPHILL FROM THE CHARRED remains of the house and after a few moments of climbing through the stand of red pines saw Vanessa Cole in the clearing a short ways beyond. She was seated on the ground at the grave of her mother. She was still wrapped in the sheet, sopping wet from the rain, and was visibly trembling from the cold, and as he entered the clearing and drew near her, he saw that beside her on the ground lay a shovel—the same shovel that he and Hubert had used to bury Vanessa's mother. Next to the shovel was a thick, brown, cardboard file folder tied with a black ribbon.

Vanessa was speaking, at least her lips were moving, but all Jordan heard was a low murmur cut with static and broken hisses, the same sound she had breathed into his ear that morning at Rangeview, the day they'd dropped Dr. Cole's ashes into the lake. It had seemed intimate and erotic then, a teasing invitation. But it sounded like madness now. She stared straight at the grave of her mother and seemed to be addressing her—addressing the woman's ghost, perhaps, or Vanessa's memory of her mother from long ago, because there was a childlike tone to her voice, making sentences that ended with an upturn, a question mark. For a moment Jordan thought that she was mocking her mother in a little girl's voice—he heard her say *a great fall*, or perhaps it was *grateful*, and *together again*, or maybe it was *never again*, and *on a wall*—words that emerged from a running stream of words in a grammar other than English. Or maybe it was a childhood nonsense song he was hearing, or a nursery rhyme.

He knelt beside her and realized that she was still naked under the cold wet sheet. He shucked his heavy waxed fireman's coat and draped it over her shoulders. She stopped speaking then—it was more a noise that had stopped than speech, but a noise filled with feelings he'd never before heard articulated by her, nor by anyone else he'd known. Feelings he had no name for.

"Can you stand?" He held her by the elbows, ready to lift her to her feet.

"Yes, of course," she said, and without his help moved gracefully to a standing position.

He backed away, surprised, once again unable to distinguish between authenticity and performance, unable to know for certain if she was mad in actual fact or was acting mad, was lost to herself in pain or merely imitating it—and if imitating pain, then what was she really feeling? For she had to be feeling *something*, didn't she? No one could be alive and conscious and not feel *something*.

"Did you set the fire, Vanessa?"

"Yes."

"Was it an accident?"

"Not really."

" 'Not really.' Why did you come up here, Vanessa?"

She pointed at the file folder. "To bury that. I could have let it burn in the fire. Maybe I should have let it burn. Turn it into ashes, like Daddy. I was going to. But then I wanted to bury it with my mother. Put it in the ground with her," she said. "But I couldn't."

"Why? What is it? What's inside the folder?"

"I couldn't do it. I couldn't let them burn up in the fire, and I couldn't bury them, either. Isn't that ridiculous, Jordan? Can't live with 'em, and can't live without 'em," she said and abruptly smiled, then was serious again. "Will you do it for me?"

"What's inside the folder, Vanessa?" he demanded. He reached for the folder, but she shoved his hand away.

"Something that should never have existed! Something

that, once it did exist, should have been burned or buried long ago." Vanessa spoke rapidly now, with more anger than agony. "Something that, if it wasn't burned long ago, should be buried with my mother. I can't bury them with him, it's too late for that now. Besides, she's the one who allowed them to come into existence in the first place."

Vanessa was smiling, and Jordan took a step back and tried to see her more clearly, more objectively, as he thought of it, so that he could somehow gain purchase on what she was feeling. He couldn't know what she was talking about, what she was referring to, unless he had some idea of what she was feeling. Otherwise, she was simply raving. Otherwise, her words had no connection to reality, not even a tangled, mad connection. Unless, of course, she was acting. And if indeed she was only acting, then it was something other than madness, something maybe worse than madness.

"Daddy kept them up here at the Reserve," she went on. "Hidden in the library, of all places. Can you imagine? Hidden right there in plain sight in the old Beinecke, in the one place he knew she would never look. And neither would I. Until yesterday, when I took you into the library, which had been the nursery when I was little, and I thought, of course, 'Everything is in the library.' That's what Daddy used to say whenever I asked a question he didn't have the answer for. 'Everything is in the library.'"

"What the hell are you talking about? Am I supposed to think you're crazy, Vanessa?"

"I'm not crazy."

"What's in the folder, then."

"What's in the folder? Why, photographs."

"Photographs. Of what? Of whom?"

"Photographs of me, Jordan! Me with no clothes on, me when

I was a teeny-weeny girl, taken by my daddy, with my mommy acting as his studio assistant. Drunk or doped at the time, no doubt, but my daddy's faithful assistant all the same. Then and now. Even dead. Do you want to see them?" she said and picked up the folder.

"Yes."

"Well, you can't." She hugged the folder to her chest. "They're mine. They're me."

"Okay, fine. You want me to bury them?"

"Yes. I . . . I can't do it myself. I don't know why. I want to, but I don't want to let them go. It's too . . . hard, somehow. I feel like it's destroying evidence."

"I'll do it," Jordan said.

"But don't look at them!"

"I won't." He picked up the shovel and proceeded to dig a hole in the soft wet ground that was the width and length of the folder. "Okay, let me have it."

She handed him the folder very carefully, as if it contained sacred scripture, a gnostic revelation. "You can't look."

"I won't," he said, and he didn't. He was absolutely sure that there were no photographs inside the folder. Papers—he could tell that much from the weight and shape of it—but probably nothing more than receipts for materials and work done at the camp, or letters, newspaper clippings, possibly a half-dozen old magazines or a pack of Dr. Cole's personal Rangeview letterhead stationery. But photographs? No. Jordan lay the folder flat in the hole and filled it in and tamped down the dirt and kicked a layer of pine needles over it. "There, it's done. Do you want me to place a rock on top, some kind of ceremonial marker?"

"Don't condescend to me."

"I'm serious," he said. "In case you ever change your mind and want to come back and dig them up."

" 'Them.' The photographs."

"Yes. The photographs."

"No. No need to mark it." She stood with shoulders slumped, hands lost in the sleeves of the heavy fireman's coat, strands of soaked hair plastered to her forehead and cheeks—a bedraggled, lost child, Jordan thought.

"Come on, Vanessa. I'll take you over to my place, get you some dry clothes, and we'll figure out what to do next."

"You can do that? Fly me away from here?"

He was silent for a few seconds, then exhaled slowly, as if a quandary had at last been resolved. "Yes. I can do pretty much whatever I want now."

"What's going to happen to me, Jordan?"

"Nothing," he said. Then added, "But only if you agree to do what your mother originally wanted you to do."

"Oh! Go into that hospital? That's what she originally wanted. So they could perform the operation on my brain. The operation they learned from Daddy. The operation that will make me nice."

Jordan put his arm around her shoulders and gently moved her away from the grave and toward the woods below. "Vanessa, no one's going to operate on you. Trust me. There'll be no brain surgery. All that business about your father and lobotomies, it's not true, Vanessa. You know that. No more than your belief that he took obscene pictures of you when you were a child. You'll be fine, I promise. If you go into the hospital, nothing bad will happen to you."

"You don't know as much as you think you do."

"I do know that if you don't go into the hospital, there's going to be a thorough investigation into the fire, and you'll likely go to jail for setting it. They already know you set it. That you set it 'not really' by accident. And who knows what else will come out in an investigation and trial? Your mother's death, for example. Which might also be seen as 'not really' an accident. And that you kidnapped her. And buried her body here on the Reserve. You've still got plenty to hide, you know."

"Is it like I'm pleading insanity?"

"Yes."

"Am I insane, Jordan?"

"I don't know." Then added, "No, not to me."

They walked a few more feet, and she stopped and stuck out her lower lip and pouted. "I don't want to go."

"You'll be fine," he said again. "Trust me."

"What if they find out about what happened to Mother?"

"They won't. Not if you go quietly into the hospital. I told the sheriff and Russell Kendall that I flew her out last night and she went back to New York by train from Westport. Your original plan. They believed me. Or at least the sheriff did. Kendall went along for his own reasons, I guess. And Hubert will, too. No one will ever know what happened here. It will be just as you planned. Your mother will have simply disappeared. But now, because of the fire, you have to disappear, too. Only for a while, though. A hospital in Europe is perfect. A nervous breakdown is perfect. In a year, you'll be able to come back to New York and start your life over again."

"Start my life over. It sounds nice, doesn't it? What about you, Jordan?"

"Yeah, well, like I said, I can do pretty much whatever I want to now."

"So you're free?"

"Yes. I'm free. In a sense, you are, too. We're both free as birds."

At the Tamarack clubhouse, the overheated kitchen was crowded with local women and girls cleaning the pots and dishes and utensils. The firefighters and the Reservists who had gone out to the Second Lake with them had been rewarded with a large dinner prepared by the staff of the Club and the wives and daughters of the volunteers from the surrounding villages. Local women and girls had cooked the meal, and the wives and female guests of members had served it and cleared the dining room tables afterward. Then, a little before nine o'clock, Alicia Groves left the kitchen and walked slowly, wearily from the building, past the tennis courts and toward the staff parking lot where she had parked her car. Her mind was on her sons, Bear and Wolf, whom she had left at the house in the care of the girl Frances. Alicia needed to get back to them. They were trying not to show it, but she knew they were frightened and confused and did not believe her steady assurances that everything was going to be fine, Papa will come home soon, but then he might have to go away on a long trip to Spain.

The rain had stopped falling. As she neared the car she glanced up at the rising meadow beyond and saw flickering chartreuse lights dotting the darkness—fireflies. She stopped for a moment to watch. They were beautiful, the first thing of beauty that she had noticed in days, it seemed. The first thing that had given her pause and taken her thoughts away from the sudden dismemberment of her life. Fireflies. Their tiny lights flared against the darkness, then went out, like sparks from an invisible fire.

For a long time Alicia stood beside the car watching the fireflies dance through the darkness, until it came to her that she would survive this day and the next and the next, for in the midst of a life of loneliness and unacknowledged abandonment she had finally come to know true love, and because she had known love she had for the first time been able to see the darkness that for so many years had surrounded her. She had deceived her husband, yes, but in the end she had not lied to him about her love for Hubert, and now she was glad that she had not lied to him, glad that she had not told her husband what he wanted to hear, which would have partially healed the breach in their marriage and allowed it to continue more or less as before, in darkness, with no brilliant lights illuminating for a few brief seconds the wildflowers strewn across the alpine meadow before her. She did not realize it, so caught up was she in the glow of her thoughts, but as she got into the car and drove it from the parking lot down the road toward her home and her children and her unknown future, Alicia Groves was smiling.

But then she stopped smiling. No, she thought, nothing good or useful could come of what she had done. The undeniable truth was that her husband, her marriage, had used her badly, and she had rebelled against that abuse by convincing herself that she had fallen in love with Hubert St. Germain so that she could commit adultery with him. She had used Hubert as badly as her husband had used her. But that was not the problem she faced now. That was merely the truth. The problem she faced now was that except for her children she was alone in the world. Her marriage was ruined, and the man for whom she had ruined it was not a man she could love and live with. Hubert St. Germain, the guide, the man of the woods, a taciturn, stoical, mildly sensual man, a man who had let her be his envelope, his perfect companion and lover: Hubert St. Germain was dull and unimaginative and provincial. She saw clearly for the first time that he was not capable of knowing who she was. And he was not ignorant enough to pass for innocent. She might have learned to love him if he had been innocent. She had brought down on herself an unexpected darkness, and she could not blame him, and she could not blame her husband. She could only blame herself, and that did not matter, because it did not change anything.

What will she do now with the rest of her days? She knows the answer. She will raise her sons, and when they become men she will cling to them and want to ask constantly of them if they love her, but she will hold her tongue. Instead, over and over she will ask herself, and now and again will dare to ask her sons, if she did badly by them, and they will sigh and reassure her one more time that she did not do badly by them and they are grateful. She will not ask them if she had been wrong to betray their father after he had so many times betrayed her, because they will never know of that. Their father will have died in Spain in April 1937. Shot down by the Fascists. In their eyes and in the eyes of most of the western world who cared about that war or cared about art or both, he will have died a hero. Only Alicia, his widow, will know what took him to Spain in the first place, and even she won't know the whole story.

From the long veranda of the clubhouse, Hubert watched her drive away. She had not seen him, he knew. Then he heard the distant rattle of an airplane engine, Jordan Groves's airplane flying from the Second Lake over the Carry and the First Lake, tracing the lane to the clubhouse, and there it was in the night sky, bringing Vanessa Cole in from the Reserve. The plane flew low across the clubhouse grounds, as if it bore a load that was too heavy for it and was struggling to gain altitude. And then, as it passed beyond the clubhouse grounds, it rose up and over the tall trees and soared into the dark sky, aiming for the notch between the two mountains in the east, Goliath and Sentinel. The airplane was quickly gone from sight, and a few seconds later Hubert could no longer hear it.

Slowly, he stepped down from the porch and walked around the clubhouse to the back of the building and headed for the parking lot where he had left his truck. As he neared the truck, he saw the same fireflies dancing over the dark meadow that Alicia had seen, and at first for a moment his heart, like hers, filled with freshened gladness. I will see her again, he thought. He was sure of it. And it will be very soon, he thought, and in time we will marry, and someday we will have a child of our own.

But when he got into his truck and closed the door and sat there for a moment in the silent dark, suddenly, without reasoning his way to it, he realized that he was a fool. A goddamned fool! What had he been thinking! He felt his face heat up from embarrassment. It was ridiculous even to hope that he and Alicia would marry and have a child together. Ridiculous and arrogant. He did not know what was in Alicia's mind or heart; he couldn't. Any more than she knew what was in his. All she knew of his mind and heart was what he had been able to show her of himself. And very little of what he had shown her corresponded to who he really was. He knew it was the same for her. For months it had been as if they were both asleep and dreaming each other into existence, and now they were awake. Or at least he was. He did not know if she was awake yet or still dreaming. He couldn't. Maybe she was, maybe she wasn't. It didn't really matter. He would not see her again, except at a distance, and when he did catch sight of her he would immediately retreat or change direction so that they could not meet. Hubert St. Germain will live alone in his cabin until a very old age, and he will become legendary. A guide of the old school, people will say, a gruff throwback to an earlier era when the Adirondack guides were viewed as true woodsmen. Those who knew Hubert St. Germain when he was young will say that he was one of those twentieth-century men who resembled in every way the first Europeans to enter this vast, unsettled forest, men who learned from the Indians how to hunt and trap the beasts that lived here, men who marked the steep, switchbacking trails to the mountaintops and crossed the lakes in their guide boats and descended the rivers and streams that tumbled from the icy headwaters to the mighty Hudson River in the south and the broad St. Lawrence in the north. Those men were the true Adirondack guides. They were not the mere caretakers of the grand old summer camps and the servants of the members of the Tamarack Wilderness Reserve.

ACKNOWLEDGMENTS

The author wishes to thank his assistant, Nancy Wilson, for her invaluable help with research. The author also wishes to thank his friends, who happen to be his neighbors, Charlie Segard and Tom Smith, for the flying lessons.